Falling for an Enigmatic Billionaire

A BEST FRIEND'S BROTHER ENEMIES TO LOVERS ROMANCE

LILY CROSS

Contents

Chapter One: Alyssa

THE SENSUAL HUM of the club's music and heavy thrum of the bass thumps through me, electric and warm. I make my way deeper into the club, scanning the crowd. There's only one person I care about tonight. Damien Darino.

I push through the crowd, turning my attention to the upper balcony where the VIPs usually hang out.

Damien is my best friend's older brother. He kissed me once when I was sixteen. It was my first kiss, and it ruined me for everyone else. Then he turned cold with no explanation. I'm still thinking about the kiss all these years later.

Tomorrow, I'm heading out of state for my master's program, and I only have this one chance for a repeat and an explanation. His sister Lucille told me he's here tonight, and the second floor seems the most likely location.

Call me mad, but I don't believe he hates me like he claims. I never did anything to him, after all. I like to think I'm optimistic, not mad, though.

Finally, I spot him. He's spotted me too, his gaze locking with mine. A brief electric thrill shoots through me. Then his lips press into a tight line of disapproval. I grin at him and then turn to the nearest guy for a dance. Time to put my plan into action.

Tonight, I will test my theory about his true feelings for me.

If I'm being honest, I'm not just here to test my theory. I'm also hoping to drive him past his steely, cold control. Maybe then, just maybe, I might get past that brief kiss I've been dreaming of for twelve years. Or I might just end up stuck on a whole new moment in time with him. That seems more likely.

Damien doesn't like to be teased or toyed with. So, what I'm about to do is guaranteed to get him down here, if only to send me home because he still treats me and his sister, Lucille, like wayward teens.

The guy I've chosen is reasonably attractive. I grab his arm and lean in to shout over the music. "Hey, buddy, wanna dance?"

He looks me over with a slow grin and then runs a hand down my arm before putting it at my waist. "Only if you think you can handle it."

I keep a smile plastered onto my face. This is for Operation Damien so that I can put up with it. "Maybe it's you who won't be able to handle it," I suggest.

The two of us find a place nearby to dance, and I play up the way I press against him as I move slowly and sensually. I can feel Damien's eyes on me, and when I look up at the balcony, he's clenching the railing so hard I think he might snap it in two. Jealous? I hope so.

It only takes a few more minutes before I feel a warm, firm hand on my shoulder. Then I hear Damien's smooth voice behind me.

"Mind if I cut in?"

The guy looks at Damien as if he's going to protest for a minute, and then he pales and stammers out an excuse. He stumbles off.

I turn to Damien with a flirtatious smile and hook my arms around his neck.

He scowls, his hands going to my hips as if to push me away.

We face each other in a silent standoff, but I'm going to have my fun with this one way or another, and I'm going to drag him with me.

Finally, he breaks eye contact and leans in to murmur in my ear. "What are you doing here, Alyssa?"

"I'm here to have fun."

His grip on my hips tightens. "You're going to go home."

"No..." I tap my chin. "But I'll have my fun with someone else, so you aren't bothered, grumpy."

He growls. Actually *growls*. "You're treading on thin ice. Are you drunk?"

I look him in the eye and grin. "Haven't had a drop. I wanted to be sober for this."

His expression is a mix of shock, fury, and—if I'm not mistaken—a hint of naked lust. "You don't have any idea what you're playing at."

"Actually, I do." I press closer to whisper in his ear. "You, on the other hand—"

His grip on me flexes. I'm getting to him, but it's not enough to break his self-control. So, I pull him closer and run my nose along his neck. "Dance with me."

He hisses. "Stop it, Alyssa."

"I could always just go ask someone else..."

He pulls back and grabs my chin. "Why me?"

I smile innocently. "You know, that kiss on my sixteenth birthday was unforgettable, particularly since it was my first. I want an encore."

His jaw tightens, and he curses under his breath.

I watch in fascination as the cold facade begins to crack.

He closes his eyes to regain his composure.

"What's wrong? It's just a dance."

"Are you going to touch me the way you touched him?" His eyes snap open, and his steely gray eyes look wild and ravenous. "That won't stay *just a dance*, love."

I shiver and drop my gaze to his broad chest. "And?"

"Do you know what you'll unleash?" His voice is a low hiss in my ear now. "Can you handle that?"

"I love a good challenge."

He laughs, rough and low. "Fine."

I pull away and tangle my arms around his neck with a triumphant smile. "Fine?"

His hands shift over my hips to my butt, pulling me against him. That leaves no doubt in my mind that I've done just what I meant to. I've broken Damien Darino's infamous self-control.

The minute we start dancing, though, it becomes clear I haven't won anything. My cheeks flush at the smirk he gives me when I realize he's taken control and is teasing me instead. Not five minutes in, and I'm the one who's near begging.

I turn my back and slowly move against him, a fire igniting deep inside.

His hands come to rest low on my belly not quite where I need them. Then his lips skate over my neck, and I gasp.

"Still sure you can take it?" he asks.

I tremble a little and close my eyes. "I ...." My throat goes dry as he slides his hand just a bit lower. "Damien, please."

"Please what?"

"More," I groan and drop my head back onto his shoulder.

"Hmmm...." He sounds unaffected. "I don't think you can take it."

"Please, don't... don't stop." I wiggle against him, desperate not to lose whatever was building between us.

He sighs. "If I'm going to continue, I'm not doing it here. I won't share what's mine."

Mine. The word sends another shiver through me.

"Just for tonight," he adds.

I don't need more. I'll be leaving tomorrow, so I turn and wrap my hands around his neck. "Tonight's enough."

He nods and takes my hand.

He escorts me away from the dance floor to the upstairs level with a hand on my lower back and leads me down a hall of closed doors to one at the end that has his name on a card by the door. He produces a key card and swipes it before ushering me inside.

The space is a small office and, off it, a bedroom. He must sleep here fairly often if he had a room set up with a bed. It isn't anything luxurious. It's pretty Spartan. But it'll do.

He shuts and locks the door before scooping me up and carrying me to the bed. When he drops me onto the mattress and stares down at me, I get the sense I've unleashed a beast. He was right. I didn't know what I was unleashing, but I can't find it in me to regret it.

"Strip," he orders.

I bite my lip. "Maybe you should make me."

He laughs sharply. "You aren't ready for me to do that, so for your sake, you'd better obey."

I decide it's better to listen. He has a look in his eye that's daring me to disobey him now, and I don't want him to end this before it even starts. Or worse... I don't know what would be worse, but I'm sure Damien would find a way to make me pay for my defiance, and I don't want to find out what it is.

That doesn't mean I can't take my time, though. I start unbuttoning the front of my blouse slowly.

He stalks closer with a razor-sharp smile. "Are you still teasing, sweetheart?"

I swallow hard and shrug.

"Let me help you out, then." He reaches for me and yanks the half-open blouse down, his gaze turning openly feral as he examines me. "Did you dress up for me?"

There's zero point pretending I hadn't come here to do exactly what I've done, so I nod. My cheeks warm at the look he levels on me, but I'm not backing down.

"I suppose it's only fair I repay you for the effort, then." He strokes his knuckles down my cheek and over the swells of my breasts. "Take the rest off and do it quickly before I decide I'm going to move just as slowly as you were earlier."

I do not want to find out what that means, so I quickly shuck off my leather pants and pull the blouse off. He nods, and then he removes his shirt, revealing swirling tribal tattoos across his pecs and a lithe torso.

I can't believe this is happening, but he dispels any fears I'm having when he pulls me up into a kiss that's every bit warm heat and demand like the one he gave me twelve years ago.

I'm lost in that moment. I'd give up my soul to have him, and the gleam in his gaze tells me he knows it.

"Just remember..." He tugs me down onto my back and hovers over me, trapping my arms above my head. "You asked me not to stop. Now I'm not going to, so don't regret this later."

***

I STARE DOWN at the two pink lines on the pregnancy test in disbelief. I can't be pregnant. This is the first month of my master's program, and I can't afford to have a kid right now. What am I supposed to do?

Worse still, I know exactly whose kid it is. I really should've been more careful with Damien that one heated night of passion. He asked me if I was on anything, and I was. Except I'm not always consistent about it, and it's a low dose.

I groan and drop my head into my hands, tears welling. What am I supposed to do? I don't want to be one of those girls who's a statistic, but I always wanted kids, and the idea of getting rid of the baby makes me sick.

Lost, I decide to call Lucille. She always has good advice. I just have to make sure I don't tell her who the father is. She'll flip on me if she finds out now like this. Over the phone is not the way to break it to my best friend that I've done it with her brother.

She picks up on the first few rings. "Hey, girlfriend. What's up?"

"L-Lucille...." I burst into tears, overwhelmed.

"Hey, what's wrong?" She sounds concerned now. "Alyssa?"

"I messed up," I tell her past the sobs. "I'm... I'm pregnant."

She's silent for a long while. Then, "What?"

"I'm pregnant." Tears spill down my cheeks.

"Oh... okay. Umm... well, what do you want to do?"

"I don't know. That's the problem."

"Listen, you don't have to make choices now. How far along is it?"

"A month," I say miserably.

"Then you have time. Just don't make any rash decisions."

I close my eyes and nod. "Okay. Okay, I can do that. I'll call you later, Lucille, okay?"

"Okay. Take care of yourself, hon," she says.

"I will. Promise." I hang up and bury my face in my hands.

I have never regretted a moment so much in my entire life as I do now.

Chapter Two: Damien

A Year Later

I HEARD THAT Alyssa had come back to town a few months before the end of the semester. She and I haven't spoken since the night at my club, and I've been keeping it that way. It's best for her if she isn't around me. I spell nothing but trouble for her. I'm everything she isn't—grumpy, demanding, and connected to people who would as soon kill as bargain for what they want. Not that I chose the last, mind you, but it is what it is. We don't get to choose our family.

When my sister, Lucille, showed up to tell me Alyssa needed work, I figured she wanted the job I had open for a secretary just to make enough money to finish her degree. Why else would she come home before the end of the semester? Her parents owe my dad a lot of money—a constant source of argument between me and my father, who wants me to collect it—and I'm willing to bet the money her parents had to help her is gone.

At first, I argued with Lucille about it.

Given the fact that I'm now sitting at my desk staring at the blonde-haired, blue-eyed woman I'd taken to bed a year ago, it's probably plain I didn't win that argument. Alyssa looks more tired than she did the last time I saw her. She still has a sweet, gentle demeanor about her, but her blue eyes aren't quite as bright as they used to be, and she's filled out a bit since last I saw her. She doesn't look railthin anymore.

It doesn't make her any less attractive. I haven't been able to forget that night with her any more than I'd been able to forget the kiss I'd stolen from her when she was sixteen and I was nineteen. I knew it was wrong then, and it still seems wrong of me to think of her this way now, especially given what my family is like. They'll never approve of her, and she doesn't deserve to be stuck with someone as jaded and ornery as I can be.

But it doesn't stop me from wanting her just like I wanted her when we were teenagers, and just like I wanted her when she showed up in my club wearing those tight leather pants and nearly sheer blouse with the borderline goth makeup, she knew I preferred on my women. The woman sitting in front of me is a menace, plain and simple. A sweet, biddable, surprisingly stubborn menace, but a menace, nevertheless.

"Are you sure you're up to the task?" I finally ask, my tone rougher than it needs to be. "You know I'm not an easy man to please." She shifts in the chair, her gaze lowering to her lap. Her cheeks flush just a bit. It's all I can do to keep a lid on the desire that ignites. "Because the Alyssa I knew couldn't have handled it," I say.

Her gaze snaps back up to mine. "I can handle it."

I was expecting tears, but I don't find any. Just stubborn determination and hope. Maybe she can handle it. I'm a jerk for pushing her like this, but she needs to understand that being my secretary isn't an easy job with good pay. It's a hard, demanding job with good pay. She's been away for a year. She could've forgotten what I'm like. "I don't think you can. I don't think you know what you're getting into. I'm going to push you and demand a lot from you, Alyssa."

Her lips curve into an innocent smile so much like the one she gave me in my club that night.

I'm the one tensing now, the look she's leveling at me sending fire through my stomach and then lower. This isn't how I planned for things to go at all.

Then she says, "I love a good challenge. You should know."

I swallow, my throat getting dry. I absolutely know. Memories of that night wash over me. Hiring her for this job is such a bad idea. I'm going to have to fight not to go back for seconds with her, to treat her as an employee like any other rather than as a former lover I'd very much like to have again. "Okay. Go by HR and tell them you need to fill in the new hire forms for the secretarial position."

Her eyes brighten for the first time since she sat down. "I'm hired?"

"No," I drawl, unable to help teasing a little. "I just want you to fill out new hire forms for my own sadistic pleasure. Then I'm going to tell you I've decided to find someone else."

She ignores my sarcasm and offers me a bright smile, getting to her feet. "Thank you very much. You won't regret it, Damien."

I have a good view of her full hips and waist. Even with the little bit of extra weight, she's still tiny, delicate. I am a cad for doing this. I'm also already regretting my decision, but

I'm not going to tell her that. It's not her fault, after all. I wave toward the door. "See that you don't. Now, out you go. I have work to do."

There's a brief rustle of fabric, and I force myself not to look up. When I finally do, the door has swung closed, and she's making her way down the hallway in her usual easy, carefree stride. I groan and scrape my hand over my face. What have I just gotten myself into?

***

MY DAY KEEPS getting worse. My father shoves his way through the glass door to my office in the complex I've built for my real estate offices. He doesn't knock—why would he when he thinks he owns me as his heir? —and just comes straight in to flop into a chair across from me.

I stop what I'm doing to level him with a flat stare. "Dad. What are you doing here?"

"We need to talk."

I never like hearing those words. Usually, it means he wants to lecture me or demand something I'm not willing to do. Something illegal, mostly. "No, we don't. I have work to d o."

"You always do. Put it away for a minute and listen to your old man. This is important, Damien." He has a deep New York City accent, something I didn't pick up entirely thanks to the time I spent at boarding schools as a younger child.

Realizing I won't get rid of him by pushing this off, I sigh and close out the reports I was reading. "Make it quick."

"You need to come back into the fold. People are starting to talk. What you've done here is admirable, boy. But it isn't the family business."

I fold my hands in front of me on the desk with a cold smile. "No, it isn't. That's what I like about it."

"Yeah, well, it rubs the wrong way with a lotta people in our world, son. You gotta come back." He spreads his hands in a placating gesture, smiling innocently. "All this, it's worth a lot. You can use it. We can really use it. It's time for you to take your place at the top of the food chain in this city, boy."

"I've told you before, and I'm going to tell you again. None of the businesses that I run—especially not ones I've purchased with my own hard-earned money and my labor will be used for crime. I'm not coming back to the family, Dad. It doesn't matter how much you beg. It isn't going to happen."

His smile fades and is replaced by a scowl. "You don't know what you're turning down, kid."

"I do, actually."

"No, you don't. And when you someday figure it out, you're going to come crawling to me for help. Whether I give it or not is going to depend on whether you're willing to make amends and beg me to take you back. Then we'll see if you still think you understand what you're turning down right now." He pushes himself up out of his chair with an angry little laugh. "I'm willing to bet you'll change your mind and think that you were a fool in this moment."

"I'm willing to bet I won't," I said. "Now, if that's all?"

"That's all for now." He heads for the door. "Just remember what I said. Come back before it has to hit that point, boy."

It isn't going to happen, but I'm not interested in prolonging this discussion, so I stay silent until he finally slips through the door and leaves me in peace. Maybe now I can get some real work down without interruptions. I know he'll be back to hounding me over this soon enough, but for now, he's said his piece, and I can safely put it out of mind.

Chapter Three: Alyssa

I CAN'T BELIEVE I got the job working for Damien. That interview might have been one of the hardest things I've ever had to do. Second only to giving birth to my son, Timothy. Damien Darino hasn't aged a day since that night in his club. He has the same piercing, demanding gray gaze and chiseled jawline, and he still fills out those crisp white dress shirts of his perfectly.

He isn't any less grumpy, either. The way he treated me during the interview was downright hostile, though I knew that for Damien, it was just a little irritable. Still, I'm not one to back down from a challenge, and I need this job if I'm going to support myself, my son, and my education without help from my parents. The money from them dried up at the end of the semester, and I wasn't able to pay my bills at the school, so here I am. Working for Damien Darino.

I walk into the little space in front of his office, admiring the polished wood and chrome surfaces of the reception desk that guarded the way to his office door. How I am going to keep him from noticing how attracted to him I still am, I don't know.

Worse, working for him will make it more complicated to keep Timothy a secret from him. If he finds out he has a son, I don't know what he'll do, but I doubt he'll let me keep custody. He won't want his kid growing up in poverty. I know that much. He'd take it as an affront to his dignity and a clear indication to the rest of the world that he's not able to care for his own.

"Are you going to admire your pretty face in the chrome all day or sit down and log into your laptop?"

Damien's low murmur in my ear startles me. I screech and jump, spilling the coffee I'd brought with me from home all down my pink blouse. It's not hot coffee—I like mine iced, and thank God for that—but now my shirt is indecent, and the polka dots of my bra are showing through it. My cheeks flame, and I whirl to face him.

His gaze drags from my face over my breasts and the soaked blouse. "You scare easily, and now you've made a mess. A wonderful start to your first day, isn't it? Go clean up, and hurry up about it."

"Yes, sir," I manage, setting the half-full mug of iced coffee on the desk.

I need to invest in a mug that has a lid with a working closure. Mine dumps way too easily. I hurry to the bathroom I saw down the hall. There's no way paper towels will clean this mess up entirely or make the shirt less see-through, but I don't have a change of clothes, and I can't go back home. It's too far of a drive in city traffic.

Tears prick at the corners of my eyes, and I can't help thinking Damien's crueler than he used to be. He didn't even offer me a change of clothes or time to go home for them. He all but made fun of me instead. Maybe he was right.... Maybe I'm not ready for everything this job will require of me.

I hope I can make myself push through it and put on a brave face. I can't let him rattle me, however nervous and bothered he makes me. I'm here to do a job, and I intend to do it well. It's not like I need to like Damien to do my work, and if I can keep my crazy hormonal brain in check, I should be able to manage.

Or maybe that's too optimistic. I don't know, and right now, I don't care. I have to keep my chin up somehow, and if telling myself lies will help, that's what I'll do.

***

THIS HAS OFFICIALLY been one of my worst weeks ever. On my first day on the job, I didn't just spill coffee all over myself. I also managed to send some of Damien's mail to the wrong spot, so it didn't go out with the post like it was meant to. I sent copies of his reports to printers across the building somehow, which left me walking ten minutes to get them after IT finally explained where they had gone.

The rest of the week was more of the same, and with each mistake, I felt worse and worse. At this point, at the end of the day on Friday, I'm wondering when Damien will fire me. He made a big deal out of every little mistake, showing zero patience as I struggled to get a grip on my emotions, my nerves around him, and the job itself.

It isn't like the work is that hard in and of itself. I think I'll do well in the job if I can just make it past the constant chiding from Damien every time I make the smallest error due to not knowing the ropes.

Sighing, I turn on the baby monitor and flop onto the couch. I've fed Timothy and put him down for the night, so with any luck, I can try to unwind. I grab the wine I poured earlier and take a sip. The taste is heavenly after a long day, and I take a slightly larger swallow to forget my woes faster. Maybe next week will be better instead of more of the same.

I'm just starting to relax when the doorbell rings. Groaning, I get up and step over the toys Timothy was playing with on his little floor mat to go answer. Who can be ringing my bell at seven at night? This is ridiculous.

I yank the door open and force a pleasant smile onto my face. Whatever they want, if I'm nice, I can probably send them on their way quickly without any hurt feelings. Those ideas fly out of my head when my brain registers who it is that's ringing my bell.

Damien stands there, a finger poised to press the bell again. He drops his hand and shoves it into his pocket when he sees me. "Hey. Is now a bad time, Alyssa?"

I bite my lower lip. "What do you want?"

He grimaces at my tone. "I guess I deserve that. Look, Alyssa, I came to apologize about this week. I've been harsh on you. Too harsh. I know you're trying and that most of the mistakes are little, unimportant ones."

I blink at him, stunned. Damien Darino apologizing? Hell has a better chance of freezing over. But here he is, so maybe it already has. "Excuse me?" I manage weakly.

"I'm saying that I'm sorry," he mumbles. "I've had a lot on my plate, and I know that's no excuse for how I behaved, but that's why I'm here. To explain and to apologize. You didn't deserve the behavior I gave you to put up with this week."

"Oh...." My brain seems incapable of forming any good responses now. "Oh, well...,"

"Have you eaten? I brought a casserole. Your favorite if I remember. Well, it was when we were kids. Maybe it isn't anymore. It's store-bought.... I'm not much of a cook."

A casserole? He is sorry if he's bringing me food. And he still remembers my favorites from childhood? That's odd, but I don't have time to parse it out because he seems to think he should bring it in.

He holds up the grocery bag he has in one hand and moves to step inside. "I brought you wine too. A housewarming gift. I realized I never brought you one when Lucille first let me know you'd come back into town." He pauses. "I guess I was just really busy."

I don't doubt he was busy, but the way Lucille put it, he was avoiding me, not just too busy. She was confused by the behavior since Damien and I always butted heads but had never avoided one another. I, on the other hand, was not confused. He probably didn't want to see me after we both said that one night was it.

Now I have to keep him out of the house because I can't let him see the evidence of what that "one night" resulted in. "Umm, now's not a good time...." I try to push him back out the door, reaching for the bag. "I... I was, uh... in the middle of something."

He raises a brow at me.

Good going on my part. It sounds even more suspicious than his claim he was too busy to even bother sending a housewarming gift with his sister. "Yeah, I was... I was watching something, and I think you could probably just leave the food with me. Thanks, Damien. Apology accepted, and I'll see you at work on Monday."

His eyes narrow, but after a minute, he nods and hands over the food. "Okay. See you Monday."

I take the food and hurry to shut the door behind him once he goes. Sagging against it, I let out a sigh of relief. I don't think he saw anything. My secret is still safe. That was way too close for comfort, though. This might turn out to be harder than I anticipated.

Chapter Four: Damien

ALYSSA'S BEHAVIOR WHEN I stopped by to give her my apology and the food has been weighing on me all weekend. She seemed desperate to keep me out of the house, and I find that odd. What was she hiding in there?

She claimed she was watching a movie, so maybe she was watching something she was embarrassed by. I think it's more than that, though, and I'm determined to get to the bottom of it. With that in mind, I call her into my office on Monday morning.

Alyssa steps inside hesitantly.

I nod toward the door. "Shut it, please."

She obeys, biting her lower lip. She always does that when she's nervous, though she's gotten better at hiding it over the years. "Did I do something? I didn't send the reports to the wrong printer again, did I?" She hovers at the door, as if prepared to make a quick getaway if I'm angry.

I stand and walk over to her, reaching past her to close the shades on my office's front window. "I wanted to talk to you about Friday night."

She freezes and stares up at me like a deer caught in the headlights. "Why?"

There's something she's hiding. I'm not going to play games about this, and I want answers. She can keep her private life private if she wants, but she's being cagey in a way that makes me wonder if there's more to it. "You seemed keen to keep me out of your house," I remark, eyeing her.

We're both standing close enough to touch now. I still have my hand on the rod that closes my shades, and her head is right next to it. My body is almost flush against hers, just like it was that night a year ago. I try to shake that mental image out of my head. It won't help anything.

She wiggles a little.

I'm not expecting it, and a little hiss escapes me as her movement presses our hips together momentarily. This whole situation already has me turned on, and that did not help the situation.

Her gaze flies to mine, and her cheeks go red. "S-sorry."

I'm not going to let on that I'm also embarrassed, so I smirk and turn to my usual fallback when a situation's uncomfortable. Fake it until I make it. "Sorry for what?"

She drops her gaze away from mine, as tense as a violin string. "Umm... I...."

Her reaction intrigues me. I've never seen her face so red before, and I'm starting to think she's flustered, not embarrassed. If I'm wrong, then what I'm about to do could get me in a whole lot of trouble, but I decide to risk it. I know Alyssa pretty well, and I knew all those years ago she had a crush on me just like I know now the telltale signs that she's getting bothered by this in the same way I am.

I lean in and put my other hand on the doorjamb next to her head, caging her in. "Sorry for what, Alyssa? Do tell."

She shivers but still isn't looking at me. "Damien...."

The single word is a plea, but it's one I'm not going to heed. I want to know if I'm right if she is still interested and turned on right now. "Alyssa...." I bend my head to whisper in her ear. "What's wrong, *love*? You seem a little flushed."

She sucks in a sharp breath, but we're so close now that all that does is press her chest to mine.

Her warmth seeps into me, and I'm finding myself more and more aroused by the second. This might have been a bad idea. But I've started, and now I don't want to stop. I want to coax the truth from her full lips. I'm not sure why I need to hear her say it so badly, but I do. "Well? Do you need a sick day, Alyssa?"

She shakes her head, her whole body tight and tense against mine.

I'm willing to bet that she's as turned on as I am right now and that I'd easily find evidence of it if I took a few layers off, and stripped her of her armor. I'm not going to do that here, though, however much I want to take her into the small bathroom of my private office suite and remind her of what happens when people tease me.

Not that she's trying to tease me. I think this time she's holding back the answer because she knows where it will lead and is worried about what might happen after. Not something I can blame her for, but I also need the answer.

"Alyssa," I growl. I'd like a little transparency. So, you can answer one of two questions for me." It isn't fair of me to do this, to use the knowledge that whatever she was hiding in her house is something she doesn't want to share. I do it anyway. "Either tell me what you're hiding in the house that you didn't want me to see on Friday night or tell me why you're tomato red right now."

Her lower lip quivers like she might cry. "You know why I'm all red right now," she hisses.

I raise a brow at her. "I wouldn't ask if I knew for certain. Indulge me."

"You're standing too close."

"And why does that make you go red?" I coax.

She shakes her head.

"Then what were you trying to hide on Friday night?" I reach down and take her chin in one hand, tipping it up so she's looking me in the eye. "I was being nice, for once, and trying to make things right, and you shut the door in my face."

She licks her lips.

I follow the movement with my eyes, and when I look back up at her gaze, it betrays her. It's a look of longing and need, and she sags in defeat against the glass.

"B-because it reminds me of that night a year ago," she whispers.

I didn't think I could get any more worked up, but that does it. I'm thinking about that night and how it felt to claim her, to make her mine like I dreamed about doing so many times before that night, and I want so much more than just the one night I got. I don't care that we said just one night. I want it to last longer. "And what do you remember about that night?" I ask roughly in her ear.

She shivers, and her hips move against mine just a bit. "Damien, don't make me—"

"You chose which topic to discuss," I remind. "How do you feel when you remember what happened that night?"

Her eyes close, and she drops her head back against the window. "Needy," she whispers. "I know I shouldn't be, but I am, and you're a damn jerk for making me admit it."

I allow myself the luxury of dropping my hand to her hip, knowing I'm treading on dangerous territory doing this here, or really at all. "You shouldn't be ashamed of wanting or needing something."

Her eyes open, and she stares back at me, tears swimming in her eyes. "It isn't fair how badly I want you when I know you're off-limits. Why couldn't you just leave it be so I could do my job and try not to think about it?"

I lean in closer and capture her mouth with mine. It's foolish. I shouldn't give in to that temptation, to the need to release the tension building inside, but I give just one small outlet and hope it will be enough.

She moans, half in protest and half in need.

I plunder her mouth with mine, making it clear in no uncertain terms that I need as much as she is right now. I'll never admit that out loud, of course, but when her hands tangle in my hair, I know she's understood anyway.

I grip her jaw in one hand, tilting her head to get better access. The way she feels against me, her tongue on mine, is intoxicating, and if I don't want to take this further in my office, I need to stop.

I pull away, my breath coming in shorter pants than I'd like, and shake my head. "We're not doing this. Not here." I straighten my dress shirt and adjust the cuffs. "I had an errand for you to run. Could you take this down to the post for me?" I turn and collect a FedEx envelope from my desk. "For two-day delivery. Use cash from the petty cash stash in the safe."

She takes it from me, swallows hard, and then nods. "Okay."

After that, she leaves the office. I stand there, struggling to get a grip on myself and wishing there were a shower in my suite so I could take a nice, long cold one. She is trouble, and I'm falling headlong into it.

Chapter Five: Alyssa

I CAN'T GET the moment in Damien's office out of my head. It's been three days, and I desperately need a distraction. That man is going to be the death of me. Maybe not literally, but figuratively speaking.

I'm still angry that he managed to drag the truth out of me. That night was meant to be it, and I can't afford to get tangled up with him again, no matter how he manages to heat my blood or coax me into saying things I'd never say otherwise.

The doorbell rings while I'm putting Timothy down for a nap. I settle him into his crib, glad he's finally fallen asleep, and pray that whoever's at the door won't wake him.

When I open the front door, my dad is standing there on the front step, glancing around nervously. I frown. "Dad? What are you doing here? You should've called."

"Can I come in?" He sounds as nervous as he looks.

"Yeah, sure. What is it?"

He comes inside and shuts the door behind him, pacing to the counter and taking a seat. He's up again a moment later, walking up and down the length of the counter. "I am sorry to disturb you like this."

"It's not a disturbance," I promise.

It is, but he's my dad. I'm not going to tell him that after everything he and Mom did for me when Timothy was still in my womb or after he was born. Besides, I'm worried now. He doesn't normally get this cagey or jumpy.

"I came to ask if you have an in with Damien. Since you're working with him, and all."

I don't know what to make of it or why he's asking. "Why do you want to know?"

"I'm being an inconvenience, aren't I?" He groans and drops onto one of my kitchen stools. "I'm sorry, hon. I shouldn't have come in like this to ask you about your boss."

I'm getting a little freaked out now. I don't know what my dad's connection to Damien could be, but it seems weird my dad's so desperate to know if I have an in with him. "I don't have an in with him, really, Dad."

"Oh... well... I need to speak to him, if possible, sweetheart. Would you at least relay the message?"

"Yeah, Dad. Of course. What's going on?"

"Nothing you need to worry about," he promised. "It's nothing. I just need to talk to him."

I want to ask him how he and Damien know each other. My mom knows Damien a little because he used to bring Lucille over to play sometimes, but as far as I know, Dad hasn't met him. Though, somewhere along the way, he has. Otherwise, why ask to speak to him?

"Can you let me know if anything changes? Anything at all?"

"Of course. I wouldn't pin your hopes on it, though. Damien and I aren't close."

It's a bit of a white lie. We aren't exactly close, and the man gets on my last nerve sometimes, but we do know each other beyond simple business, and after what happened in his office a few days ago.... Well, I'm pretty sure it's safe to say he wants to take it far beyond simple business for the moment.

I probably could put a bit of pressure on him to talk to my dad. I'm just not willing to do so when things are what they are right now. I need this job, and aside from asking Damien to consider meeting my father, I'm not going to push my luck and risk my job.

"Okay, honey. Thanks for helping as much as you can. Your mom told me to tell you to call and set up a time for dinner. We miss you." My dad got up and hurried toward the door.

"I'll give her a call, then. I'm sure I can find a good night, and I'll bring Timothy over with me."

"That would be wonderful, darling." He kisses me on the cheek. "I love you; you know."

I do know that, but my dad's never been one for telling me or my mom, so it worries me even more. He isn't going to die or something, is he? "I know, Dad. I love you too."

"I'll see you later, then. Maybe when you come for dinner." Then he's gone.

I can't begin to imagine what that might've been about, but I know who I can ask if I want answers. I'm going to see him tomorrow, and he won't be able to escape me.

***

THE FOLLOWING MORNING, I make my way into Damien's office with his usual mail. Instead of leaving like I usually do, though, I sit down in a chair across from his desk.

He raises a brow and sets aside the pile of mail I handed him. "Is there something else, Alyssa?"

"Yes. My father came to visit me yesterday."

His expression turns to neutral boredom. On him, it's the closest to wary that he gets. He knows something. "So? Your family matters aren't my concern."

"He wanted me to relay a message."

Damien crosses his arms. "Is that so?"

"He says he wants to talk and is hoping you'll meet with him."

The look on Damien's face tells me he knows something. I just don't know what, and I don't know why he doesn't want to let on that he knows more. I'm also not sure why he's pretending he doesn't know my father.

"Why would I meet with a man I've never met if he isn't bringing business to my firm?" Damien inquires. "Did you bother to find out what he wanted?"

I flush and drop my gaze to my lap. "He didn't say. He just insisted he needed to talk to you and asked if I'd get that message to you. Besides, you can't be a stranger. Not if he knew you and wanted to talk to you."

"On the contrary...." He waves a dismissive hand and turns his attention to the mail. "It's entirely possible he knows me from the newspaper or who knows what else while I know nothing of him."

"Then what do you think he wanted?"

"A prime piece of real estate in the city?" Damien drawls. "How would I know?"

I know I'm being dismissed now, but I fight to hold onto my usual sunny demeanor and smile brightly at him. "I can assure you; real estate is not what he's looking for. My dad doesn't have that much money."

Damien grins. "Then who knows? Maybe he wants some sort of favor and thinks I can grant it. I can't see inside his mind. Maybe you should ask him."

"I did ask." I can tell I'm not going to get anything further from him, though I want the truth of the issue. "He didn't say. Look, Damien, he looked scared. I've never seen him that way. He thought to talk to you for a reason. Can't you tell me anything?"

His grin fades. "Alyssa, maybe it's better not to know. He didn't tell you for a reason."

"So, you do know something. You're just not going to share?" I'm starting to lose my ability to pretend I'm not angry. "He's clearly in some trouble.... Maybe he's been gambling again or something." I'm rambling, but I'm just trying to figure it out. Even if I can't help, I want to know. It could be something that'll affect me and Timothy, after all.

"And how would I have anything to do with that?" Damien looks at me like I've lost my mind. "You're grasping at straws, love. I know you're worried about your father, but he's a grown man. If he wants a meeting, tell him to call and set one up. If he doesn't want to do that, then you've done all you can. Now, if you don't mind, let's stop wasting my time, please?"

I don't like being dismissed like this, but he's right. There's nothing I can do for my dad as long as he doesn't want to tell me what's wrong, and I've done what I promised him I would. If Damien doesn't want to meet him without my dad calling to make the appointment, then I'm under no further obligation.

It doesn't make me feel any better about this, but Damien's not going to tell me more if he even knows anything. "Okay." I stand and head for the door. "I'm sorry I inconvenienced you. I'll let him know to call if he wants an appointment."

"You do that. You have my office number." Damien turns his attention back to the mail I brought in.

My heart sinks, and I push through the door. He really can be grumpy and emotionally inept at times. I guess I'm on my own if I want to figure out what's going on with my dad.

Chapter Six: Damien

AFTER THE CONVERSATION with Alyssa, I realized that things must be desperate for her father if he's asking to meet with me. He must know I'm the one who's been told to collect the debt. What he seems not to know is that I have no intention of doing so. I've told my dad repeatedly that I have zero interest in being part of the family's illegal activities. Just because he doesn't listen doesn't mean I'm changing my plans.

I've let a few days pass to think about what to do. The best solution would be to get him into the program for recovery from gambling. I've set the charity up to help addicts recover and stay clean from gambling addictions, and it helps pay debts—to a point—if the case is determined to be a candidate for it. I could get him onto the list as a candidate, and we could handle this problem.

I would pay for it with my own money, but I know full well my father won't accept it. He'll see it as yet another refusal to get involved as heir to his crime empire, and he'll refuse the money. I can't get Alyssa's father out of it that way.

As I'm looking at what hoops I'll need to jump through if I want to help her father, there's a knock on the door. I look up to find Alyssa standing there, a stack of folders in hand and a nervous expression on her face. "What is it?" I ask.

"Your father's here, and he's demanding to see you. He doesn't have an appointment. Should I tell him to come through or to wait?"

I'm tempted to tell her to have him wait, but I know that'll just make this that much more obnoxious, so I sigh and nod. "Tell him he can come through. I have an hour free, but no more."

She smiles faintly and hurries out, her gait faltering. He probably makes her nervous. My father has that effect on people.

My father comes in a moment later and storms across to my desk. "Didn't I tell you to collect on Mr. Jones's debt, boy?"

I frown at him. "You didn't give a timeline, and as you can see, I'm a very busy man, what with running three different legitimate businesses. Send one of your lackeys if it's so important."

His jaw clenches, and he scowls at me. "I will do no such thing. You're going to collect it, and you'll do it soon."

"I have a conference to attend in a few days, and I'm a very busy man." I turn to my computer and open it to check my email. "Send someone else. I've made my stance clear. No criminal activity."

"You are sorely trying my patience, boy," he hisses. "This is not a discussion. It's an order. Take care of it and take care of it quickly."

I grind my teeth, frustrated. What did I have to say to him for him to understand that the answer was 'no' regardless of what he said or did? "I'm not going to help you with illegal activity. Unless you're willing to accept my money to pay his debts and to leave him alone permanently—by which I do mean ban him from your casino—you won't see a dime from my hand."

"You will not pay his debt with your own money. He owes it, and he'll pay for it. You'll collect it." My father's eyes narrow. "Why do you care so much about helping him, anyway? Why offer to pay his debts?"

I tense. My father's scented blood now, and I should've been more careful not to give him anything. The truth is, while I will never help him collect money from illegal gambling debts, I'm not one to offer my money to settle anyone's debts either. This isn't the first time he and I have been in a standoff. I've won the previous times. This time, he's cracking down harder, determined to win.

"Well?" He crosses his arms. "What is it this time?"

I glance at the door.

Wrong move. My father's gaze follows mine, and it lands on Alyssa at the front desk. He grins knowingly. "Alyssa Jones. His daughter, if I'm not mistaken."

I look away as if bored and return to my emails, but I'm focused entirely on what he's saying. If he goes after her to push me into this, he'll regret it. I have my connections, and I'm not afraid to use them to protect the people I've taken under my protection. "And? Get to the point, Dad. I have work to do."

"And she's very pretty." He leans in closer, putting one palm on the desk's polished surface. "I bet you're screwing her."

I clench my jaw by reflex and glare up at him. "Get out. I run my office with ethics. We're not screwing."

"Oh, but you'd like to. I can see it in your eyes. Do you think that'll convince her sleeping with the boss is a good idea?" He grins. "Oh, wait... you haven't told her about your family, have you? You haven't." He scoffs. "Good luck with that one, Romeo. Get me my money within the month, or her father's not the only one who'll pay."

I know better than to engage him on the threat, though I want to tear him to pieces for suggesting he might hurt Alyssa to get back at me for refusing to collect illegal money. I'm not going to do it, and I'm not going to let him hurt Alyssa either. I don't know if he'll try, but my stubborn refusal to rejoin the fold might push him to it. If it does, I'll be ready for it.

He shakes his head with a grimace. "Damn disappointment, boy."

Then he walks out, leaving me to stew. There's no way I'm collecting that money, but there's also no way I'm letting her get hurt. It'll happen over my dead body. She's mine, even if I can't admit it to her yet and can't act on it. Even if she doesn't know it yet.

***

I'M RELAXING AT home when my doorbell rings. Groaning, I push myself up out of my easy chair and go to answer. If it's my dad or one of his goons knocking to tell me he'll make me pay if I don't collect Mr. Jones's debt, I'm going to rearrange somebody's face. I can call it self-defense, probably.

Instead, I open the door to find Stewart on the other side.

My best friend holds up a pack of beer and grins. "Thought you might need some cheering up."

He's probably heard, through whatever grapevine he still has in his family and mine, that my father's pissed at me for refusing to come back to the fold. It's been an ongoing thing.

Stewart ditched his family a long time ago, severing all ties and taking with him the legitimate businesses he started while he was still in the family. We were best friends back then too, since our families have strong connections. At one point, his dad and mine arranged for Stew to marry my sister, Lucille, but that fell through when Stew abandoned the family to strike out on his own.

Someday, I'm going to do the same. He's an inspiration to me. I haven't yet because I'm still hoping to convince my father to take things legitimate with the business, but I know deep down it's unlikely he will.

"You heard he paid me a visit?"

"One of the guys in security at your firm mentioned it to a guy at mine. Anyway, thought you might want a drink."

I usher him in and take one of the beers before flopping onto one half of the couch. "Thanks, Stew."

"We both know you're not going to cave, so I'm here more as support than anything." Stew grabs one of the beers and takes up the other half of the couch with a sigh. "That and I hear Alyssa Jones is working for you now."

I tip my head back with a wry smile. "Have you, now?"

"How are you doing with that one?" Stew sounds amused. "Given you slept with her and all."

Frowning, I glance at him. "The truth?"

"When do I ever ask you to lie to me, Damien?" he drawls. "Yes, the truth."

"Okay." I heave a sigh and sit up to face him. "The truth is I'm interested in her, and I want more than just that one night. We... there was a moment in the office. I know she's interested in me too, but I feel like it'd be stupid to act on it"

"Why? If you both like each other...?" Stew cracks his bottle open.

"I just about screwed her right there in my office, Stew. What I want from her isn't healthy. Not for her. She's too innocent and sweet."

"She wasn't too innocent and sweet to sashay into your club that night and tease you until you snapped and took what you wanted from her."

He has a point, but I still can't. "Her family and the debt they owe mine is in the way too, Stew. If I take her, my father's going to use her against me."

"You think he won't do that anyway?" Stew laughs. "You're naive if you do. He probably already knows. She's safer if she's warming your bed if nothing else. Let people know she's yours, and a lot fewer will come after her for fear of angering you or your father."

"That's not going to stop my father," I mutter.

"No, but it'll still put you in a better position to protect her. Why are you hesitating?"

"Because she shouldn't be dragged into my world."

"She's already in it thanks to her father's gambling. Damien, you might be her one chance of coming out of it alive and whole on the other end if he's in bed with anyone else besides your father." Stew shrugs. "Not saying he is,

but there's a good chance. You know how these gamblers a
re."

I sigh, realizing he's right, and nod. "Okay. I'm trying to
figure it out. I just don't have a solution yet. And I'm not
sure she wants anything permanent with me. Admitting
she wants me isn't the same as saying she wants to be with me
."

Stew nods. "You're right. Figure it out fast, though, man.
This pickle with her family could drag her in faster than
you know what hit you."

And he's right. I do need to hurry because there's only so
much time to pull her out of the fray. I just need to figure
out a way to do it that won't leave her furious with me for
what my family's doing to hers if I want to hold on to her.
I do get myself into some of the worst pickles.

Chapter Seven: Alyssa

DAMIEN CALLS ME into his office a few days after his father's visit. I go hesitantly, the last time I was called into his office on my mind. If he's going to pin me to a wall and practically grind confessions out of me again, I'm not sure I wouldn't prefer being fired for insubordination. As much as it left me hot and incredibly turned on after he did it, it also left me wanting and knowing full well every reason why it can't ever go the rest of the way. Pure torture.

I go anyway because I still need this job.

"Sit," Damien directs me.

I do, biting my lip nervously.

He watches the motion like a hawk, a knowing smirk on his lips. "I need someone to go with me on my next conference trip. It starts next week, so we'll fly out over the weekend."

Immediately, my nerves disappear to be replaced with confusion and concern. I can't just leave. Timothy needs me, and I don't have anyone I can leave him with. My parents are always off doing something, so they can't be expected to take him, and I can't leave him with the daycare overnight.

Maybe Lucille?

Damien snaps his fingers at me. "Alyssa? We're in the middle of a conversation. Pay attention."

I wince and return my focus to him. "I don't know if I can on such short notice."

"Why? Is Sparky at home waiting?" he drawls. "You're my secretary, Alyssa. It's part of the job description."

"It's just... I expected I'd get a little more notice," I whisper, feeling bad.

"Did you have other plans?" The sarcasm is gone now.

"Well... I need to arrange for someone to... to house sit."

"House sit?" His tone drips with disbelief.

"Maybe Lucille could," I mumble. "I'll ask her and get back to you."

"Call her now. She's not usually busy."

"Oh, umm... okay. I'll just... my phone's at my desk."

He waves impatiently. "Go make the call and tell her whatever you need to. She'd probably be thrilled for an escape from my parents, anyway."

I bite my lip and get up, rushing out to my desk. I hope he doesn't decide to follow and listen in on this because I need to explain to Lucille the real reason for asking.

Not that she doesn't know about Timothy. She does, and she's known Damien was the father since she saw Timothy in the hospital. It clarified for her all the times I begged her not to tell Damien about my pregnancy. I swore her to silence, but she's been nagging me to tell him, and she's going to tell me now is the perfect time to do it.

She's more likely to wonder why I'm asking her. Godmother or not, she's not exactly the babysitting auntie type. I dial her and close my eyes, begging for her to pick up and just say yes when I ask.

"Lucille," her bright voice chirps.

"Lucille, hey!" I glance over my shoulder and spot Damien sitting in his office chair watching me like a hawk. I sag into my chair with relief. "I need you to help me out with something desperately, okay?"

"Oookay...." She drags the word out and then pops the gum she's chewing. "What's going on?"

"Damien is. He's demanding I go with him to his conference this upcoming week. We have to leave over the weekend and stay all week."

"And?"

Sometimes Lucille is a bit clueless. "And Timothy," I hiss.

"Oh!" Her voice drops. "Oh... you still haven't told Damien?"

"No! Are you kidding me? Good God, no. He'll kill me if I tell him now. He can't know. I need you to take care of Timothy for me. My parents aren't reliable enough to keep an eye on him. They'd probably forget they have to get him from daycare for me. Please, Lucille?" I don't hesitate to let a little bit of a whine creep into my voice, knowing she's a sucker for begging. "Please, I'll owe you big time, but I'm stuck. Damien didn't give me enough notice to sort out anything else."

Lucille groans. "The things I do for you. Fine. Go tell him you've got someone to cover whatever stupid excuse you gave him. Someday, you have to tell him the truth. I'm not going to keep doing this."

"Thanks, Lucille! I owe you. Like, big time." I hang up and run back to Damien's office with a bright smile. "Okay, it's sorted out. Just tell me when to be at the airport."

***

DAMIEN'S CHOSEN A suite, not a set of rooms. My bed is in a smaller room across the hall from his, but we're sharing the same living space, and I don't know what to do with it. It's driving me crazy.

We're three days into the conference and having him across the living room from me is slowly driving me crazy. He's not even trying to pretend to be professional either. I know I told him I wanted him, but he doesn't have to make it so damn hard to refuse to act on that desire.

He walks around in shorts and a T-shirt before bed and in the mornings, and he's not exactly shy about taking off outer layers when we get back to the hotel suite after a long day of conference speakers. The man is going to be the death of me.

So, when I wake up in the dark with a sob after a nightmare where Timothy is taken away from me by strangers—a dream I think is a subconscious manifestation of my fears of telling Damien the truth about our son—I don't think before I'm leaving the room and knocking on his door.

I wake up enough to realize what I'm doing right at the moment that he opens the door in shorts and nothing else. Gasping, I turn around, intending to run back to my room.

He grabs my wrist before I can. "Alyssa?"

"S-sorry," I manage. "I shouldn't have woken you up. I thought I heard a...." I rack my brain for a suitable reason I'd wake him up in the middle of the night. "A mouse. I thought I heard a mouse."

He tugs me into his room and presses me down onto the corner of his bed. "A mouse?"

I watch one corner of his full mouth tug up in a slight smile. He doesn't believe me, and after a delivery like that, why would he? "Umm. Yeah."

"There aren't any mice. We'd have heard it before now, love. Why were you knocking on my door?"

I can't stop staring at his biceps and pecs. The man is built like he spends hours in the gym every day. Hasn't lost any of the muscle he had last time I saw him in a state of undress like this. I swallow hard and meet his gaze. "Okay, not a mouse," I whisper. "I had a nightmare."

He nods. "I'm sorry you did."

"It was silly for me to wake you up. I can go back to bed now. Alone. I don't know what I was thinking."

He grabs my chin and gently presses my mouth closed. "You were thinking you were scared and wanted reassurance, and you were probably thinking you didn't want to sleep alone. Am I right?"

My cheeks warm, and I'm glad the light is dim in here from the night light at the sink in his small bathroom. "I... yeah."

"Then lie down." He climbs in on the other side of the bed where his things sit out on the nightstand and holds the blanket up for me to slide in with him.

I hesitate. This is a bad idea. It probably won't lead anywhere good. My rational thinking isn't in control at this hour, though, so I slide in next to him and curl up close, putting a hand on his chest.

He drops the blankets over us and slips his hand down to run it over my arm.

My arm is not where I want that hand, though, and suddenly my mind is back to that moment at his club when he threw me down on his bed and took what he wanted. My whole body tingles, and I shiver.

His hand glides a little lower, teasing along my fingers and brushing against my thigh where my shorts are too high to cover me.

A surprised gasp escapes me, and I tense, but I don't pull away.

Damien doesn't break eye contact. "I could distract you from whatever woke you up and sent you scurrying into my bed."

He does fit his namesake. He's pure sin and temptation when he speaks in that husky murmur, and I'm running out of strength to keep refusing.

He leans in and runs his nose up my neck to my ear. Then he nips my earlobe before soothing it by drawing the spot he'd bitten into his mouth.

I should push him away. My hand is on his chest in a perfect spot to do it, and I know he'll stop if I do. Instead, I close my eyes, my breathing becomes shallow. "Damien...." I don't know if his name is a plea for more or a plea to stop.

His breath tickles my neck. "Do you want this or not, Alyssa?"

I shiver. He already knows the answer. I want it so badly I'm barely able to remain still against him, but I shouldn't I really, really shouldn't.

"Alyssa." His tone is a warning now.

I swallow back a whimper. "You know already."

"I want to hear you say it." His nose trails along my neck, and then his lips find the hollow of my throat. "Do you want this or not?"

"I do," I whisper. "But I shouldn't—"

His teeth graze my throat, nipping at my skin.

I yelp and then groan as he soothes the sting with the tip of his tongue, moving it in slow, lazy circles. This is bad. So bad. But I'm no longer in any state to refuse what he's offering. I want it too badly.

He grabs my leg and pulls me closer, hitching my leg over his hip so that my legs are forced open, and my hips are flush against his. I whimper when he grinds into me, and I realize he isn't just doing this to provide a distraction. He wants me too, and the proof of that is pressing against me as he kisses a lazy trail down to the *v* of my pajama top.

His head lifts, and he tugs me up just enough to yank the shirt off me. I'm left entirely bare to his gaze, and he grazes his knuckles over my breasts with a wicked grin. "As beautiful as I remember," he murmurs.

I shiver. "Damien...."

"Yes, love?" He settles back down and slides his hands down my back to the back of my pants' waistband.

"This is a bad idea."

"Deliciously so, maybe," he agrees.

I'm about to say more, but he dips his head and trails his mouth along the tingling path his knuckles had followed. I arch into him with a startled groan. Maybe he's right. This might be a horrible idea, but it feels amazing, and what's the harm in it? "This is the last time, then," I manage.

He hums but doesn't say anything to confirm his agreement with the sentiment. Instead, he works my pants off and pulls my bare body into his.

He still has too much clothing on compared to me, but I know better than to rush him. Damien's the one in charge of this, not me, and while I know he'll always stop if I ask, I also know he makes it so worth it to surrender. So, I do.

I surrender to the moment. I'm going to regret this later, but right now, I decide I don't care what the consequences will be.

Chapter Eight: Damien

I PROBABLY SHOULDN'T have done what I did last night with Alyssa. I wake to find her limbs tangled with mine and her hair fanning across her pillow. My chest aches at the sight, and I realize that I wouldn't mind waking up to this sight every day for the rest of my life.

Man, I have it bad. I should be putting her and the mind-blowing sex from last night out of my mind for her own sake. But then again... Stew advised me to make her mine to protect her. Maybe he's got a point. It's not as though it would be a hardship.

Maybe she's the right one. I've never found a woman that made me want to settle down before, and this one... I haven't been able to let this one go since I kissed her behind the bleachers after her school play on her sixteenth.

Even then, I knew I shouldn't do it, but I had, and I never forgot how it felt to finally claim her mouth with mine. I know now, just as I did then, that I'm never going to forget how it feels to take her like I have, and I can't let her go. Maybe I should, but the truth is, I can't.

I'm ready to admit that to myself now. I haven't gotten as far in life as I have by lying to myself about my ambitions, needs, or reality.

Still, I can't shake the sense she's hiding something. I don't know what it is, but I'm not ready to claim her when I don't know what she's keeping from me. I need to know first, and I have a suspicion it has something to do with what she was hiding in her home and her need for a house sitter for this little trip.

Getting up, I leave her sleeping in bed and go to take a shower. A few minutes in, and no answers coming to mind, I hear the bedroom door open and then shut. She's woken up and left. Well, I suppose it was too much to hope she'd be brazen enough to join me in the shower.

Alyssa isn't the brazen type. She's shy, sweet, and sunshine to my bold, gruff, and grumpy. She won't join me in the shower unless she knows it's not going to upset me, and right now, I need to be alone to think, even if I don't want to be.

The best thing to do right now seems to be pretending that nothing's wrong. Once I sort this out, I can approach her about it, but I'm not going to worry her about my withdrawal until I know for sure what I need to confront her about. Besides, I don't want her stressed or on high alert. That'll just encourage her to keep secrets.

Twenty minutes later and feeling no better about the situation, I grimace and step out of the shower, toweling off and dressing quickly. Then I take care of my usual morning routine before stepping out into the common area.

She's curled up on the couch with a cup of coffee, already dressed and hair up. She applied a touch of makeup while I was in the shower. She didn't need twenty minutes to shower. Her hair's not wet, so she must have skipped that part of the morning.

"Coffee?" She waves to a steaming mug on the coffee table by her feet. "I thought you might want some given the night we... umm, you know."

I raise a brow. She still feels the need to avoid saying what I did to her last night. I grab the coffee and take a seat across from her, sipping it in silence.

She fidgets for a while before saying anything. "Damien, are you upset? I mean, you were up before me, and you're sitting far away compared to normal. I wasn't... I wasn't that bad, was I? I know I'm not exactly experienced, but I didn't think I was that bad...." Hurt colors her voice.

I shake my head. "Nothing's wrong. You were perfect, Alyssa."

"Then why do I feel like you're trying to distance yourself from me?" she asks quietly. "I mean, it was the last time, so we can just do things like we always do."

I have no intention of doing things like we always do, but I know better than to say that now. I must not be doing a good job of hiding how I'm feeling this morning, though, if she can sense it. Feeling out of my depth, I push back. "I said I was fine, Alyssa. When I say that, I mean it."

She wilts visibly into her spot on the sofa. "Okay. Sorry... I'll leave it be."

I didn't want to push her to this response, but I do want to be left alone on this one until I figure out how to pull a confession out of her. There's no sense putting her to the fire before I know what to ask and what buttons to push. "It isn't anything important. When it is, I'll tell you." I get up and take my coffee to the sink. "We should leave for the conference."

***

I SETTLE ON a way to find out what she's hiding at home a few days before the conference ends. Without telling her, I have our plane tickets switched. I wake her up at the crack of dawn with the news.

It's cruel. I know that. And I know she's probably going to be furious when she figures out my game. Just to make sure she can't alert Lucille; I remove the batteries from her phone.

It's a jerk move. I'm well aware, and I'm going to have to work to make amends later. I'll do whatever I need to to make it up to her, but right now, finding out what she's hiding is more important.

I want to go the next step with her, and I can't do that if I don't know what I'm dealing with. She's never going to tell me. I figured that out when she chose to admit her attraction to me over telling me what she'd been hiding at the house that day. I need to know before I can decide what's best when it comes to a relationship, though.

"Come on, love," I murmur, giving her shoulder a little shake.

She groans, the sound causing my stomach to tighten. It reminds me of the sounds she made for me a few nights ago after her nightmare sent her running to my arms.

"No time to sleep longer," I tell her.

When she still doesn't move, I scoop her up out of bed and drag her to the bathroom.

She comes awake a bit and starts to struggle. "Damien! Damien, put me down! What are you doing?"

I dump her into the tub and start stripping her. "We have a flight to catch, and I need you showered and dressed in ten. You weren't moving, so I'm getting you started on it."

Her confusion deepens. "What flight? There's another day left to the conference."

"I've decided to go home early. I'm done with my speaking engagement, and I'm tired of all the people. So, I changed the flight last minute last night."

Her gaze flicks from the faucet to me. "I can just change."

"You'll be grumpy without your shower. You've complained about being rushed every time I've made you skip it so we could leave on time. If I have to, I'll shower you myself."

I have her down to her bra and panties. She was too distracted to stop me, but now she snaps to attention, her cheeks blazing with color. "No, I'll do it myself! Get out! What the hell is wrong with you?"

I raise a brow and let go. "A lot. Which item on the list are you asking about?"

Her flush deepens. "Just get out. I'll be done in ten. My stuff's almost packed. Do I have time to pack, at least?"

"I can give you ten for that too," I tell her. "We just need to leave in about twenty. I'm going to hop into the shower myself."

I need it. Seeing her like this has me all kinds of turned on, and that's not at all appropriate at this moment, especially given what I'm going to do when we get back home.

Leaving her to her shower, I take a shower of my own, trying to take the edge off my need and my tension. I manage to at least take the edge off, so I'll be less grumpy and impatient. She doesn't need me to make the flight and getting through the airport an ordeal too.

The two of us manage to leave on time and get to our flight with time to spare. She doesn't talk to me the whole flight back to New York City. We've barely spoken since the morning after I took her to bed. I pushed her away, and she knew it. She's kept her distance since.

It's just one more thing I'll have to apologize for, but right now, I'm more focused on finding out what she's trying to hide so we can move on and figure out what the future looks like. The fact that my father's threat to use her to force me to cave to his demands is still hanging over my head only makes me more eager to claim her, so he knows, in no uncertain terms, that hurting her is declaring war.

When we touch down, I'm strung so tightly I'm afraid I might snap. "Come on," I tell Alyssa. "I'll drop you at yours."

"I left my car in the subway lot, though," she protests.

"I'll have someone come pick it up, Alyssa."

"But work tomorrow...."

I press a finger to her mouth, wanting to stop it with my own instead of a finger but knowing it's a bad idea. "Alyssa, we're home a day early. We're both taking a day off. Just let me take you home. You're exhausted, and I'm not."

It's true too. She looked ready to drop, and halfway through the flight, she fell asleep on my shoulder and didn't wake until the flight touched down.

Her shoulders sink. "Okay. Well, let me just make a call to Lucille so she knows I'm coming."

I wait while she pulls her phone from her pocket. She hasn't used it since last night because I kept her too busy, and she was too tired. She spent most of the flight fighting sleep until I quietly told her to just sleep if she needed to.

She tries to turn it on. "What the hell? I thought I charged it last night…. It won't turn on."

"Maybe the charger was broken?" I offer innocently.

She groans. "Maybe. Can I borrow yours?"

"It's dead. I used it up on the plane…" I shove my hands into my pockets. "I figured I have a GPS in my car, so I don't need it."

That's nothing like me at all, but I'm banking on her not knowing that.

She pales. "I need to call Lucille."

"It's fine," I tell her. "Lucille won't be upset we arrived early. I'm sure she's sick of house-sitting. Come on."

Given no other choice, she follows. Our ride to her place passes in long, tense minutes without a word exchanged between us. She's fretting about the situation.

When I pull into the driveway, she jumps out and makes for the trunk. "Okay, I'll just say goodbye now. Thanks for the ride, Damien."

I climb out and deliberately let the trunk stay closed. "I'll take your suitcase in for you."

"No, I can do it. Really." She wrestles with the trunk's lock.

I stride over and press the button on my key fob, grabbing the suitcase first. "Please. I insist."

Her shoulders tighten further, and she looks at me like she's equally ready to cry or fight me on it. "I can take it, Damien. Please."

The door opens as we're staring at one another in a silent standoff. I look away and see Lucille standing on the doorstep with an infant in her arms.

I stare in shock, unable to believe what I'm seeing. She has a baby. A baby who's the spitting image of me.

Chapter Nine: Alyssa

I WATCH THE shock and disbelief play across Damien's face, and my stomach drops. He's spotted Lucille, who is now trying to backtrack into the house, realizing her mistake. More importantly, he's spotted Timothy, and the look on his face says it all.

He turns to me, a thunderous expression replacing the shock. "I think we need to have a long talk, little girl," he snaps. "Let go of the suitcase handle now, and then go inside. I'll be along. If you lock me out, there is going to be hell to pay."

I flush because the thought was just crossing my mind when he issued the warning. Maybe there's still some way out of this? Maybe he hasn't realized Timothy's his and is just angry to discover I've been involved with someone else.

His gaze drops pointedly to my hand, and I realize I'm still holding onto the suitcase. I didn't even realize I grabbed it to begin with. When it registers, I let go of it like it's burned me and bolt for the house.

Lucille is inside. She stares at me wide-eyed as I dart into the house like a pack of wild dogs are on my tail instead of one very pissed-off man. "You think he knows?" she whispers, eyeing the door.

I burst into tears.

"Oh, jeez." Lucille hurries to put Timothy down in his little rocker by the sofa and comes back to me. "Hey, hon, it isn't that bad. Right? It's not. I mean, Damien has a temper, but he's never, ever hurt me or any other woman. Ever. He might yell a bit, but that's it. Even then, I don't think I've heard him yell before."

"He's going to hate me," I sob. "He'll probably fire me."

She wraps me up in a big, tight hug. "He will not. I won't let him fire you."

The thought of Lucille, who's tiny and petite, going up against her bear of a brother when he's in a grumpy mood makes me laugh past the tears. Then I'm crying again because as stubborn as she is, I know she won't win this if Damien's determined.

The door opens. I should get ahold of myself, but I can't seem to stop the waterworks.

"Lucille, go home," Damien says quietly.

She hugs me tighter, and I'm guessing she's giving him a defiant look. The two butt heads often enough that I'm pretty sure of my guess. I'm still crying on her shoulder and too afraid to look.

"Go home," Damien says.

He's still quiet, but his tone brooks no argument. Lucille pats me on the back. "Sorry, hon. Just be honest with him. I'm sure it won't be that bad. Damien." She marches up to him. "You hurt her, and I will make you pay. I have my ways, and you know it."

He gives her a flat look before locking gazes with me. I can't see him through the blur of tears very well, but I can tell his jaw is working and that he's upset.

Lucille leaves. It takes a long while before Damien moves. When he does, he walks right past me to the baby seat where Timothy is sleeping soundly despite the sobbing coming from me.

Seeing him move towards my baby snaps me out of my state. I sniffle and hurry to stop him, grabbing the sleeve of his shirt as if that might keep him away from Timothy.

"Let go, Alyssa." His voice is still that deathly quiet tone that makes me afraid a storm is coming. "I'm not going to hurt a defenseless infant."

Something about the way he says it lets a little of the knot in my chest unravel. I let go of his sleeve, letting my arm drop to my side.

He goes to the bassinet and kneels to look at my sleeping baby. Watching him look at his son for the first time leaves me equal parts terrified and enamored. His expression softens, and when he looks at me, there's a mix of pain, anger, and hurt in his gaze. "Whose is he?" he asks softly.

I look away. "Damien—"

"Whose?" he demands more firmly.

"I...."

"How old is he?" Damien stands and stalks towards me, backing me into the sofa. "Answer me, Alyssa."

My whole body warms even as a tremor of fear shoots through me. "He's about three months."

I can see the wheels turning as he does the math.

"You had him when you came home. Before the end of the semester."

The pain in his face as it hits him crushes me. I'd expected anger and a demand to take my son away, but I didn't expect the soul-crushing pain mingling with the expected fury in his gaze.

"He's mine."

It isn't a question. It's a statement. He knows the truth, and I know I can't keep it from him anymore. It's written all over my face anyway. "Yes," I whisper.

"He's what you wanted to hide that day I came over." He sounds equal parts angry and hurt. "Why, Alyssa? Why didn't you tell me? I would've helped."

"Because you said one night only, Damien. You told me no regrets once I told you yes." I wrap my arms around my middle. "Forgive me for thinking you wouldn't want me to keep him."

He goes back to the bassinet and drops to his knees, reaching out tentatively to touch Timothy's tiny fist. "How could...?" He swallows hard, his throat working. "Of course, I'd want him. You never even gave me a chance to make that choice, Alyssa."

"I figured the one-night stand bit made it pretty clear," I said bitterly. "I did what I thought was best."

"And you hid him from me when you came home. Why?"

"Because I was afraid you or your family might decide to take him once he was born. It can't be undone, and I know your family's rich. I was just—" My voice cracks. "I thought you'd take him away, and I'd never see him again."

He gets up and walks to the door. "You thought wrong. I didn't realize you thought I was a monster as well as a grump. Maybe I misjudged you in thinking that you knew you could trust me."

My voice is small when I answer. "I would've told you. Eventually. I just didn't know how to do it."

"I'll give you a hint. The way not to do it is this. Hiding it from me and refusing to tell me when I've given you every opportunity is the way not to do it." He shakes his head and opens the door.

"Where are you going?" I whisper.

"Home. I need some space because I'm far too angry at you to deal with this the right way right now. I'll see you at work on Monday."

With that, he stalks out, shutting the door behind him. I crumple to the floor beside the sofa and burst into tears. This isn't how I wanted things to be. And if I'm being honest, a part of me thought maybe something more could come of us. Whether that was a pipe dream or a possibility, I've ruined it now.

***

I'M AT HOME on Saturday when the doorbell rings. I jump up to answer it, hoping it might be Damien returning to tell me he wants to talk things out. When I open the door, though, it's my dad.

"Dad?"

He careens onto the top step of the stoop, and I catch a whiff of alcohol. He's been drinking. My dad doesn't do that often, so something must have driven him to it. Still, I can't have him in the house like this. He's not nice when he drinks.

"You have a connection with Damien." He slurs half the words, and he sounds angry. "I know it. You need to set up a meeting."

I push him out of the way a little so I can step onto the front stoop and shut the door. "Dad, I don't know what you're talking about, but you need to go. I can't set up a meeting. I told you already. Damien said you needed to set up the meeting yourself."

He scowls. "No. You set up the meeting... I need it. You have to set it up."

"Dad, I can't," I insist. "Please, just go home and sleep this off. Does Mom know you're here?"

That only gains me a scoff. "No. Not going anywhere until you"—he hiccups— "get me my meeting."

I don't know what to do. He's getting red in the face, and I can tell I'm about to have him melt down in fury if I keep telling him I can't do what he's asking. It's starting to scare m e.

He grabs my shoulder and drags me in close. "Get him on the phone. Set up the meeting. I need to talk to him. It's... urgent. Really urgent."

I wrestle free of him. "Okay, okay. I'll go inside and call him, Dad. Can you just wait here? I'll tell him he needs to come by."

It's not like Damien's likely to come, but at least if I make the call, my dad might leave me alone.

"No. Make the call here," he snaps, his cheeks bright red. "You always have your cell."

He's right, but my phone's still not working. It hasn't been since the airport. I pull the phone from my pocket and show him. "Dad, it's not working. Okay? I'll call him from the kitchen so you can watch me do it, okay?"

He shakes his head. "I'm coming with you."

I don't want him in the house, but I have a feeling he'll force his way in after me anyway. "Fine, but Timothy's asleep, so you have to be quiet."

He nods. I open the door and go inside, letting him follow. Then we head to the kitchen. Thankfully, I have Damien's business card on the fridge from when I had to call for an interview. I find it and give him a call, hoping he'll pick up. If he doesn't, there's no telling what might happen. The phone rings and rings and rings some more.

Then I get the voicemail tone, and my heart sinks. "Hey, Damien." My voice is shaking now as my father starts to scowl. "It's me, Alyssa. Umm, my dad's here, and he wants to meet with you now. He's... he's pretty upset about whatever business you two have. Please call me back."

I hang up and meet my dad's eyes, and I know that if Damien doesn't show up, my dad's not going to keep asking nicely.

Chapter Ten: Damien

I CAN'T BELIEVE she kept my son from me. She didn't just fail to tell me about him. She actively hid him from me. At any point, she could have told me about him. She chose not to.

I'm still fuming when I show up at Stew's place on Saturday morning. He has no idea why I asked to hang out, but I'll tell him when I see him. I need someone to vent to because even after tossing and turning all night on Friday evening after trying to drown myself in work all day, I don't feel any better. I'm still furious and hurt.

While I won't say that my dream has always been to be a father, I do want that white picket fence most Americans dream of. I want a wife, and in the last year or so, I've thought about kids too. If Alyssa had told me about her pregnancy back when she first found out, I would have told her to keep it. I would have helped, and I would have wanted it. She gave me no say, though.

Stew opens the door, takes one look at my face, and tugs me inside. "You look like a truck ran you over. What happened?"

"Alyssa happened." I clench and unclench my fists.

"Okay, let's sit down and talk this out. Start at the beginning, maybe?" Stew leads me to the living room and pushes me down onto the sofa. "What do you mean, Alyssa happened?"

I scrape my hands through my hair. "She has a kid."

Stew drops into the chair across from me with a whistle. "That's a real bombshell.... Whose?"

"Mine." I lift my head and meet his gaze. "It's my kid, and she didn't tell me."

His shock turns to understanding. "Hell...."

"Yeah," I mutter. "He's... he's perfect, Stew. Tiny, adorable... and she didn't tell me. She tried to hide him."

"Did you ask her why?" Stew asks.

"Yeah."

"And?"

"She told me she was afraid I'd take him. Damn it, Stew! Am I that much of a jerk that she had reasons to think I'd rob her of her son?" I look him in the eye. "For the love of God, tell me I'm not that awful."

Stew grimaces. "You can be pretty grumpy, but I don't think you're that bad."

"You want to know the worst part?" I ask morosely.

"Not sure, but you're going to tell me anyway, so let's have it."

"Lucille knew too. She told Lucille, and they both kept it from me." I clench my hands on my knees. "I want to be a part of his life, but I don't know if she wants me involved. She went out of her way to hide him from me. I only found out because I pulled strings to get home early to find out what she didn't want me to know."

Stew whistled again. "Does she know that, man? Because that's not exactly the sort of behavior that makes a woman think, 'Hey, prime father material, right there.'"

I glare at him. "I'm not an idiot, Stewart. I didn't tell her, and she thinks I just got sick of the conference. I do need to find a way to replace her phone's battery. I stole it so she wouldn't call Lucille and alert her."

"Damn." Stew shakes his head. "That's messed up. May I recommend that you never do that again if you do want things to work out with her? Or any woman."

I wince. He's probably right on that one. "Recommendation noted. But what do I do?"

"You talk to her. Tell her you don't want to take the baby but that you do want a part of his life. See what she says and figure it out from there. You can't let your anger at her for keeping secrets prevent you from working things out. She had her reasons, and you might not understand them, but she was trying to protect her son, Damien. You do have to try to understand that." Stew clasps his hands between his knees. "Don't make her feel like a terrible person for that."

Sighing, I try to let go of the anger enough to see it from her perspective. Stew is right. If I'm going to make this work, and if I love her enough to stick around even though she's lied to me, I have to realize she didn't lie to me because she wanted to hurt me. She lied because she wanted to protect her baby, and she was right to do that even if he didn't need protection from me. "Okay, thanks, Stew. I'll think about it and then talk to her. Now, how about we watch some football and unwind?"

***

WE'RE IN THE middle of a football game when my phone goes off. I ignore it until it beeps to tell me a voicemail has been left. When I feel that buzz in my pant pocket, I get up to see what's going on.

I unlock my phone to find a missed call from a number I don't recognize, and I pull up the voicemail.

"Hey, Damien." Alyssa's voice comes through the speaker, shaking like a leaf in the wind. "It's me, Alyssa. Umm, my dad's here, and he wants to meet with you now. He's... he's pretty upset about whatever business you two have. Please call me back."

My blood goes cold. I didn't think her dad would hurt her, but men can do crazy things when pushed to the brink. If she's that scared, he must be doing something.

I shove my phone into my pocket, my mind going to my son and whether he's safe. "Stew, I have to go."

Stew joins me in the kitchen with a worried frown. "What's going on?"

"That was Alyssa. Her father's harassing her. She sounds scared. I'm driving over there now."

He nods. "Keep me updated. I hope everything's okay."

I do too. I grab my keys and race outside. The drive from Stew's apartment to hers at this hour on a Saturday will take ten minutes, assuming traffic isn't worse than usual. It's not long, but I feel the seconds racing by as I drive it.

I've never known fear like this. My heart's racing, and I'm hurrying along the route as quickly as I dare with what traffic is about. My mind keeps looping over every possible scenario, and I worry that he might hurt her.

Alyssa's father is a weak, cowardly man. I know he loves his wife and daughter, but it hasn't stopped him from gambling away all their money or taking on debts to men like my father to pay off his gambling losses. I never thought he would hurt anyone, but what if I'm wrong? Why else would Alyssa sound scared?

When I pull in, his car is in the driveway, but I don't see any sign of him or her. I rush up the steps after parking and bang on the door. "Alyssa?"

She answers almost immediately, and her shoulders sag with relief. "Thank God. Damien, he's drunk, and he's angry.... Angry and scared. He keeps mumbling about owing people and people coming after him. Please... please, just get rid of him." She sounds close to tears.

I nod. No matter how angry I am at her, I don't like seeing her scared or upset. "Okay. Just wait here, okay?"

She drops onto the porch's swing and curls her feet under her.

I don't have time to worry about her. She's safe for now, even if she is shaken up, and I have damage control to do. Going inside, I find her father standing at the counter.

When he spots me, he straightens. "Thank God. You showed up, you piece of work! You and your father are making my life hell. My wife's worrying, and I've had to go to my daughter twice now to try to meet with you."

I cross my arms and stare him down. "You've terrified your daughter. She's out on the porch nearly in tears, and you're in here calling me names. If I wanted to make your life hell, I'd let you suffer the consequences for your gambling by collecting the money you can't pay and letting his men break a few bones. Fortunately for you, I have morals my father doesn't have, and I won't get involved in it."

"So instead, you'll just watch him crush me," her father says bitterly. "You know, I thought with your kid in the picture, you might have mercy and not put Alyssa through watching me ruined or even killed. You know that when you don't collect, they'll go after her and my grandson, don't you?"

Then her parents knew whose baby Timothy was before I did. Yet one more betrayal, but I don't have time to think about that. Stew's given me good advice on it, and I'll follow it. For now, I have this drunk to deal with. "Look, you need to go home and sleep this off. You'll regret this later if you don't. I've never known Alyssa to be frightened of you, but she is right now, so if I were you, I'd go before you can make it worse."

"Look, I just wanted her to bring you here so we could talk. I need help, and I thought you might show some leniency. I know he's told you to collect."

I stalk over to him, grab him by the shoulder, and propel him toward the door. "I can't help you yet. When I have decided if I'm going to and how, exactly, to do it without alerting my father that I paid it for you, then I'll be in touch. I know where to find you."

He deflates at that and lets me shove him through the door past Alyssa. At the bottom of the porch steps, he turns to look at Alyssa. Her expression is heartbroken and frightened, and he seems to realize he's at fault. "Alyssa, sweetheart, I'm sorry... I'm sorry. I shouldn't have scared you like that."

I pull my wallet out and give him a few bills. "Get a taxi or an Uber, Mr. Jones. Your daughter doesn't need to get a call about an accident involving you due to drunk driving."

He takes the cash with a grimace and manages to make it down the driveway to the sidewalk. I watch him pull his phone out and hold it to his ear a moment later. Satisfied he won't be driving home himself, I turn to Alyssa.

She's in tears watching him. "I'm sorry, Damien. I didn't know who else to call."

I nod. "We have things to sort out. Right now, though, I want to hold my son. Can I do that?"

Her expression turns wary.

"Alyssa," I murmur, crouching in front of her. "He's mine too. Not just yours. He's ours. I don't want to take him away. But I do want to be around and be a part of his life. Please?"

She bites her lower lip and eyes me for a moment. Then she licks her lips quickly and nods. "Okay. But just for a bit, and I'm not telling you I'm going to give you full license to hang around all the time."

We'll have to deal with that one later because I'm not going to be denied the ability to see my son, but for now, I nod in agreement.

We head inside, and she leads the way up the stairs to the room next to hers, which she's converted into a little nursery. The baby is lying there, wide awake and starting to whimper.

She picks him up. "Hi, Timothy," she murmurs.

"That's his name?" I come closer and look at the baby over her shoulder. He has my eyes, but his nose is all Alyssa's, cute and pert.

"Yeah." She eyes me hesitantly. Then she slowly hands me my son.

I gather him up in my arms, memories of holding my little sister when she was a baby coming to mind. I can't believe I missed his birth and the chance to hold him during the first hours of his life in the world outside of his mother's womb. "Hi, Timothy," I whisper to the baby.

He grabs my finger and giggles a little.

"Yeah, hi, kiddo. I'm your daddy. It's nice to meet you."

When I look up, I find Alyssa watching us with tears in her eyes.

"You aren't going to take him away, are you?" she whispers.

I smile and draw closer, bringing her to my side and cradling Timothy in one arm between us. "I'm not."

Chapter Eleven: Alyssa

THE THINGS MY father let slip when he came over drunk and angry have been bothering me for days since the encounter. I heard some of what he said to Damien through the thin walls of the house, but I didn't catch all of it. Only enough to know that Damien knows something, and my dad thinks he can help.

I need answers, and I know that Damien can give them to me. The trouble is, I don't think he wants to. Still, I'm hoping I can wheedle the answers out of him. It won't happen at work, so I make a trip out to his house in the suburbs.

It's the weekend, so I'm hoping I'll catch him at home. Luck is on my side. When I ring the bell, he comes to answer the door almost immediately.

"Alyssa?" He looks confused. "What are you doing here?"

"Can I come in?" I hook a thumb over my shoulder at my running car, knowing what I'm about to point out is a bit of a bribe. "I brought Timothy along."

Damien's smile catches me off guard. He rarely smiles over anything, and it's at odds with his usual grumpy demeanor. At the same time, I know I have to see more of it. The smile leaves my whole body on fire and melting. "Bring him in. Do you need help?"

"I can get him."

He's going to be angry at me in a few minutes, I have no doubt, and I don't want to feel bad for taking advantage of his good mood.

Jogging back to the car, I make quick work of getting Timothy's car seat out of the car and shutting off the vehicle. Then I come back to the door.

Damien reaches out and takes the car seat without asking, relieving me of the heavy, unwieldy object. I let him, but I keep a close eye on him as he carries Timothy inside.

We walk through the austere, crisply decorated halls of his house to a living room that looks pristine and barely lived in. He sets the car seat down next to an armchair and bends down to coo at Timothy, who laughs and coos back.

Seeing him with our son does funny things to my insides. It leaves me feeling warm and fuzzy, but it also leaves me inexplicably turned on and needy. He's so gentle with Timothy, and I've never seen him like this. I like this side of him.

When I take a seat in the armchair next to Timothy's car seat, he looks up. "What did you come about? I'm sure you didn't come out here just to let me spend some time with my son."

"I didn't," I admit. "I came about my father."

His jaw tightens. "What about him?"

"I overheard bits of your conversation, enough to know he's in trouble. It's about money, isn't it? Damien, what's going on?"

He rises and comes over to stand between my knees, bending over to put his hands on either side of my head. "Alyssa, I told you before when you asked—"

"He's gambling again, isn't he?" I press my palms to his chest, but I don't push Damien away. "You know something, Damien. Or he thinks you do. Why?"

He dips his head so that our foreheads touch, and his breathing is heavier than usual. "We aren't going to talk about this. You're better off not knowing what's going on, Alyssa. Your father is a grown man, and you're not dependent on him. His problems are his own, and when he chooses to tell you, then you can ask whatever questions you want."

I scowl up at him. "But you're not going to answer those either, even if he does tell me, are you?"

He tips my chin up and looks me in the eye. "I'm trying to protect you."

"I never asked you to."

"I'm doing it anyway. For you and for our son. Don't fight me on this, Alyssa."

Anger rises. Whatever's going on with my dad is already affecting me, and I don't believe that this is the end of it. It's clear Damien doesn't see it that way and isn't willing to discuss it further, though. I shove at his chest. "Let me up. I'm leaving."

He backs off, tucking his hands into his pockets. "Fine. I'm sorry if you're upset about it, Alyssa, but I'm not going to budge on this, and you need to understand that. You need to understand—"

"I understand just fine," I snap. "You think it doesn't matter to me and that it doesn't affect me. You're wrong, but

I can see I won't get anywhere trying to reason with you, so I'll see myself out. I'll see you Monday."

With that, I storm back the way we came and out the front door. I put Timothy's car seat back into its place in the car, get in, and pull out of his driveway. If he won't give me the answers I need, then I'll speak with my parents myself and get the truth out of them.

***

I START WITH my mother. If my father's gambling again or worse, she might know. My father doesn't tell her those kinds of things, but she figures them out. He's not as good at hiding things as he thinks he is.

I knock on the kitchen door of their little, broken-down house in one of the poorer sections of the New York suburbs. My mom opens the door right away and smiles broadly when she sees me and Timothy.

"Darling! You should have phoned. What brings you out this way?"

"Mom, can we talk?" I ask.

"Of course." She ushers me inside and shuts the door behind me. "What's going on?"

I sit at the table and set Timothy's car seat on the floor by my feet. "It's about Dad. He's been acting weird. He showed up at my place drunk a few days ago, and he said some stuff about owing money. He thinks Damien Darino can help him. What's going on, Mom?"

My mother sits down at the table with a heavy sigh. "I don't know, honey. I mean, I think he's been gambling again, but I haven't had a straight answer from him, and he swears he isn't anymore. I don't know why he'd think Mr. Darino could help him."

A sigh escapes me. I guess it was too much to hope this would be easy.

"Why don't you talk to him yourself, sweetheart?"

"Maybe because he freaked me out when he was drunk?" I scrub my hand over my face. "And I'm still a bit angry he showed up at my place like that."

"If you want answers, he's the only one who has them here, Alyssa. He's in the workshop. You can leave Timothy with me until you're ready to go home. If you like, you're welcome to stay for dinner."

"I can't. I need to go home and get to bed early today for work tomorrow. Thanks, Mom." I get up and leave her with Timothy to go talk to my dad.

I walk across the backyard to the small shed he uses as a workshop. He's back there tinkering with the old car he's had since I was a kid. "Hey, Dad," I call as I approach.

He slides out from under the car and gets up, coming to greet me. "Hey, kid. Listen... about a few days ago, I wasn't myself. I shouldn't have said what I did, and I'm sorry."

The apology is nice, but I know he'll do it again if he drinks too much. It's one of the few situations where I don't like my dad. "It's fine, Dad. I came to talk to you about what you said while you were there. I'm worried about you."

He glances around with a frown. "About me? Hon, I appreciate it, but I can handle myself."

I cross my arms. "Then why did you come to my place drunk and threatening me if I didn't get you a meeting with Damien?"

He shifts his weight from one foot to the other and laughs shakily. "I was drunk, Alyssa. I didn't know what I was doing."

"Are you gambling again, Dad? You said you owed money, and from what I could catch, it sounded like you thought Damien could help you with the problem."

"It was nothing, sweetheart. Nothing at all. I'm not gambling again, and I just wanted to talk to Damien about a

loan his father gave me. Nothing is going on. Nothing at a
ll."

It doesn't sound like anything at all. Why isn't he willing
to tell me what's going on? Has Damien paid him to keep
quiet?

More importantly, what would Damien's father have to do
with this? Why would he lend my father money to begin
with? Damien's father is wealthy, and they grew up in a
practical mansion with twenty-four-seven guards posted
around the property on the Hudson. It's a beautiful, high-
ly expensive bit of property, and I'd always been envious of
Lucille for getting to live there. I just couldn't imagine my
dad being connected to Mr. Darino in any way.

"Why would Mr. Darino give you a loan? He's not in the
banking or finance business, is he?"

I thought my father couldn't be more uncomfortable than
he was a few minutes ago, but those questions have him
sweating and glancing around again.

"Dad?" I asked. "Why?"

"It doesn't matter. Nothing is going on. It's not something
for you to worry about."

"Then why go to Damien?"

"I thought he could talk to his father." My dad's tone is impatient now. "I needed an extension to pay this month. It doesn't matter, kid. I can handle it, and besides, you're living your own life making good money now. You don't need to worry about me or my finances."

"I worry anyway."

What worries me most right now, though, is why he won't talk. Did Damien pay him not to tell me what's going on? If so, I'm beginning to think I've gotten into bed with a man who's not what I thought he was, and that worries me even more.

"I know, and I appreciate it, but I'm telling you, there's nothing to worry about this time." My dad cleans his hands off on a rag. "Are you staying for dinner?"

I shake my head. "Not tonight. I'm going to head home now. I just drove out to check on you and Mom and to talk to you both about what happened at my place."

He looks guilty at that. "I am sorry about that, you know."

"I know, Dad." I sigh. "Look, I have to get home. Just... please be careful with whatever it is you're doing."

"Always, kid."

My heart sinks. I know that's not true, and whatever he's gotten himself into this time is bad. I can tell by how dodgy he's being about it. I just don't know yet if it's something I should worry about or not.

Chapter Twelve: Damien

ALYSSA IS GETTING too close to sorting out what's going on with her father for comfort. This isn't the first time she's had to find out what is going on with him and sort it out. That makes me angry, but my bigger concern for now is what she's going to learn if she keeps digging. I don't want her to know what her dad's gotten mixed up with for her own safety and health.

She doesn't believe me on that, of course. It's going to be a big problem, and I know I need to do something about her father's debts before it can become a worse problem than it already is.

Stew's set to come over for a game or two of pool for the evening, so I decide I'll ask him when he shows up. It's been weighing on me, and I'm no closer to a solution. Stew was in my position with his own family a few years back, and he'll understand how I feel about my dad's demands, the danger posed to Alyssa, and the problem of finding a way to pay the debts so that he won't be a target anymore.

When the bell rings, it's a relief because it pulls me from my bleak musings. I answer gladly and find Stew standing on the other side with a bottle of wine. I pull him in and shut the door. "Good. You're here. You might want to pour some of that wine."

"Another crisis?" Stew strolled into the kitchen and found the ice bucket I'd set up for the wine. He always brought wine with him when he came to visit. "With Alyssa, no doubt?"

"Not really *another* one," I mutter. "The same one only exacerbated. Her father's debts have come due, he can't pay them, and my father's demanding I collect them. He let a few things slip with Alyssa around, and now she's demanding answers.

"What are you going to tell her?"

I scoff and head for the living room.

He follows. "I'm serious. What will you tell her?"

"I don't need to tell her anything. This isn't her burden to bear. What I need to do is make sure my father's paid back for the money her father owes so he won't go after Alyssa or my kid."

Stew grimaces and flops into a chair. "That's not a good idea, probably. At some point, she'll probably figure it out, and then you'll be in trouble because she'll be angry that you didn't tell her the truth."

"Look, I can't tell her the truth. It's dangerous, and I don't want her exposed to this."

"She's already exposed just by being his daughter, Damien, and you know it. You need to run damage control is what you need to do. Pay the debts quickly if you're going that route so your woman can be free of it."

"That's just it. I can't get the charity involved in time to pay it off and get him into rehab by the deadline my father demands. Plus, it goes against every fiber of my being to hand that man any money at all. He'll use it to fund the family crime operations."

"Your father isn't a pretty man to behold when angry or out of patience. I recommend you sort out some way to pay him and fast. And don't do it in a way he can trace back to you."

"Oh, thanks, Stew. I hadn't thought of that," I drawl. "He's refusing to accept anything that doesn't end with the full sum paid up in a few weeks, at most. You know he gets what he wants. He's threatened to drag Alyssa into this too."

Stew scowls. "That's low. If I were you, I'd pay it off before it's too late."

I realize he's right. If I don't find a solution somewhere fast, things are going to go sideways, and Alyssa may pay the price. There's no time to waste finding a way out of this, and I can't keep putting it off thinking it'll sort itself out because it won't.

***

I'M IN MY office trying to sort out what I can do to help Alyssa's father when the office door opens. My father barges in as I look up to tell Alyssa I'm not to be disturbed. I scowl when I see him. "I have a secretary to set appointments and announce visitors, Dad," I grumble.

"Make time," he snaps, stalking in. "You're delaying in collecting the debt that's due, and I won't continue waiting around without payment."

"I told you," I say coldly. "I'm not going to help you collect on an illegal debt like this. I'm not going to get involved in anything illegal. If you haven't sorted that out by now, I don't know what else to say to you."

"I don't want you to say anything else. I have something I want you to do! You have responsibilities to this family, Damien." He paces the room. "You can't abandon them just because doing something a little illegal makes you uncomfortable."

"It is illegal, Dad. There's no such thing as a *little* illegal. It either is or isn't legal. In this case, it isn't. I'm not getting involved to help you out with it." I turn back to my computer. "Now, if you'll excuse me, I have work to do."

He scoffs. "Fine. If I can't get through to you the nice way, we'll do it the hard way. That cute, sweet little girl who's friends with Lucille.... What's her name? Alyssa." He grins wickedly. "If you don't want to collect her father's debt, fine. I'll send someone else, but Damien?"

I glower at him. "Leave her out of this."

"I'd love to, but if I have to send someone else, I can't promise how they'll handle it. They might go after her to get his cooperation, and really, I couldn't blame them for it." My father's gaze is sharp and cunning. "If you don't want to collect, I can't promise they won't hurt her. Maybe they'll even screw her before they hurt her or kill her to get their point across to him. My men aren't known for being the kindest with women."

That's a fact I know all too well. Growing up in that household, I saw plenty of terrible things that left me scarred and wanting no part of the work my father did. I knew exactly how wicked and dreadful the people who work for my father are, just as I know how evil he is.

"I said to leave her out of this," I growl.

"I can't if you bring her into it by continuing to resist and refuse me, Damien." My father spreads his hands in a placating gesture. "So, what'll it be?"

I swallow hard, seeing my window to protect Alyssa closing. If I don't find a solution, it could very well mean her death. "Give me time."

"You've had enough time." My father strode to the door. "The debt payment hits my desk by tomorrow evening, or I'll put someone else on the task and make you watch whatever they choose to do to your little pet in their efforts to collect what you should've."

Then he's gone, and I realize I'm shaking. If I don't find a solution, I'm going to lose her, and that's not acceptable. I have to find a way out of this before it's too late.

Chapter Thirteen: Alyssa

I TRIED TO stop Damien's father from barging into Damien's office, but he's through before I can interpose myself between him and the door. When the door slams shut in my face, I take it as my cue to go back to my desk.

The argument that ensues between them is muffled by the door and the glass windows of the office, and I only catch bits and pieces. They're arguing about debts and money. Something about Damien collecting a debt.

I don't catch anything else, but what I've heard worries me. It doesn't seem related to my dad's situation, but something about it niggles at me and won't let me rest easy.

As soon as Damien's father stalks out of the office and disappears onto the elevator, I get up to go to Damien. Perhaps he'll answer my questions about this. More importantly, I should apologize for letting his father through without an appointment.

I push open the door.

Damien looks up and groans. "What now? Can't I be left in peace to work?"

"Sorry," I murmur. "I just wanted to check you don't need anything and... sorry for letting him through. He didn't give me a chance to stop him."

He sighs and pinches the bridge of his nose. "You couldn't have stopped him anyway, love. He's bigger than you, and he wasn't going to take no for an answer. I'm glad you didn't try."

I flush. "I still feel bad... Damien sounded angry. I mean... is something wrong? Are you in trouble? I heard something about debts."

Damien stands and comes to where I'm hovering in the doorway. He pulls me inside gently and closes the door. "You may as well come in if you're going to distract me anyway. Why do you want to know about this so badly?"

"I don't know," I mumble. "I was just worried about you."

He presses me close to the door, glancing at the shades, which are closed on both windows into the main office. Then he pushes his hips against mine with a smirk. "Worried about me, sweetheart? I'm flattered, but there's nothing to worry about."

His fingers play lazily along my bare arms, leaving me shivering and struggling to focus on the conversation. "There's nothing to worry about?"

His head dips, and he buries his face in my neck. His teeth scrape over the juncture between my neck and shoulder, and then his tongue laves over the spot to soothe the sting. "Nothing at all. I can think of better things for you to think about, anyway, love."

I whimper, trying to force my mind back to what I wanted to ask. He's doing an excellent job of distracting me, but I still feel like something more is wrong. "Damien, please... he sounded angry."

He bites me harder this time.

I squeak, and then I moan as he sucks on the spot he bit. This is getting well out of hand.

"That was a cute sound," he murmurs against my neck. "Should I try to get you to make more of those noises?"

A shiver racks my body. "We... this is too much. Not in the office."

"So, if I wanted to take this further elsewhere, you'd do it?"

That isn't what I meant at all, but I also don't have the presence of mind to refuse him right now, either. We really shouldn't be doing this.

He slips the shoulder of my blouse off, exposing the swell of one of my breasts, and makes his way down from my shoulder with his mouth. "Then come to my place tonight for drinks. You can bring Timothy. I have room enough for him to sleep in his car seat or on the floor of the bedroom while we have a little fun."

I gasp. "Damien! He's a baby. We can't... we can't do that with him in the room."

"Can I tell you a secret?" he whispers against my skin.

"What?" I whisper back.

"I bought him a crib and had it put in yesterday. I wanted to have a place for him. I was hoping you'd bring him over more often, maybe." He stills against me. "Is...? That wasn't too much, was it?"

I shake my head, squeezing my eyes shut. He's making it impossible to keep things to the few nights we've had, and after that, I don't want to say no anymore.

"Then will you come for drinks? He can sleep in the crib. I'll set it up before we get too tipsy."

I swallow hard and nod. "Okay... I'll come over for drinks, and I'll bring the baby."

Maybe in the process, I can drag the truth out of him about my father. Maybe the night can be productive in more ways than just spending time with Damien. A girl can hope.

***

DAMIEN IS FINISHING up the crib, which is a solid oak affair that I'd never be able to afford myself. I'm busy putting together the cocktails at his request while he finishes the crib and puts Timothy down to sleep. I was reluctant to leave my son, but I doubted Damien would hurt him, so eventually, I agreed.

I'm just putting out glasses and mixing up a few cocktails when I feel strong arms snake around my middle. I didn't hear Damien come downstairs, but he must've finished the crib.

"You know, I kind of like having you here in my house like this." Damien trailed his mouth down my neck. "It's nice."

I shiver. "Do you want a drink? I made cocktails. Is Timothy still sleeping?"

"I got him settled into the crib for you. He barely woke up, so he must be pretty tired. Don't worry about him anymore, love. He's fine."

I'm grateful for the help. It was kind of him to do that instead of leaving it for me to do, and I realize that Damien might make a better father than I initially thought.

He reaches around me and collects one of the cocktail glasses. "This looks good. I haven't had one of these in ages."

"What do you usually drink?" I turn to face him.

He grins. "Whiskey. Neat or on the rocks, but not mixed with anything else."

"Oh. If you'd prefer—"

He takes a swallow of his drink and slips an arm around my waist, pulling me into him and then kissing me. I whimper and open for him when he prompts me to deepen the kiss.

The taste of the cocktail and some of the cold liquid I'd prepared slides over my tongue and burns its way down my throat. Then his tongue is on mine, and I forget all about the drink.

He groans and tangles one hand in my hair, setting aside his cocktail. His free hand slides down my body to my hip and then up to splay below my rib cage, dangerously close to cupping my breast.

I whimper. This isn't what I planned on. "Damien, wait... wait, I had a question."

He pauses, but his hand inches closer to my breast. "What?"

"I know you know what's going on with my father. Please, just tell me. He won't tell me, and I'm worried."

Damien's grip on my hair tightens, and he pulls my head back to nip at my throat before meeting my gaze again. "We're not going to discuss this. I have other things I want to do right now, and I told you, it isn't my place to tell you. You don't need to know at this moment, and I'm not going to tell you."

I bite my lip, meeting his gaze. "Damien... I just want to know I don't need to worry."

"You don't. It will work out."

I think he believes it will, or at least, wants to. His gaze is steady, and he looks determined. "Because you'll make it work out?" I ask quietly.

A growl rumbles through him. "If need be. Alyssa, stop worrying about it. Stop thinking about it. Just agree to let me distract you from it all and put it out of your mind."

I shiver. That's all I want. To know I can leave it to him or someone else to deal with. But I'm afraid, and I don't know if I can trust him that way yet.

His fingers play along the column of my throat, and he leans in to whisper in my ear. "You're going to have to trust someone at some point, love. I'd like to think I'm a good first start."

Closing my eyes, I wonder if he's right. It doesn't matter if he is or not, though, because I do trust him enough to let him distract me and have me, at least. I think I can trust him with this too, if he's involved. "Okay," I whisper.

"Okay?"

I nod.

He smiles at me, a genuine, warm smile that I see so rarely on him. Then his fingers close lightly around my throat, and his mouth is on mine again. His hand at the top of my rib cage slides up to cup my breast.

I groan. He's so good at distractions. This time, I don't bother to tell him it'll be the last time. I've said that every time, and it's never been true.

His answering groan tells me I'm not the only one who's losing myself to this. I tip my head back, bracing myself against the counter behind me as he presses into me gently. His hands drop to the hem of my blouse, and he undoes the buttons before sliding it off me and staring like he wants to devour me.

A shiver works its way through me again. "Damien," I whisper. "Please."

His gaze snaps up to mine, hungry and eager. "Upstairs to the bedroom. Now."

I spin around, leaving my blouse with him, and dart upstairs. I can hear him following, though he doesn't seem to be in any hurry. Then we're in the bedroom, and he has me on my hands and knees. He unzips my skirt and tugs it down. Then he strips off my undergarments too, leaving me entirely exposed to his gaze and shivering in the cooler air of the bedroom.

"This won't be gentle tonight," he murmurs. "I'm going to make you forget about it for tonight, and gentle isn't going to do that."

My arms tremble, and I quiver as he touches me. He's already making me forget, but I'm not going to argue with him. He pulls me back against him, and I'm lost in the moment, grateful for anything that will let me forget my troubles for a while.

He trails his fingers down my spine to my lower back and then over my legs. His warmth seeps into me, and I feel the cold I've been living with since my father showed up at my house drunk starting to fade. His fingers trail down to my inner thighs, and I fight the urge to clamp my legs closed at the sudden wave of sensations.

That draws a chuckle from him, and he leans into me, his breath tickling my ear and neck. "Need something, sweetheart?"

"You said it wouldn't be gentle."

"I did." He delivers a pinch to my inner thigh. "But I didn't say you'd get to set the pace or that there wouldn't be any teasing. I'm trying to distract you, remember?"

I close my eyes with a moan. "Please, Damien...."

His mouth closes on the side of my neck, hot and wet. I can't help the shiver that it elicits, and he laughs at the reaction.

However maddening the teasing is, though, he's most certainly good at distraction. I can't think of anything besides where his hands and mouth are, and for once, I don't feel like I'm going to regret this later.

Chapter Fourteen: Damien

I'M TRYING MY best not to think about how good it felt to tangle Alyssa's limbs with mine and drive her to distraction all over again this morning when my office's phone rings. Frowning, I glance at the number and pick up. "Damien Darino."

"Damien, it's Marcello."

"Marcello." I sit up a little straighter.

Marcello is my contact in the Giovanni family. They're technically allies, but we're in constant competition with one another, and the peace between us is uneasy. I like to keep tabs because my connection to the Darino family means I could be at risk, and it pays to know what's going on even if I refuse to get involved.

"Hey, man, I thought you should know what's going on here. Word is on the street that Alyssa Jones works for you now, and her pop owes my don a lot of money."

I drop my face into my hand with a low groan. "Of course he does. How much?"

"Sixty grand. It's not a little debt." Marcello clears his throat. "Look, I thought you deserved a heads-up, but the Giovanni family's going to go after him for it. He hasn't been paying. Probably can't, but all the same…."

That's going to get ugly fast. I've been keeping my dad at bay for now, but he's wearing thin on patience too, and the Giovannis don't have anything to restrain them. "Is that it?"

"No. They're planning to go after his wife and daughter to make him pay up. Sorry, man, but they're not going to let him continue dodging payments. They know you have a connection to the Jones family through Alyssa. They found out about the kid, and they know you're likely to step in. They also know you're on the out with your father, so they know they can put pressure on you without starting a war.

I curse under my breath and rake my fingers through my hair. "How soon? And what do you mean, put pressure on me?"

"I don't know that much. Just that they're planning. The word is that they're going to go after his daughter and wife, but not the kid. I've been told to tell you that if you get involved in protecting either of them, they're going to release documents proving you're involved in the criminal aspects of your father's business."

"We both know I'm not." My voice is hard and curt now.

"It won't matter when they're through with you. You'll be tied up in legal battles for years to come, and we both know the only way you'll get out of it is to work with your dad."

"And we know what he'll demand." My return to the fold to get involved as heir of his criminal empire. "How close can I get to the line, Marcello?"

"They don't want you two together. She doesn't have your family name, so as long as she doesn't, she's fair game."

"If she had my family name, they'd leave her be?" I ask, a chill slipping down my spine.

"I can't guarantee it, man, but they'd hesitate. Listen, though... Just stay out of it if you know what's good for you. They're going to be ruthless on this."

"I can't stay out of it." I close my eyes with a sigh. "I'm not going to leave her defenseless. She's the mother of my child. I love her."

"If you want her not to hate you when this is over, you might want to avoid doing anything that will get my side riled up. If they think you're going to get in the way, they'll go after you. She'll think you're part of the criminal organizations that her father's in trouble with." He sighs. "I'm sorry about the mess, my friend, but there's not much I can do."

"And if I provide protection for her or move her in with me to keep them safe?"

"I don't know what will happen, Damien. The best I can tell you is to wait and see. Hope her father comes up with the money when they go after him first."

"I won't leave her unprotected if the winds shift and they're going to hurt her."

"Then you'd better sort out some way to do it without making it apparent that you're protecting her. Otherwise, you're going to end up losing her anyway."

"I'll sort something out." At the end of the day, I won't let them hurt her, even if I do have to lose her over lies they'll tell about me. I hate the thought of being pushed to that, and I'll try to avoid it, but in the end, I'll do what I must.

"Hope you do. Listen, I gotta go. Make sure you don't tell anyone what we've said. My don told me to warn you that if you do, it'll be much, much worse than some documents implicating you in illegal activities. Good luck." He hangs u p.

I stare down at the phone in anger and frustration. The timing isn't right to tell Alyssa what's been going on, and now I really can't tell her, even if I want to. I can tell I'm barely starting to gain some of her trust, and if I tell her what I'm involved in, what her father's involved in, she's going to go right back to pushing me away. And now, there's even more reason not to tell her because if I breathe a word of what's been threatened, all of us will be in a lot more danger than we are now.

It won't matter that I'm not responsible or that I don't partake in the criminal behavior the rest of the family does. She'll feel betrayed and lied to, and I'm not looking forward to it.

Unfortunately, I also have no choice but to tell her some of what's happening. She needs to know now about her father because I can't place her under my protection if she doesn't know why she needs it. Alyssa isn't stupid. She'll never let me have that much control without knowing why. Not right now. Even the small amount of control I can take to protect her without setting off the other side isn't going to go over well. I'm going to have to walk a very fine line here if I want any chance of things working out.

Groaning, I lean back in my chair. I can feel the start of a headache coming on, but I need to deal with this sooner rather than later. She's at work, but this isn't the right place to discuss it. I'll take her to lunch, and I can explain everything then. This is going to change everything between us in ways I never planned for, and I'm dreading what comes n ext.

***

LUNCH DIDN'T WORK out. Alyssa had plans with Lucille. So, I revised my plan. I stand on her front step and hope she's home as I ring the bell.

She answers a few moments later, and I don't know if I'm glad she did or disappointed because I could've postponed this longer if she hadn't. Her expression is surprise and wariness all in one, but she offers me a smile, ever the sunshiny sort. "Damien?"

"Can I come in? I need to tell you something."

She steps aside, her smile dropping. "It sounds serious."

"It is," I tell her. "It's about your dad."

Her whole body stiffens as she closes the door behind me. "I thought you weren't going to tell me anything."

"The situation has changed."

She turns to me and crosses her arms. "Changed how?"

"Can we just sit down and talk, please?"

Sighing, she waves towards the living room. "Okay, fine. Let's sit and talk."

We move to her little living room, and I take a seat, eyeing her and trying to decide the best way to approach this. I decide on full honesty.

"You're not going to like most of what I'm about to tell you," I inform her. "Please, just wait to say anything until I've finished."

Her lips press into a thin line, and she fiddles with the drawstring on the sweatpants she's wearing.

"Your father is in trouble with two major crime families operating in the area. He's racked up some really bad gambling debts, and they're eager to collect."

Her face pales, and her eyes are wet, but she doesn't say a word.

This is the hard part. Explaining how I know and why he thinks I can help. "One of the debts is owed to the Giovanni crime family, and they're looking to collect by using his family... you... to get to him."

I watch her grip the arms of her chair until her knuckles turn white, but she doesn't ask the question showing so clearly on her face. How. How do I know? That's what she wants to ask.

"The other is owed to my father, and he's been trying to make me collect it."

Her breath escapes in a harsh rush. "What?"

She's breaking her promise, but I've said the part that's most important now, so I don't object.

"Your father... you?"

"My father's don of the family. I'm the heir, but I don't want the position, and I don't want anything to do with all the crime. Unfortunately, while I've been postponing it with my dad, I can't do anything to stop the other family."

"So... so Timothy and I are in danger?" Her grip tightens a little more.

"I think you will be."

"You promised me it was nothing to worry about, that you'd handle it!" Her voice rises an octave. "Now you're telling me this whole time he's been in bed with a bunch of crooks, and my son and I are in danger?"

"Our son," I correct. "Alyssa, I'm telling you this because you need to know if I will protect you."

She shakes her head and pushes to her feet. "Get out."

"Alyssa—"

"Get out!" Her voice grows louder and stronger. "You don't get to lie to me and keep secrets and then try to pretend you're going to protect me. Leave, and I don't want you to come back. I'll see you at work tomorrow, and only because I do need the job."

I contemplate trying to stay and convince her, but I know it won't do any good when I take a look at her face and see the stubbornness and the hurt there. She's trying not to cry. She trusted me, and I've now broken that trust.

"Okay. I'm going."

I turn and leave, not wanting to think about what might happen to her or my son if I can't win this war with her and with the others who have set it into motion.

For a long time, I just drive, needing to think and be free from additional pressures. When I find my way to a spot on the Hudson outside the city, near my vacation house on the river, I pull over to park. Tugging the phone from my pocket, I give Alyssa a call.

She doesn't pick up.

I didn't expect her to.

"Alyssa, I know you're angry with me, but please... just give me a fair hearing. You and Timothy are genuinely in danger, and I'm trying to protect you both. Please, call me back when you get this."

I hang up and drop my phone onto the passenger's seat with a low curse. It's going to be a long road ahead to convince her to give me a chance, and I may not have that kind of time. By telling her the truth today, I may have doomed her to the very fate I was trying my hardest to save her from.

Chapter Fifteen: Alyssa

I GET DAMIEN'S message the same day he sends it, but I don't reply. I can't handle it right now. He might think he's doing what's best with me and this situation, but I'm not sure if I think it's best.

Mostly, I feel betrayed. His choice to finally give me answers has left me questioning everything, and I'm questioning whether I can trust him or, by extension, his sister. I'm freaked out and running scared, and I know it, but I can't seem to help it.

Which is how I find myself on Lucille's doorstep with Timothy in his car seat at my feet. I ring the bell and wait, my throat tight and tears threatening. Does she know about her family? Has she known all along and chosen not to tell me the truth?

Lucille answers the door with her usual bright smile. It dims when she sees the look on my face. "Alyssa, what's going on?"

"Can I come in?" I ask faintly.

"Of course." She steps aside to let me in.

I pick up Timothy and step inside, my heart thudding wildly against my rib cage. What if she does know about this, about my father, about all of it, and never told me? What will I do if I can't trust my best friend either?

"Why don't you come sit down in the living room?" Lucille suggests. "You look shaken. Is this about Damien finding out about Timothy? I'm sorry, Alyssa. I didn't mean to—"

I shake my head. That's just one more mess to deal with. I'm not sure I want to let Damien have any part in my son's life if he's in any way involved in the family business. He says he isn't, but can I trust him on that? "It's not. It's about something else." I take a seat. "My father's in trouble, and it turns out that your family has something to do with it."

Lucille doesn't seem to understand my meaning. She drops into a seat across from me and shakes her head. "I don't know what you mean. My family? How?"

"I've been pestering Damien for answers ever since my dad let slip that Damien could help him with his situation somehow. You know my dad gambles."

She nods. "I thought he was clean, though."

"He was. He isn't anymore. I don't know how long he stayed away either. It doesn't matter now." I slide my fingers through my hair with a groan. "I got the answers I wanted from Damien. Did you know that your family is involved in crime and a whole lot of other illegal, shady stuff?"

Lucille laughs. "Alyssa, have you been drinking? Smoking something like we used to do in high school and undergrad?"

I shook my head. "No! I'm serious. Damien told me that's why my father thought he could help."

Lucille's laughter dies. "You're serious...."

"Deathly."

She begins chewing on a nail, eyeing me while she does. She must be processing. Lucille always does this when she's thinking. Maybe she didn't know.

A little bit of relief washes over me at that small sliver of hope. Maybe she didn't keep it from me and let me think that getting tangled up with Damien was a good idea when it wasn't.

"I don't know what to do with this," she murmurs at last. "I mean... this is a lot."

"You didn't know, then?" I need to hear her confirm she didn't.

She shakes her head. "Not a thing. My dad doesn't talk business around the women in the household, and as you can see, I'm living in my own apartment now. I mean, I know my family's wealthy, and I knew the wealth had to come from somewhere, but I thought it was just old family money.... There have been expectations...."

"Expectations?" I prod.

"Well...." She falters and stares down at her hands. "My dad's always been particular about who I can and can't date, and they've been pushing a match with a man from another family that has money. You don't think... I mean, you don't think the guy he picked is also part of the criminal enterprises, do you?"

"I don't know, Lucille." I sag back into my spot on the sofa. She didn't know. "I'm just relieved that you aren't in on it too. I trusted Damien! I let him start to pull me in, and then he finally gave me my answers, and it turns out he's a conniving, lying bastard whose family is connected to crime."

Lucille flinches. "Alyssa, you're being a bit hard on him. I don't think Damien's involved. It was terrible of him to try to keep this from you, but I can understand why he would. He probably thought it would protect you. A lot more things suddenly make sense about our home life, though."

I frown. "What do you mean?"

"Well, Damien never got along with Dad. Still doesn't. The two clash all the time. My dad keeps complaining he won't step up and do his duty to the family. I always thought it was because Damien didn't want to help him run the businesses my dad started before we were born, but maybe he meant more." Lucille's eyes fill with tears. "He didn't mean legitimate businesses. He meant the family business. If my family—"

I watch her choke off as the reality of her situation and mine hits. She's just realized what I have—all the extra security for her and the fuss about familial bonds and ties was to strengthen the crime family's foothold in criminal society. I don't know how it all works, but I have enough of an idea to guess.

"Dear God," Lucille whispers, eyes wide. "So many things make so much sense now. How did I ever miss this?"

"No one likes to think their family is involved in criminal organizations and crime rings, Lucille." I reach out and take her hands in mine. "I'm sorry you had to find out this way. I thought you might know, and I was upset. I didn't think."

She shakes her head. "You didn't do anything wrong. I just... I think I need time to process. But Alyssa, if Damien told you, it's because he's genuinely concerned and believes that if he doesn't tell you, it will result in more harm. Give him a fair hearing."

I bite my lip and nod, getting to my feet. "I'll give him a fair hearing. Thanks, Lucille."

She sees me to the door, and I hug her before leaving. Deep down, though, I'm still as worried as ever. Can I fulfill the agreement I've just made? Can I give Damien a chance?

***

EVEN AFTER TALKING to Lucille, I can't wrap my head around what I'm learning about my family or hers. I need someone else to confirm it, someone who won't lie to me, sugarcoat things, or try to pretend they're not what they are. For all his faults, my father has never been one to lie when asked direct questions, even on things he might prefer not to discuss.

I drive over to my parents' house after leaving Lucille's apartment. My dad is out front weeding the flower beds when I pull in. I take Timothy out of his car seat and lock the car, walking over to where my father's kneeling in the grass.

He looks up and smiles broadly when he sees me and Timothy approaching. "Sweetheart, you didn't tell us you were coming to visit! You should've phoned."

"It was a bit short notice for me too, Dad. Look, I need to ask you some questions, and I need honest answers."

His smile dims. "What kinds of questions?"

"Do you owe exorbitant gambling debts to the Darino family and others?"

He stands slowly, brushing off his knees and taking his time. "Why would you think that?"

"Because Damien told me," I hiss. "Damien told me because you didn't. You've put yourself in a bad spot with the others you owe, and you don't have Damien to provide a buffer in the other family."

His face drains of color. "I... yes, I do. I'm sorry, sweetheart."

A combination of betrayal, rage, and pain swells in my chest. How could he do this to me? "You did this knowing full well these people were dangerous and might come after me or Mom to get to you?" I snap. "Tell me you at least weren't that stupid!"

He flinches and looks away. "I didn't think it would get this far. I thought I could handle it, manage everything... it wasn't supposed to go this way."

"Yeah, well, it did! I can't believe you did this to us. Now, I'm in danger, and so is my son, all because you chose to rack up debts with the wrong people. What happened to getting clean?"

"I... sweetheart, I thought I could manage it. I didn't think a few times would do any harm, but before I knew it, I was spiraling out of control like before. I just didn't think it would go this way."

How had he possibly thought it would go any other way? "It always goes this way!"

Timothy starts to cry at the harsh tone I'm taking. I bounce him on my hip to soothe him as I glare at my father. "I hope you're proud of yourself for this! Damien's the only reason I know I'm in any danger to begin with. You could've told me, and you chose not to."

"Please, sweetheart." His voice breaks. "Please, forgive me. I didn't mean for it to get out of hand."

"Well, it did." I glance at the house and see Mom peeking through the drapes. "Does Mom know? Did you tell her what you did?"

He lowers his gaze. "No. Please, don't tell her yet, Alyssa. I'll tell her. I promise. Just not yet."

"You better tell her soon, Dad." My tone is bitter and cold, but I don't care anymore. He's put us all in danger, and I don't know if I can forgive that. "She's in as much danger as I am now, thanks to you, and I think she deserves to know that."

His shoulders hunch, and he looks broken as well as devastated by my words. I should feel bad, but I don't. Instead, I feel a mixture of pain, sadness, and fear as well as the anger that has been simmering under the surface since he first confirmed his gambling addiction was back.

"Will you ever forgive me?" My father meets my gaze.

I can see that he knows the answer might be no. Right now, I can't even answer that question because I don't know. I don't know if I can forgive any of them. Him. Damien.

Damien's father. The people who took advantage of my father's weaknesses.

"I don't know," I murmur.

He nods. "Please be safe, Alyssa."

I don't even know if I can do that. Doing so might mean trusting Damien again, and I'm still unsure if I should. I promised Lucille to give him a fair hearing, but it leaves me sick to consider talking to him again so soon. "I'll do what I can," I tell my father.

Then I turn away and walk towards the car with Timothy on my hip. I can't handle anything more right now, can't bear to look at him. I just need to get away.

I put Timothy into his car seat, buckle him in, and drive for home. But instead of going home, I drive out toward the countryside. The city feels too claustrophobic right now. I find myself driving the route to the small countryside cottage that Damien owns. It used to be the spot where his father took them for vacations until Damien bought it.

Unsure why I'm going there at all, I pull off into a park with miles of forest. We used to walk in this park and play in the woods as kids. It feels familiar and in some strange way, safe. I get out of the car and take Timothy with me, locking the vehicle behind me.

Then I just start walking. The tears start to fall, and eventually, I can't see past the blur, so I stop. There's a bench just up ahead on the path, and I find my way to it. My legs give out, and I drop onto the bench, clutching Timothy to me as I sob.

I have no one to rely on now. Lucille can't help me with this. Damien can, but I don't know if I can trust Lucille's hunch that he's not involved. I feel lost and overwhelmed, and I don't know where to turn anymore. How am I ever going to get through this when the one person who might be able to protect me is involved in the very thing putting me at risk?

Chapter Sixteen: Damien

I NEED TO cut past the red tape and get Alyssa's father into my charity's rehab program now. A few days have passed since I called Alyssa after our spat. She hasn't replied, and I know time is of the essence.

If I give her father the money to pay the debts off, I'm going to be in hot water with my father. Not that I'm not already, but I don't want to be in worse shape with him. My father can be petty, and if he thinks it will force me back to the fold, he'll do anything he deems necessary. He might go after Alyssa anyway or refuse to take my money to pay him off for her father's debts. I don't know, and I can't take the risk. At least through the charity, the debts will be paid off anonymously.

The trouble is that he owes sixty grand to the Giovanni family, which is enough to make them want to go after him on principle, and I have no idea if I can get him out of all of it. I can handle what he owes my father through the charity, but the additional sixty grand might not be possible, and then I'll need a backup plan. Maybe I can pay them off to disappear.

First, though, I'm going to have a chat with her father. I pull in at their home address, which I got from Lucille, and park. The lights are on to ward off the creeping darkness following dusk, so I know they're home.

Getting out of the car, I go to the front door and knock.

A small woman with Alyssa's warm smile and cheerful demeanor answers the door. "Yes? Can I help you?"

"Mrs. Jones?" I smile as best I can. "How are you?"

"I'm well. What is it you're here about? We don't want to buy anything if you're selling something." She wraps her arms around her waist.

"No, I'm not here to sell anything. I'm looking for your husband. Is he home?"

She frowns. "Why do you ask? Who are you, anyway?"

"Damien Darino. I'm Lucille's older brother. Please, it's urgent," I say.

After a moment's hesitation, she steps aside and sweeps an arm out to usher me in. "He's in the kitchen. I'll show you there."

I follow her, thankful she didn't make too much fuss. It would surprise me if he told her anything, and I don't want to be the one to break the news to her that her husband's been gambling again.

Mr. Jones is in the kitchen, sipping on a hot cup of tea. He glances up when we enter and goes pale. "Damien?"

"You know him?" his wife asks.

"Dear, could you give us a few minutes alone?" He doesn't answer her question, and he won't meet her gaze.

She glances at me, her lips pressing into a thin line of distrust. "Maybe I should stay."

"I'm not here to do him any harm, ma'am," I assure her. "I just wanted to talk to him about a business matter."

"A business matter?" She stares at me in disbelief.

I can understand why, but there's nothing else I can tell her that would be more plausible. Nothing but the truth, and I can't tell her that right now. I don't want to frighten her or drive a wedge between them both when there's a possible danger to her life and safety too.

"Fine." She throws up her hands with a sigh and walks out of the kitchen.

I wait until she's well out of earshot before sitting and meeting Mr. Jones's gaze. "Mr. Jones, you know why I'm here."

"My gambling debts," he mumbles.

"I'm trying to find a way to save you from the problem you've created, but it can't be by giving you the money to pay off my father. He's running out of patience with my refusal to collect, and he's going to send someone else. He won't let me pay it for you." I steeple my fingers in front of me. "However, there might be a solution. You could apply for aid from the charity that I started to help gambling addicts."

He spears me with a scowl. "I'm not a gambling addict. It just got a little out of hand and then got away from me this time. That's all."

Already this is going wrong. If he's not willing to admit he's an addict, we may not get anywhere with this. I try anyway. "The charity requires you to do rehab and to stay clean, but they'll pay debts, up to a point. If it isn't enough, then I'll pay the remainder for the other family, if they'll allow it."

"Why would you do that?" he asks, sounding suspicious.

"Because of your daughter. Because it's my son and the woman I care for on the line now because of your choices. I'm trying to save them both."

His jaw tightens, but he looks a bit surprised in the brief moment when he meets my gaze. Maybe he thought I didn't care about saving them from his bad decisions. I would think my choice to step in to help her when he showed up drunk on her doorstep would've been a dead giveaway, but he was pretty drunk, so maybe he doesn't remember that. Whatever the case, he knows otherwise now.

"I'm not going to some rehab program. I'm managing it fine." He looks away.

"No, you aren't." Bluntness is the last resort here for me. "You aren't, or else you wouldn't owe my father and this other crime family enough money to make them want to break your legs and hurt your family to get it back."

His throat works, and he stares down at the table's pock-marked top. "I'm not going into rehab."

I shake my head. "Don't you get it? If you don't go to rehab, you won't be able to pay off the debts. I won't be able to help you."

When he meets my gaze again, there's nothing there but stubborn denial. "I'm not a charity case. I racked up the debt, and I'll find a way to pay it. I just need more time."

"You don't have more time!" I snap. "You're out of time, and because of that, your wife, daughter, and grandson are in danger. I can't fix that if you won't help yourself."

"I said no," he replies firmly. "And I mean it. I'm not a charity case."

I know I'm not going to win, and I slump down in my chair in defeat. I'm going to have to find some other way, some path forward that lets me protect Alyssa and Timothy.

The trouble is, I don't know what options or paths forward I have left, and I don't know if I can put them into action in time. Is this the end of the road for me? Have I failed this, and, in doing so, failed as a father to protect my son? I hate thinking that's possible, but what if it is? I'm at a loss, but I get up and head for the door.

"Then I hope you're willing to accept the blame when they pay the price," I snap in parting.

***

I HAVE ONE last thing I can do that might help. It won't stop my father, but it will buy me time to figure something out without the immediate threat to Alyssa hanging over my head. I've never been one to feel fear or terror, but right now, I'm experiencing terror for the first time in a long time. I'm terrified that Alyssa and Timothy will pay for her father's foolishness and that I won't be able to protect them from it.

So, I did the only thing I could think of. I set up a meeting with my contact from the other family to have lunch at a restaurant near my company's headquarters. If they'll accept my money to pay for this, I'll gladly pay to protect those I've decided are mine. I can't let anything bad happen to my son. Maybe I haven't had a lot of time with him, but I already adore the kid, and I can't stand the thought of failing him. I also can't stand the thought of losing Alyssa.

I step into the dimly lit interior of the restaurant that we agreed to and glance around. When I spot my contact, I stride over to the table he's taken and sit across from him. "Marcello."

"Damien. How are you?"

"Well. And you?"

Marcello grins. "As well as can be expected."

Marcello and I came to be friends after I saved his life in a drug deal gone wrong. I wasn't supposed to know about the deal, but I had been in the wrong place at the wrong time. So had he. We were teenagers at the time, but he never forgot.

"Good. The wife and kids?"

"Doing well too. The oldest will be off to college soon." He leans forward. "But I know that's not why you're here. You said you needed to talk."

I glance around the small restaurant and then lean in and lower my voice. "I need to ask you a question, and I need a straight answer, Marcello. It could be a matter of life or death."

His smile fades. "What is the question?"

"If I pay Mr. Jones's debts to your don, will he leave the man and his wife and daughter alone?"

Understanding lights in Marcello's eyes, and his lips press into a grim line.

I know the answer will be 'no' then, but I need to hear it anyway, just to confirm it.

"I'm sorry, my friend.... Handing him cash won't make the problem disappear. It's a matter of reputation now, not just the money." Marcello shakes his head. "The don can't let everyone think they can get off easy when they've snubbed him, stabbed him in the back, or failed to pay up for as long as Mr. Jones has."

I swallow hard and look away. "What can I do?"

"Marry her or pray he finds a way to pay?" Marcello's tone is light.

My gaze flies back to his face. It's a mask of grim determination. He means it. I don't know how I could go through with what he's suggesting, though. Alyssa's still angry with me, and I know such a suggestion would be foolish.

Besides... I want her, but I'm not sure if she wants me. Tricking her into marrying me....

"You don't want to coerce her or use the circumstances to pressure her into a marriage." Marcello recognizes my hesitation for what it is. "But if you don't, worse may happen. Anyway, I can see it in your face, my friend. You want this woman. You just don't like the line you might cross if you gain her this way."

I clear my throat and shake my head. "It's a crazy, reckless suggestion. It won't work."

"They won't go after the wife of another don's son, Damien. The Darino name holds weight, even if you don't live the lifestyle like the rest. They don't want to tangle with your father, and they know tangling with you is tangling with him."

I know he's probably right, but we don't have the kind of relationship where we give each other this sort of advice much. Stewart's always been the one I talked to when I needed advice on things like this. "I'll think about it."

"Think fast," Marcello suggests. "Because you may not get more time before too long."

I know that too, and it scares me. Not many things do scare me, but this does. The thought of losing Alyssa or my son makes me ill. "Thanks for the answers and the advice, Marcello." I rise.

"Don't you want to eat?"

"Lost my appetite," I admit. "You enjoy. The food's excellent."

He nods. "That it is."

I leave him there and head out into the bright sunlight, heart heavy and mind swirling. I can't let them hurt her, but there's every chance that doing as Marcello has suggested will hurt her just as badly. What if in trying to save her, I ruin her beyond repair?

Chapter Seventeen: Alyssa

I'M STILL FURIOUS with Damien after a week of thinking things over, but I also know I need answers. First and foremost, I need to know he's never been involved with his family's illegal activities and never will be. I can't trust a man who's been involved in crime.

I leave Timothy with Lucille at my place and drive out to Damien's to talk to him about the things I've been struggling to work through. Only he can answer my questions, and I desperately need answers.

When I knock on the door, he answers it quickly. Seeing me, he steps aside and ushers me in. He must know I'm here to talk.

We haven't spoken outside of work and work-related matters since he told me what was going on. I haven't been able to bring myself to broach any of the things hanging over my head. Today, however, I'm going to. I have to, for my sake and my son's. So, I step inside. "Are you involved in your family's illegal dealings? And were you in the past?"

Damien shuts the door softly behind me. "I was never involved directly when I was younger, and I'm not involved now, though I know that the money my father poured into my first business or two was likely blood money. I didn't have a choice, and he never confirmed if it was or wasn't. I chose not to ask. These days, I want out of any connection. He pressures me to come back to the fold and to take up my position as his heir, something I never did."

"And?"

"I won't do it. I never got involved then, though I couldn't avoid seeing things, and I won't get involved now." He falls silent, seeming to be considering his next words with care. "I think I may have to cut ties with him entirely soon. He's trying to force me to come home to take my place in the family. You're a part of that. It's why he wanted me to collect from your father and why he's threatened to give someone else the job with instructions to go after you if I refuse."

I shiver and close my eyes. "Why haven't you cut ties already?"

His warm hand takes my elbow, and he draws me away from the door. "Come sit down. We'll talk in the other room where it's not as chilly and has a little more comfort."

Reluctantly, I follow. I want answers now more than I want them in comfort and ease later, but I can tell from his look that he's not giving me a choice to argue. So, I let him lead me to the living room and take a seat on the large sectional. "Why haven't you cut ties already?"

"Because it has to be done the right way. If I don't do it when the timing's right, it'll come back to haunt me. By extension, it'll come back to haunt you and Timothy."

"Us too? Why?"

His gaze bores intently into mine. "You know why."

"Pretend I don't," I shoot back.

He sighs. "Because he knows you're my weak spot, and he thinks that if he uses you against me, I'll cave."

"Is he right?"

He meets my gaze with a firm, glittering look of pure regret. "Yes. He's right."

I swallow hard. That wasn't the answer I expected. I'm not sure what to do with it either. "Damien—"

"I'm not going to lie to you, Alyssa. I haven't so far, and I'm not starting today."

Biting my lip, I look away, ending our stare down. "Okay... so now what? What do we do? Because I can't let you put Timothy in danger any more than I could let my father do it knowingly."

"I'm working on a solution. I just need to know you still want one that includes me."

I frown down at my hands. Did I want one that included him? I couldn't deny my attraction to the man. The number of times we've ended up in bed "just one more time" is proof of that. Still, I don't know what I want. Not yet. I'm not sure if I can handle having a relationship of any sort with him when I know what his family is involved in.

He sees the decision in my eyes before I can put it into words and nods. "You don't."

"It's not that," I murmur. "I just don't know yet. I need time to think about everything to decide if I can handle having any sort of relationship with you given what your family does."

His gaze drops to his hands. "I'm not my family, you know."

"I know, but they've defined parts of who you are today, for good or for bad. And your world is dangerous in ways I never thought it could be... I don't know if I can bring my son into that."

"Our son," he corrects quietly. "Timothy is ours, not just yours."

I tense and look away. "I'm his mother."

"I'm his father." His voice is still quiet, but it's firm. "I said I wouldn't take him away from you, but I didn't say I didn't want any part in his life, and I never said I wouldn't try to protect him just as much as you do. You're not alone in making these decisions anymore. Not when it comes to him."

Technically, I am. I have sole custody. I don't have the heart to rub that in his face, though, because however I feel about him and his family, I can tell he means what he's saying. He cares about Timothy, even with this short of a time, and he's not going to let any harm come to our baby if he can stop it.

"I respect your need for time, Alyssa, and I'll try to give you what I can, but I can't promise you an indefinite amount of time to think. If it were up to me, I would, but it isn't up to me. There are outside forces—" His voice cracks. "You have no idea how much I wish it were otherwise, but life is what it is, and I can't change the way it is."

I feel bad for making him feel he has to, but at the same time, I also hate the fact that our relationship is dragging me into a complex, dark reality that I'm not sure I know how to navigate. Standing, I nod. "Then I need time to process everything and come to a decision. Can you give me that, at least?"

"I can," he agrees. "But I can't promise you how much time I'll be able to give you before I need an answer if I'm going to save you and Timothy."

I smile sadly. "Whatever time you can give is appreciated. You're a better man than your father for giving it and for trying to let me have choices even when you may not like the outcome."

He smiles just as sadly and looks away. "If I were a better man, I'd walk away from you both. But I'm not. I'm selfish, and I don't want to let go. If you tell me to, I will, but I don't want to, Alyssa."

The words shoot straight through my heart and warm my core. I know he's telling the truth even if I'm not sure yet if I can accept the words or admit to myself that I don't want to walk away either. Instead, I just nod again and turn, walking back to the front door alone.

***

I MANAGE TO hold in the grief, fear, and crippling uncertainty until I get home to Lucille. The minute she asks me if I'm all right, the dam breaks, and I'm sobbing on the couch.

She wraps her arm around me without a word and holds me close while I cry.

When I finally stop, she clears her throat. "What happened?"

I sniffle and bury my face in my hands. "This is all too much... all of it. Everything I've learned about my father, about Damien, about your family, and what goes on around here."

It isn't fair to put this on her now when she's struggling to come to grips with the same facts about her family and brother as I am. Still, I can't stop the flood from pouring out of me. "And I'm scared, Lucille. I'm scared about so many things.... What will happen to Timothy if I die? What will happen to me if I lose him? "And then I learned what your father's doing to Damien. How your father is using me to pressure Damien into a life he doesn't want."

Lucille squeezes my hands. "I'm sorry, Alyssa. I can sort of imagine, but not really.... I mean, I'm only dealing with discovering my family's full of criminals. I don't have to deal with the imminent threat of violence and pain. I wish I could take it all away."

I start sobbing again. "The worst part is, I do like him, Lucille. I do. I think he means everything he's saying. I just don't know if I can live with the way his family is."

"Hey!" Lucille gives me a playful punch and tries to offer a smile, though it doesn't reach her eyes. "That's me you're talking about!"

"Okay, everyone but you," I amend.

"Better. But really, I think he does want to do what's right and genuinely cares for you. You're just too afraid to see it."

Puffing out my cheeks, I stare into the fireplace even though it isn't lit or running. "I never imagined he'd want to be part of Timothy's life, but he keeps insisting he does, and I've seen him with Timothy. He's a natural."

"Maybe you're staying mad at him for something he can't control and that's why you feel wrong about the situation," Lucille suggests.

"You think your father isn't the heart of the problem?" I challenge.

"He's part of the problem. Maybe even *the* problem. Still, Damien has been refusing to take his place with the man for decades causing him grief. He won't hurt you if you tell Damien you're willing to give him a chance, and I think that's all he needs to hear."

"What if I tell him I'll give us a chance and something terrible happens?" My voice is a bare whisper.

"What if you don't and something horrible still happens?" She crosses her arms. "You can't live your whole life in fear. You shouldn't make decisions from fear either. Instead, you have to face your fears. What might happen is one fear, and you won't overcome it if you choose to hide from the future you don't know yet."

I groan. "When did you get so wise?"

She grins. "Oh, stop grumbling. I've just seen enough to know you two are perfect together. Don't throw away a good thing just because you're afraid. I promise you'll regret it."

Is she speaking from personal experience, or just from a general advice standpoint? It wouldn't surprise me if she knew it from personal experience. "So, you think I should give him a chance?"

"I do. He's the father of your baby, and I know my brother. He's protective and wants the baby. You couldn't have a better man. His family doesn't have to define him."

"But his family will touch our lives."

"If you let them," she agrees. "But you don't have to let them. You can choose to fight back and shape destiny instead of just living through it."

I sigh and hug her. "Thanks, Lucille. It makes me feel a little better."

"Or the crying did." She laughs and pats me on the back. "Now we're going to figure out how to get through this. You just have to be patient until we do."

I appreciate that she thinks I will, but I'm not as convinced. Damien seems convinced he can find me an out too, if I'll just tell him how I want to do this—with him or without him in the picture romantically. I'm just not sure I believe he can rescue me if we're not involved.

I'm not naive. I know what mob bosses are like. Ruthless, deadly killers when necessary. I'm not under his protection

if we're not involved, and that means I'm sitting bait. Can
Damien find a way to save me if I tell him I don't want to
be with him?

Chapter Eighteen: Damien

THE FIRST PLACE I go as soon as Alyssa and I are done talking is Stewart's. I know he'll be able to talk to me straight and tell me what I need to hear.

The thing is, I'm not sure if I can save Alyssa without pressing her into a relationship with me, and equally, I'm not sure if being my girlfriend will be enough. It's probably going to be seen as a violation of their demand I stay out of it. Moving her in with me is a trial to see if they're going to follow through. I meant it when I decided I would do what it took, though. If that means trying to convince Alyssa to marry me, not just to date me, so be it. Doing this won't protect Alyssa from my father if he decides to harm her, but I don't think he will when he wants me back in with the family, and it should be enough to keep Giovanni's family away from her for a bit.

Stewart greets me with a raised brow in silent question.

I step in and shut the door behind me. "We need to talk about Alyssa."

"Oh, do we?" Stewart chuckles. "Word from Lucille is that Alyssa's pretty angry with you. And shaken up."

I sigh and find my way to his rec room where he stores the liquor. "Yeah... you and Lucille talk?"

He flashes me a grin as he passes me and goes to the sideboard to pour the drink I'm craving. "We do. I knew Lucille when we were kids, remember? Your sister's certainly grown up from when she was a little girl with pigtails following us around."

I hold back a warning glare. Stewart is a good guy. If anything is going on, Lucille could do worse. Granted, I doubt my father will let Lucille marry Stewart willingly. She'll do it without his approval if she does. Stew doesn't play the game the rest of them do, and my father will try to marry Lucille off for more power and money.

If Stewart does hurt her, though, my father will be the least of his worries.

Stewart turns back to me and hands me a drink. "Wipe the glare off your face, Damien. I won't hurt Lucille. She's a big girl, anyway, and Lucille knows what she's doing." He takes a sip of his drink and watches me without much concern.

I thought I was keeping the glare off my face, but apparently, I haven't been successful. I cough and look away, taking my drink. "You're right. And I'm here to discuss Alyssa, not whether you and my sister are screwing around."

Stewart's expression turns dark. "Screwing around is not a term I would use for what I'm doing with Lucille. I'll thank you not to put it that way."

I realize I'm treading on thin ice. Stew cares a lot more about Lucille than he does about most of the women he's been with. "Sorry... you're right. I just—"

"Assumed." He gives me a faint smile. "Lucille is different." His tone says we're done discussing Lucille.

I nod. "Okay. About Alyssa.... The group her father owes money to is going after Alyssa and her mother, not just Mr. Jones. I tried to pay them off, but it's a matter of pride now, and they're not going to accept a payoff. Alyssa's angry with me, get I must find the best way to get her out of danger. They've blackmailed me. If I try to protect her, they're going to release false documents and photos that implicate me in illegal activities. Even if I persist in protecting her, they'll make sure she hates me for what she thinks I've done. They warned me that if I breathe a word to her or anyone else, they'll do worse than what they've threatened to keep me out of this. I'm only telling you because I know you won't say a word to anyone. But I'm going to be tied up in massive legal issues for years if I push too far, and I'm in a bind. Moving her in was my first step in an attempt to see how far I can push it, but she's fighting me on it." I sigh. "She has my son, Stew. I can't let them hurt her or him, but I also can't tell her the full truth, and eventually, the lies are going to catch up with us."

Stew takes a sip of his drink, his expression turning contemplative. Then he meets my gaze and nods. "Marry her, then. You can rescue her if you do that. They won't go after the wife of the heir to the Darino family."

I've thought that before, but the idea doesn't hold much appeal when I still won't be able to be honest with her about what's going on or why marrying her is the best way out. "First, I won't be able to tell her why I'm marrying her. I can't tell her I love her... I do, but if I tell her the truth and ask her to marry me, they'll follow through on releasing those documents, and she'll think I lied just to manipulate her into doing what I wanted. She'll question everything about me, and I doubt she'll appreciate the love of a man she thinks is a monster. They may not go after her, but she'll hate me for the rest of our lives, and she'll think I'm doing it out of a sense of duty or to get my hands on Timothy. She's already worried I'll take him. Besides, I'm not the heir, and they know it. I've made it clear I won't take my place."

"Your name still matters. They don't want to tangle with you or your father. But you and Alyssa haven't been together before, and you're not putting her in the public eye. No one's going to believe she's your girlfriend, and it won't protect her well. They may or may not release the blackmail material they have on you if you move her in with you under the guise of protecting your son, though. You can have Marcello tell them you've decided to do it as a precautionary effort to protect Timothy because you don't want him alone or caught in the crossfire if they go after Alyssa. That should buy you time to convince Alyssa to marry you."

"It won't protect her from my father, though," I grumble. "If he decides he's had enough playing nice, we're going to have another fire to put out."

"Your father? What's he got to do with her?" Stew frowns. "That makes it more complicated."

"It does." I drain my glass. "My father's determined to force me to collect the debt Alyssa's father owes us, and since I've been refusing, he's told me I either collect, or he'll send someone who will go after Mr. Jones and Alyssa. And I'll have to watch whatever my father does to Alyssa. If my father helps me out with any legal issues protecting Alyssa ends up causing, he's not going to do it without demanding my return to the fold."

Stew coughs. "Damn... the man's a real piece of work. I'm sorry, Damien. But if that's true, then marrying her may be the only choice. Your father won't go after your wife. If he does, he's dumber than I thought. Going after your wife would only make you fight back instead of refusing to get involved."

I clench my fingers around the cool glass of ice. "Damn right, it would. But if he goes after my woman at all, wife or not, that's what's going to happen."

"Is Alyssa your woman, then? Even with the fight?" Stew's gaze remains calmly fixed on me.

I meet his gaze. "Alyssa may not know it yet, but yes. The only way it won't be that way is if Alyssa tells me she won't have me. I don't force women. I don't think I'll have to worry about getting that response, though. It's after the wedding I'm worried about, because once I go through with that step, they're going to start the hell they promised, and I'm not sure Alysa will stay."

Stewart nods. "I don't think you're going to be left with any other choice, though. Not if you want to protect Alyssa. So, you'd better figure out how to suggest something else that's going to make her upset because I don't think she's going to like this way out. But it is the only way out for her."

I know he's right. How am I going to break the news to Alyssa, though? And what will I do if, after all of this, Alyssa wants to leave because of the cost I'll pay?

***

I'M RELAXING AT home a few days later, trying to sort out the best way to tell Alyssa about the solution I've found. She's not going to like it, and I sigh, tilting my head back to stare up at the ceiling. The only question is how upset she'll be when I finally find a way to tell her what the solution is.

The doorbell rings, pulling me from my stupor. I get up and answer to find Alyssa standing on my doorstep. She's hugging herself and shifting from foot to foot like she's nervous. I don't see Timothy with her.

"Where's the baby?" I ask her.

"With a babysitter this time. Someone I trust."

I'm not sure I do. Not with a bunch of murderous thugs looking to take what's owed them from both her father and the rest of the family. "You should've brought him," I say quietly. "Things are dangerous for all of you right now."

"They won't hurt a defenseless newborn." She doesn't sound certain of it.

"They might or might not. I can't say for certain they wouldn't. But what's done is done. We'll call to check in if we need to. Do you want to come in?" I'm hoping she'll be here for a bit rather than leaving quickly.

Alyssa nods, avoiding my gaze.

I step aside to let her in.

Alyssa enters, the vanilla of her perfume tickling my senses as she passes by me. Her arm brushes my chest, and I close my eyes, relishing the contact. With her as angry at me as she's been, we've only spoken when necessary, and we certainly haven't ended up in bed together. I miss her.

Alyssa finds a spot in the living room and curls up in a chair as far from my spot on the sofa as she can get. "I'm... this is hard, Damien. All of it. I don't even know where to start."

I take a seat in the spot I abandoned to answer the door and pick up my drink. "Start with why you're here, then, love."

Alyssa nods. "I'm here because I've made a decision after a lot of thinking. I'm willing to overlook your family's activities and connections as long as you promise me you aren't involved. I... I need to know that much."

"I'm not involved," I murmur. "I never will be, and I never have been."

"I need to know your family's illegal activities won't affect us."

After I propose, if she accepts me, that's not a promise I'll be able to keep, and I won't make any more promises I'm going to break. "I can't promise what will happen if they're caught and splashed on the news, but I'm clean, Alyssa. I can't swear to you we won't get caught up if something happens out of my hands or someone tries to tangle me up in my family's troubles, but I can promise you the truth will come out eventually. I haven't done anything that I can go to jail for."

She bites her lip and lowers her head. "Okay... okay."

I know I need to tell her the plan for saving her from the other crime family, but I can't bring myself to do it now. She's been through so much. And I'm selfish. I want to have this time with her without adding to the reasons she wants to leave this house and not look back.

I'm not sure what she'll think about marrying me, and if she wants to have a relationship with me, give us a chance, that's a step in the right direction. I want to control but not push things. Especially since when I do ask, I can't tell her the real reason I'm asking—love. I have to keep that out of it because I won't be the sort of cruel man who would tell a woman he loves her knowing that in a short time, she'll learn to hate him and doubt if he ever really loved her at a ll.

She stands and walks over to me, standing just in front of my knees. "Damien, I'm scared... I'm scared of what they might do to me... to Timothy. I'm scared your father might hate me enough to try to separate us if I trust you and we end up... I just... I'm scared."

I set my drink on the end table and reach out to take her by the waist. "We'll figure it all out together, Alyssa. I promise. You don't have to be afraid. I'm handling it."

She bites her lip. "But what if... what if—"

Standing, I tip her chin up and cut her off with my mouth on hers. "No what-ifs," I whisper when I pull away. "Only what is right now."

"Only what's right now?" she whispers back.

I nod.

She leans up, threading her fingers through my hair. The whole length of her body presses to mine, and I feel my own body tighten in response. Blood rushes to my core, and I can feel myself getting painfully aroused. Her mouth comes to the hollow of my throat, and I stay perfectly still, afraid if I move, she'll stop.

Her tongue flicks over my skin.

I can't help the groan that follows. She's usually the one letting me lead and taking what I give. Tonight, it seems she's more interested in taking what she wants. I decide to allow it for now to see where it might go.

Her mouth trails up to my jaw in hot, open-mouthed kisses that have me clenching and unclenching my hands on her waist.

Then she grinds her hips softly into mine, and all notions of waiting to see where she goes with this flee. I growl and hoist her up by the hips.

She wraps her legs around my waist with a moan, still rubbing against me. There's no hesitation or moment where she reminds me it's the last time this time. She seems as desperate for me as I am for her, and she's not holding back anything.

Her fingers dig into my upper back as I carry her up the stairs to my room.

I toss her onto the king-sized bed and waste no time in dragging my shirt off over my head. My sweatpants follow in short order, and then I'm stripping her too. I've missed her and this more than I ever have with another woman, and I'm not willing to wait this time.

She whimpers when I drag her panties down and unhook her bra, but she doesn't object. Instead, she lays still, staring up at me while I stare down at her, ready to devour.

I trail my fingers from her clavicle down to her navel, smiling when she trembles. "Don't you want to remind me this is the last time I'm going to take you, little girl?"

She closes her eyes with a breathy moan. "No... not this time, Damien. Not this time. I want... I just... not this time."

I smile and lean in to trail my mouth along her neck, nipping and sucking as I work my way up to her jaw and ear. "Good. Because this is not going to be the last time, love."

As I press closer and continue to tease, though, I wonder if it will be. Will my desire to let her choose me of her own volition instead of forcing marriage on her end up being our undoing? Will I lose her?

I force the questions aside to focus on the moment as I instructed her to do, to focus on how it feels to claim her again, her warm body welcoming mine and giving me a moment without worries. I can worry about whether I'll lose her when this is over and we're both satisfied.

But even as I take her and make her sing for me, the question sits in the background. What if I lose her? What will I do then?

Chapter Nineteen: Alyssa

I WAKE WITH Damien's arm draped over my waist and his fingers splayed against my rib cage, the fingertips of his long fingers brushing the underside of one breast. His deep breaths press his warm chest against my bare back, and I close my eyes, wanting to bask in the moment.

Part of me wants to wake up like this every morning. That part has grown louder since last night and making my decision. Caution tells me to be careful. I've been burned before, and I'm not eager to repeat the experience.

He stirs behind me, and then his mouth trails along my bare shoulder. "Good morning, love. Do you want to call the babysitter? I'm sure she's wondering where you are."

I gasp and bolt upright. "I forgot all about her last night! Damn it, Damien! Why didn't you say something sooner?"

He smiles. "I'll pay the bill. It's only fair since I was the reason you were distracted."

"But why didn't you say something?"

"Because I wanted you, and I wanted you in the moment with me. You said you trusted her. You hired her to watch him for the night."

"But I told her I'd be back late, not that I wouldn't come home!" I sift through my clothes until I find the phone in my jeans' back pocket. Dialing the number, I cross my fingers and hope she won't be too upset.

Her groggy voice answers the house line. "Alyssa? Is that you?"

"Haley, yes, it's me. I'm so, so sorry! I didn't mean to leave you with him all night. Things took longer than expected, and then I...." I trail off, realizing I have no plausible excuse to offer besides what I was doing.

Damien reaches out and plucks the phone from my grasp. "Haley, she was out all night because her boyfriend is very good at distractions. I'm sorry about that. We'll pay double your usual rate, and it won't happen again."

My cheeks burn, and I hurry to grab the phone from him.

He hangs up with a grin. "She says it's not a problem as long as it doesn't happen again."

"Why did you tell her what we were doing?" I hiss, burying my face in my hands as it burns.

"Because you don't have an excuse that's believable." He leans in and kisses my neck softly.

"Stop!" I push him away. "We have to go pay her and get my son before we make it worse. If you do that, I'm not going to leave this bed."

He grins like the idea has merit, but he gets out of bed and goes to find clothes. I try my best not to stare, but it's clear he spends a lot of time in the gym and working out because he has the physique to show for it. I end up staring. Just a little.

When he comes back out, I'm changed and ready to go. More or less.

"Let me drive you," he says smoothly.

"No, I shouldn't. You have work. *I* have work." I scrape a hand over my face. "Damn, I'm sorry... I'm not normally this irresponsible."

"Well, since you're going to miss work due to the boss making you scream his name a couple dozen times last night, I think it can be forgiven." He winks. "Just don't let it happen too often, Miss Jones."

I groan. "You're to blame! It's up to you whether it happens often or not."

He purses his lips and then holds out a hand. "Come on. I'm driving you home."

"But my car will be stuck here," I point out.

He gets a weird look on his face like he knows something I don't. "It's fine. We'll come back for it later."

I sigh. I'm not going to win this one. "Okay, fine. Let's go, then."

We walk downstairs and head out together. He opens my door for me and makes sure I'm buckled before he pulls out of the garage and rolls into the street. Then we pull out and head for my place.

I don't quite know what to say to him now. What we did last night was far more intimate than any of the other times. I didn't keep the buffer of "this is the last time" between us, and I was far more emotionally invested in the moment as a result. Now, I don't think I can go backward, even if I wanted to.

"Penny for your thoughts?" Damien asks.

"Last night was...." I blow out a long breath. "It was a lot."

He reaches out and takes my hand in his. "Emotionally or physically?"

"Mostly emotionally." I stare at our hands entwined. "Damien, if things go wrong—"

"They won't."

"You don't know that. And I don't know how I'll ever pick the pieces back up if they do."

He squeezes my hand. "We can only take things one step at a time, Alyssa, but I promise you that I'm in this for the long term. It hasn't been a one-night stand for me since the second time I claimed you. I was a fool to let you go that first time at all, but I told myself you wanted me to and that I didn't need to get tangled up with you. I convinced myself it was best for you anyway, given my family."

"And now I'm being sucked into that mess whether I want to be or not, so it doesn't matter," I say softly.

He shakes his head. "It always matters to me what's best for you. But you're right.... There's no way to keep you out of it now. Which means right by my side is the best thing."

I know he's right, but I'm not sure what that looks like or where it will lead. I'm mostly afraid it'll lead to heartbreak or worse.

"You're still worrying about something. What is it?"

Resting my head against the headrest, I close my eyes. "Damien, I don't want my heart broken. And I'm scared I'm making the wrong choice just because I'm in danger and need an out. I don't want you to be nothing but an out."

"I'm not. When this is over, I'm not going anywhere unless you insist I walk away. I want to be here for you and Timothy. I can't tell you what I would've done if you'd come to me when you found out you were pregnant, but I can tell you what I want now. I want you, but I also want him. I want both of you in my life, Alyssa. You may doubt whether you're making the right choice, but I have no doubts about my choice to fight to keep you. Can that be enough for now?"

My whole body trembles and my eyes fill with tears. It might be the most romantic thing anyone's ever said to me, and I know Damien means it. It doesn't help me feel like I'm not making a poor call, but it does tell me that I can trust this man's not in it for the short term. "Okay. Let's just figure this thing out, and then we'll see."

***

WE GET BACK to my place and pay the babysitter. She's not happy about the lack of a call, but the extra money Damien hands over does a lot to make her discontentment dissolve.

The two of us go inside to find the house quiet and clean. Damien and I walk to the nursery to find Timothy sleeping soundly. This time, I don't hesitate or try to stop him when he goes to pick our son up. I know he's not going to hurt Timothy.

Timothy wakes up with a whimper and stares up into his father's face. He starts to cry, but he soon stops when Damien blows gently on his face and makes some silly faces before cradling him close and rocking him in his arms. Then Timothy settles and snuggles closer, his initial distress gone.

I watch the two, and my heart melts. I'm falling for him a little more each day, and every time I see how he is with Timothy, I fall a little faster. He's so sweet and gentle despite his usually grumpy, demanding demeanor at work and around others.

I haven't seen much of that grumpy demeanor around me anymore for a while. It leaves me feeling a little more settled to realize that he's been adapting his behavior to be there for me. No one's ever done that for me before, and I don't know quite what to do with it.

Damien looks up to find me staring and smiles. "Do you need to feed him?"

"She gave him his bottle before she put him down for a nap." I point to the rocking chair. "You could sit and rock him for a bit. I can get another chair."

He nods and makes his way to the chair, crooning softly at Timothy. I go to get another chair, and when I return, he's singing Timothy a quiet lullaby.

I stand in the doorway and listen to him sing in his deep baritone. What would it be like to have this every day without the threat hanging over our heads right now? Would we be suited? Happy with each other?

Stepping inside, I set down the chair and join him. "He seems to like you."

Damien surprises me by bending his neck to kiss the top of Timothy's head. "He's precious. I always thought I'd want kids someday, but I never thought that day would come. Seeing him, it's so much more than I thought it would be."

I bite my lip and lower my head to hide the welling tears. Would things between us be different now if I trusted him enough to tell him about Timothy? I love my son with all my heart, and seeing Damien with him like this, I can tell he loves him too.

"Come live with me, Alyssa," Damien murmurs. "At least for now. You're in danger... I don't want you two at risk, and I'd feel a lot better if you were both at my place with proper security."

I swallow hard and stare at the floor. "That's a lot of change suddenly.... We only just agreed to try making an 'us' work. Now you want me to move in? Is the danger that great, Damien?"

"Yes." He reaches out with his free arm and tips my chin up. "It is, love. I know people in the other family who have informed me reliably that they're going to come after you. I tried to pay them off, but it's a matter of criminal street credibility and honor to them now. I can't pay them off."

My eyes fly to his. "You did that? For me?"

"I didn't want you or Timothy in harm's way. But even if I could've gotten them to back off by paying them myself, it wouldn't solve the problem with my father. He'll use you to get to me in a heartbeat, and if you're under my roof, I can protect you better."

There's something in his expression that makes me wonder if there's more he isn't telling me, but he's making good points about the need to move in. I swallow and drop my gaze again. "They wouldn't do anything that bad to me or Timothy, would they? I mean, he's your father, and they're more interested in my father's money."

Damien lets go of my chin and stands, taking Timothy to his crib and setting him down to sleep. Timothy fusses for a minute and then settles. The man who tried to pay off a mob for me returns to where I'm sitting and pulls me up out of my seat. "Come with me."

I obey, wondering what he's doing.

We end up in my bedroom. Without warning, he grabs my waist, pins me up against the wall, and traps my hands above my head. Then his mouth is on my throat.

I shiver with a moan. "Damien, what are you doing?"

"This is what they'll do to you. It's me, so you like it, but when it's some man who smells like stale vodka and cigarettes? A man who just wants to inflict more pain after he's already cut, burned, and bruised you?" He bites down on my collarbone hard enough to cause pain. "When he videotapes your rape and invites his buddies to join in so they can send it to your parents to convince your father to pay up money he doesn't have? Do you think you'll like it then?"

I gasp at the feeling of his hips grinding harshly into mine.

"Do you think you're going to get wet for them when the same men who may very well also have your mother and would force you to watch her suffer first decide to take you one after another with no regard to your pleasure or any safety measures? They're not going to bother with any lubricant when you aren't wet enough to take them, and they might even make you take two or three of them at once."

I try to free my wrists, wanting to cover my ears. "Stop," I beg. "Please, stop."

His expression softens. "I don't like scaring you, little girl, but that's what those men would do if they got their hands on you. I'd never forgive myself if it happened because I failed to protect you. So please... at least until the threat is past, move in with me where I can keep you both the safest. For my peace of mind and your safety."

I sag against the wall, the motion pulling on my wrists a bit, which are still pinned to the wall above my head. "Okay," I whisper, tears pooling in my eyes. "Okay... you're right. We'll move in, at least for now."

He exhales a soft sigh and lets go of my hands to gather me into his arms, holding me close. "I'm sorry... I'm sorry I had to do that... I wasn't going to tell you, but...."

I push trembling fingers through his hair and try to get my racing heart to slow. "But you didn't know how else to convince me the danger's real?" I whisper.

"I didn't," he agrees.

We stand there together for a long time in silence. The things he's told me leave me shaking and cold because now I know what's facing me. Can we get through this, or will he be unable to protect me in the end, despite his best efforts? I shudder at the thought, and I say a silent prayer to whatever god might be listening that his best efforts will be enough.

Chapter Twenty: Damien

I GET A ring from the front door early on a Saturday morning. I groan as it wakes me up and shuffle out of bed. There's only one person who would show up this early on a Saturday. Stew. If this isn't important, I'm going to strangle him.

When I answer the door, Stewart hands me a warm take-away cup of coffee. I sniff it cautiously and realize he's brought me my favorite, mint mocha. "Okay, I guess I can forgive you for waking me up so early." I step aside. "What are you doing here at this hour?"

"It's nine. I waited an hour." Stew steps in. "I wanted to check in on you. Is Alyssa here?"

"Not yet. I'm helping her move in later today, and I have people watching her apartment until she moves in."

"Why haven't you just married her already?" My best friend wanders inside and makes himself comfortable on the couch. "You know it's the solution here."

I sigh and join him. "Stew, it isn't that simple."

"You love Alyssa, don't you?"

"Of course. I'd find some other solution if I didn't. I'd never marry a woman I didn't love, even if it was the most convenient way to protect her."

"Then I don't understand why you're hesitating. I know you want to protect her." Stew crosses his arms. "So, what's stopping you?"

"What's stopping me is that I'm not sure Alyssa's ready for me to ask that of her, especially now that she knows about my family, Stew. Besides, risks are growing. If Alyssa doesn't love me, it's a terrible idea. She needs to be in this, but I can't tell her the truth entirely, as you well know. I don't think it's good to ask it of her just yet. Let her find her bearings with the whole moving-in bit. We're still trying to navigate the whole thing with a kid in the picture. She doesn't need more added to her now. Besides, I'm waiting to see how the other family will respond to this. Maybe it won't be necessary at all. They might leave Alyssa alone and just deal with her father."

Stew purses his lips in thought. "Maybe you should give her the choice, Damien. Alyssa might surprise you. There's a chance you might not need to do any of this, but you can't be sure, and if they move, they'll move fast. So, you don't have the luxury of time. You do realize that?"

"Thanks for the reminder," I grumble. "I do realize and remember that. The situation still isn't simple, and you know it. My father's going to fight me on it, even if Alyssa cooperates. I'm not going to have any backing on this."

Stew shrugs. "He doesn't control you. You can tell him no."

"You don't understand. Things have gotten worse with my father, and I'm starting to think he's going to be just as big a problem as Giovanni."

My best friend's jaw clenches. "You can't let your father get away with it, and you certainly can't cave."

"I know that." I sit back with a groan and rake my fingers through my hair. "I know that, and marrying her will deter him from starting a war with me by going after her. Even if he doesn't like it, he won't touch her if she's mine officially."

"Then get her to agree and marry her. Don't let him stop you."

"I just haven't decided on the best way to make it clear it isn't up for negotiation. He won't like it, and I need to tread carefully. It might push the Giovanni family too far and have unintended consequences for us all. It might push her too far too."

Stew nods. "Then tread carefully. Just don't drag your feet because you're worried it'll scare Alyssa off. Otherwise, you're going to find you either have no choice left but to ask or it'll be too late, and she'll be hurt or dead."

I know he's right. I'm just afraid of losing Alyssa if I ask too soon or in the wrong way. It's already a big step that she's moving in with me, and I know it. If not for the imminent danger, I doubt she would have agreed so readily.

Asking Alyssa to marry me is a lot. Overwhelming even. She doesn't even know for certain that I love her because I haven't found the right moment to tell her that either. Not precisely, anyway. I like to think actions speak louder than words, but I also know that words are important at some point. All I've told her is that I want her and my son. Not that I love her and already am falling in love with my son too.

"You could make it a lot easier for her to agree if you tell Alyssa how you feel about her first." Stew studies my face. "If she knew you love her, she might not feel like the proposal is solely for her protection."

I stare down at my hands. "I don't know if that'll help."

"It can't hurt. Honesty is important, and she'll appreciate it from you, Damien. You two are already involved. You might as well talk to her clearly about the both of you before you go into the marriage proposal."

"Maybe... But I won't be cruel by telling Alyssa I love her before I can trust that she won't hear lies that will make her believe I lied." I smile grimly. "But you're right. Something has to be done and soon. I'll ask Alyssa, but I want to do it right, and I don't want to rush her. For now, moving in together should be enough to signal to the people planning to hurt her that they'll be messing with me, and we'll see if the Giovanni family takes issue with the move enough to release that material. If they do, marrying her might end up being a whole different ball game when it comes to convincing her."

"Do you think it'll be enough to have Marcello try to convince them you're doing it to protect Timothy?"

"For now, I hope."

He gives me a look that says he doesn't believe me. "Well, I have to go. I have an appointment. Don't wait too long, for both your sakes." He gets up. "I'll show myself out."

I watch him go, stomach tightening. Deep down, I know he's right. If I wait too long, it will put her in more danger, and it might result in harm or even death. I need to find the right moment, but I need to do it soon. I can't bear to lose her. And the truth is, I'm not sure if moving her in with me will be enough for now.

It'll be enough for the other family to tread more cautiously or to go straight to following through on their threat, I think. One way or another, it's going to put things into motion for collision with them. But will it be enough to protect her from my father's thugs, too?

***

ALYSSA AND I stand together in the guest room next to mine. I've moved all of her things into the house, and we've set up all of Timothy's things in the nursery.

"I can't believe we're here," she whispers. "I mean...." She shakes her head. "Never mind."

I draw her closer, holding her hands in mine. "It's okay to be overwhelmed, love."

She smiles and leans into me. Her head rests against my chest, her warmth flooding into me. "Overwhelmed is one way to put it."

"I could distract you."

She sighs and wraps her arms around my waist. "Thank you for what you've done so far, Damien. I mean it."

I pull back and lift her chin. "I'd do it again in a heartbeat. Your safety and Timothy's mean a lot to me."

"Still, I know this is a lot to do for a person."

I dip my head and claim her lips with mine. She still doesn't know how quickly I've fallen in love with her and Timothy, and I'm not able to tell her in words yet. Not without increasing the pain she'll suffer if the Giovannis do what they've threatened. It doesn't mean my actions can't paint the story, too, though.

She leans into my kiss with a sigh. Her hands come up to my shoulders, and she opens for me without hesitation.

I run my palms up and down her arms before moving them to her hips and dragging her into me more tightly. Her whimper tells me I'm on the right track with this. She's certainly distracted.

Lifting one hand, I tangle my fingers in her hair, anchoring her in place gently. Then I pull back from the kiss and begin to trail my mouth along her jawline. I feather kisses down from her ear to her neck and then lower.

She shudders beneath my touch with a breathy moan. I smile against her skin and then trace back over the path I'd followed until I find her mouth again.

Alyssa grips the front of my shirt tightly as if she's holding on for dear life. Her grip trembles when I delve into her mouth, exploring slowly and lazily. I wrap an arm around her waist, and she lets me pull her flush against me. Her hips shift against mine, and I groan this time, pulling back to tip her head so I can trail my mouth down the column of her throat this time.

"Wait," she gasps and shivers, but she pulls at my grip.

I let her go immediately, worried. "What? What's wrong? Did I do something?"

She shakes her head. "It isn't you... I'm just... I'm tired, Damien. We shouldn't go further with this right now or I won't be able to stop, and I need sleep."

The look on her face is tight and harrowed. She's tired, but that isn't why she's pulling away. She's afraid, and she doesn't know how to cope with it. I'm a distraction, but not enough of one to keep her from worrying about the danger she and Timothy are in. I need to take a different approach, and distracting her with sex isn't it.

"Okay. First, we're going to sit for a bit and talk. I don't like being lied to, little girl." I reach out and cup her cheek in a palm. "You might be tired, but you're pulling away because you're afraid of your current situation and you don't want it getting any more complicated with what's happening between us."

She flushes and stares down at her feet. "I... I guess that's part of it. Everything's spinning out of control, and I don't know what to do. This thing between us... I don't know what it is or what we are."

I let out a slow breath. Now would be a good time to tell her we're something more than just the moments in bed. I'm still not ready to tell her that I love her, but I can offer her that. "We're more than just the sex, Alyssa. I care about you. Otherwise, I wouldn't be trying to make this all work out like this. I'd send you off to Timbuktu and wish you the best of luck hiding until the issue with the crime bosses blows over."

Her flush deepens. "You mean it?"

"Every bit, love. I know we're not stable yet in what we are, but I promise you that the types of measures I've taken to protect you and Timothy are ones I'm taking because I care about you, and I want to keep you safe."

She bites her lip and nods. "I'm really scared. What if this doesn't work?"

"For now, we have to assume it will. I think bringing you here will be enough of a signal to the other family that you're mine and off-limits."

"And your father?" Her lower lip trembles. "What about him? Am I a target for him too?"

My shoulders tense. I want to lie to her, but I know it's a bad idea to add to the lies I'm already telling. She'll probably see through it, and there's no sense pretending things are something they're not. "He'll do whatever he finds necessary to force me back to the family and into the life of crime I always refused. He thinks that if he sends someone else to collect the debt, someone who will go after you, it might force my hand. He'll do it if I take too long."

"Will this be enough to protect me from your family, then?"

The question is soft, but it packs a punch anyway. I hate that she's in danger because of my family, not just the other family after her father. I hate that my father has threatened the woman I love, and I hate that there's no way to stop it but to press her into a marriage she may not be ready for or want at all. But I'm going to do this anyway because I know it's what I need to do. I don't have to like doing it, but I do have to convince her to cooperate with the plan. "I don't know," I whisper back. "But it doesn't matter. I won't let them hurt you. I don't care what I have to do, Alyssa. You and Timothy will be protected until this is over."

"Will you stay with me until I fall asleep?" She finally looks up and meets my gaze with tear-filled eyes. "I just want you to hold me."

"Of course I will." I scoop her up and carry her to the bed. "You only ever have to ask, love."

We cuddle up under the covers, and I hold her close until her breathing evens out. When it does, I know I could leave, but I stay anyway. I don't want to lose a moment with her. Who knows how many more I'll have when this all ends?

Chapter Twenty-One: Alyssa

I WANT TO say I'm doing well adjusting to my new situation, but that's a bit of a lie. The truth is, I'm freaked out and struggling. I'm trying to be strong because I know Damien's doing everything he can, but I'm scared out of my mind and don't know what to do.

Staying at Damien's all day is leaving me going a little stir-crazy. I only leave when I go to work with him or when I need to take Timothy to his usual doctor's appointments. It's driving me nuts.

Damien told me not to leave the house by myself. He has an alarm system to keep us safe and men on call to handle any tripped alarms before anything can happen to us, but I need a break after a week of this, so I slip out once my usual babysitter shows up to watch Timothy for an hour and disarm the perimeter alarms so I can take a walk.

I'm not planning to go far. After all, I don't want to leave Timothy with a sitter for too long, and I don't want to worry Damien. He's out for the day meeting with a friend, but it's Saturday, and I don't want to hang out in the house alone and cooped up the whole day.

It feels good to be out under the strong sunshine and in the fresh air. I feel like I've been suffocating, and being out here on a walk like I usually would be loosens something in my chest.

Halfway down the side road that borders Damien's corner property, I see two men in suits meandering along the sidewalk. It strikes me as odd, but I figure they're probably just Mormons or Jehovah's Witnesses out for Saturday morning evangelizing. We get a lot of them around the suburbs.

It's only when they approach me that I start to worry. With everything going on, even if they aren't any danger, I feel unsafe. I start to back away and turn to go back toward the house when one of them grabs my arm and tugs me back.

I suck in a breath to scream, but the blunt, cold steel barrel of a gun jabs into my side. The chill seeps through my thin tank top, and I curse myself for disobeying Damien's orders. Why didn't I just stay inside? I could have run on the treadmill like I've been doing.

"Stay quiet. We just want to talk. Let's walk nicely back to the front porch and have a little chat, girlie," the one holding my arm says.

I nod frantically. Talking is good, right? Talking means no shooting. Yet. If I can keep them talking, then maybe I won't get shot.

We walk slowly back to Damien's front porch. I take a seat as far from the men as I can get, but it leaves me with nowhere to run as they cut off the exits. I'll have to go over the porch railing, and I can't reach the front door to protect Timothy if they go after him.

Suddenly, the walk seems like the worst decision I've made in my whole life. I rub my hands over my thighs and smile weakly at the two suited men. The one with the gun tucks it into his holster just out of sight if anyone walks past.

"So... what did you want to talk about?" My voice squeaks painfully despite my attempt at nonchalance.

"We want to talk about what your father owes us." The man who grabbed my arm takes a seat on the chair across from me.

"Oh, I don't know anything about that!" My hands are shaking too now. "He doesn't confide in me."

"You don't need to know anything about it. You're going to talk to him about what he owes us, and you're going to deliver a message for us, pretty girl," the guy with the gun says.

His friend smiles in a way that makes my skin crawl. "After all, it would be a shame if he didn't pay, and we had to take payment from you and your son."

"If it's money you want, I'm sure I can scrape up something." I don't have much to spare being a single mom with bills to pay, but Damien pays me pretty well, and I have savings. "This doesn't have to end in violence."

"Your father racked up the debt, so your father pays it, girlie." The man across from me smirks. "We have principles, see? Besides, there's no way you can pull together enough of your own money to pay what he owes us. Even if you could, I hear your … protector's family also has a beef with your old man, and you definitely can't pull together enough to pay Damien Darino's father. The two are always at each other's throats. He won't accept your money any more than he accepted his son's attempt to pay your old man's debt."

I swallow hard, my stomach cramping. Damien tried to pay his father off to leave me alone. I didn't know he did that, and it leaves me feeling a little warm. Only for a moment, though. Then I'm back to the cold knot of fear in the pit of my stomach. "I don't know why you think I can make him pay."

"Because I know he loves you and your mother. His grandson too." The man with the gun put his hands on his hips. "If he knows you're in danger, he'll pay."

"He can't," I whisper. "My parents don't make much, and he doesn't have the money."

"You better hope that's not true, pet." The man across from me stands with a wicked grin and crosses the space between us.

He grabs my chin before I can jerk away and drags me to my feet. Our bodies collide, and I can feel how turned on he is by this. My stomach flips. Damien warned me about this. Deep down, I knew he was right, but it wasn't driven home fully until this moment. This man would hurt me without remorse in more ways than I can imagine, and he'd enjoy it.

"If he doesn't, pet, you and I are going to have some fun. Well ... I am. So is Petey there? You? Maybe not so much. And the baby? There's not a lot of fun to be had there yet, but there are people who would pay to have him. I'll bet that'll help cover a good chunk of what's owed to my bosses."

I shiver and close my eyes. "I'll talk to him."

He leans closer, skating his mouth against mine and biting my lower lip. "You'd better convince him, not just talk to him, pet."

My whole body trembles. He releases me with a laugh and heads off the porch. His buddy follows, and I'm left alone again. I drop to the porch floor, throwing up as what just happened hits me fully. It wasn't enough that Damien took me in. Being under his protection doesn't mean much to these thugs, and I'm still in terrible danger along with my son. What am I going to do now?

***

WHEN THE FRONT door opens, I force myself to move from my catatonic state on the couch to see who's come in. It shouldn't be possible for anyone besides Damien to come inside without a passcode, but I'm too shaken up to trust that.

I'm relieved when I see Damien in the entryway.

He takes one look at my face and frowns. "Alyssa, what's wrong?"

I break down in tears. The events earlier in the day have left me frazzled and at my breaking point, and that one question is enough to tip me over the edge.

Damien's arms are around me a few moments later. Then he scoops me up and cradles me to him, walking towards his bedroom. "Do you want to tell me what's going on?"

I bury my face in his neck and shake my head. In a few minutes, when I've had enough time to calm down, I'll tell him. I need to talk to someone. My fears are starting to eat me alive, and I need to hear him tell me it will all work out. Right now, though, I just need to be given the space to cry and feel his arms wrapped securely around me.

He sighs and nudges his bedroom door open with his foot. Taking me to the bed, he sets me down and curls up with me. "Okay. We'll take it in steps, sunshine. First, cry it out. Then, when you're calm, you'll tell me what's wrong. We'll talk about it and figure it out together. Can we do that?"

I nod miserably.

He gathers me into his chest and kisses the top of my head. "Good. Then just let it all out so you can get to a point where you're ready to talk to me."

I bury my face in his shirt and let myself cry for everything I've lost in the last few months. It's a lot of things to cry for.

I've lost my independence, my security, my home, and my trust in both of my parents. I've been left with my trust in Damien shaken, robbed of everything I thought I knew about him, and told that his family is worse than I ever could have imagined.

I'm stuck imposing on his hospitality because I'm not safe out there on my own, and the attack today has only solidified that.

The reasons I'm upset and hurting just seem to keep piling up, and my tears flow until I'm too stuffed up to breathe properly and have to sit up to find a tissue from the box on his nightstand.

He rubs my back for me while I blow my nose and fight to calm down. "Ready to try to talk about it now?" he asks gently.

I nod with a sniffle.

"Okay. Tell me what happened to make you a nervous wreck when I came in."

Rubbing away the tears, I start, knowing he's going to be furious when I tell him what I did. "I wanted to go for a walk," I whisper. "I was just feeling claustrophobic being stuck in the house lately. So, I disarmed the perimeter alarms like you showed me to do and went for a walk."

His expression goes from concerned to dangerously near fury. "You mean to tell me you went out without telling me or anyone else? You went out without someone with you?"

"I didn't take Timothy." I drop my gaze to the bedspread and pick at it for invisible lint.

"That just means he would've been abandoned at home alone until I got back to find you gone if anything had happened." He grabs my chin and pulls it up so that I'm looking him in the face. "I am beyond tempted to punish you for that, sunshine."

I bite my lip, shocked at his response. I mean, I knew he'd be upset. I didn't expect him to threaten punishment. He's never really done that before. "I'm sorry," I whisper. "Please... I don't... I learned my lesson."

He searches my face with a frown. "What else happened? You might have been worried about my reaction and feeling guilty about leaving without someone along, but that's not what had you scared until you saw me."

"Two men approached me on the walk. They cornered me and threatened me. I—" Tears well. "They're going to hurt me and Timothy if I can't find a way to get them the money from my dad. And they told me that if I couldn't, they'd be happy to make the money back selling Timothy and... and... using me." I start to cry again past the words.

His jaw tightens, and a muscle in it works. "Did they hurt you?"

I shake my head. "I'm scared, though. I can't make my father pay, and he doesn't have the money anyway. I'm so scared they'll make good on the threat. What if I have to run with Timothy and spend the rest of my life hiding?"

He cups my cheeks with his hands and shakes his head. "Not going to happen." His gaze shifts away from mine, and he seems a little uncomfortable when he says the next bit. "I can't do more right now, Alyssa. I wish I could, but for now, just know that you won't have to run. We'll figure it out."

I nod, but deep down, I'm wondering why he looks guilty even as he promises me there's no more he can do to help. It feels like he's hiding something, and that leaves me shaken. I've already learned so many terrible things. What more is there that he hasn't told me, and just how bad is it if he's avoiding telling me? More importantly, at this point, do I even want to know?

Chapter Twenty-Two: Damien

I'M SPENDING THE day with Alyssa and Timothy out in a park in Upstate New York. I needed to get them away from the things back in the city that were stressing Alyssa out, and this was the best I could think of. It's secluded, far enough away from the city to minimize the risk that she's attacked, and peaceful.

Alyssa's pushing Timothy in the swing while I get us lunch from the hot dog stand by the playground. I watch Alyssa while I wait for the food, admiring the way her hair blows in the wind and the way her face lights up when she smiles. She hasn't had many reasons to smile like that lately.

Time is running down on us, and while Alyssa is less stressed than she has been in a while, I'm going to ruin that soon. I'm going to have to tell Alyssa the only viable way out of our predicament, but I also know she may not like it. I also don't have the first clue how to go about breaking the news to her that marrying me is the only way out.

Alyssa's not only going to hate it—she already disliked the whole moving-in-with-me bit—but she's going to want to know if it's forever or temporary. That wouldn't be a problem if I wanted temporary, as I suspect she will. At least, it wouldn't be if I agreed to sign Timothy over to her in a prenup. But I don't want to let her or Timothy go when the danger is past, and with all the lies I'm already telling or secrets I'm holding onto, I'm not going to lie to her about that.

Of course, I feel like a piece of garbage for using the situation to get what I wanted from her to begin with. It hasn't just been about sex with her for me. Not for a long time. Not since I realized that she was all I ever thought about or that other women just didn't do it for me anymore. I doubt it's like that for Alyssa, though. However she feels, though, I'm out of time and the luxury of following my conscience or her wishes on the matter. Now I have to act decisively and without allowing any lingering misgivings to impede me.

"Here are the hot dogs, man." The kid at the counter shoves two hot dogs with all the condiments at me. He pushes over two baskets of fries with them. "And the fries."

"Thanks." I collect the food and take it to a picnic table near the swings.

Alyssa pulls Timothy out of the baby swing and puts him back into his car seat. Then she brings him over and sets him on the bench next to me before taking the seat across from me. "Thanks for getting us lunch."

"It's not a problem. I was happy to do it." I turn to Timothy and smile broadly at him. "Hi, Timothy. You look happy. Did you have fun with Mommy pushing you on the swings?"

"You're good with him," Alyssa says quietly.

I look up at her. "You sound surprised. You didn't think I'd be good with kids?"

"Well... it's not that." She sighs. "It's just that you're normally so uptight and grumpy. I didn't think kids would be your thing."

I shrug. "I kind of always wanted a kid of my own. Yeah, I'm a bit of a grump, but I'm a grump with a soft spot. Lucky for you."

She blushes and looks away with a laugh. "I guess. Damien, can I ask you something?"

"Anything. I just don't promise I'll have an answer."

"Is something wrong? You seem upset and tense, even when you're in a place where you should be able to let your guard down. Did I do something wrong?"

Alyssa hasn't done a thing. This is all me. I don't want to do the wrong thing by her, but I also don't want her dead. "You haven't done anything wrong. I'm just dealing with a lot."

"Will you talk to me about it?"

I shake my head. "We don't need to talk about it, little girl. I'm managing the situation fine. You don't need to worry about me either."

A slight frown furrows her brow. "So I have to talk to you about my worries, and you don't have to talk to me about yours?"

I smile and shrug. "I'm built to take a lot more. I'm a protector, love. It's what I'm made for. Trust me when I say that what I'm handling is more than you can bear. More than you should have to bear. Let me handle it and don't ask me to burden you with it."

Alyssa shakes her head. "I don't get it... why can't I handle it?"

"Because you'll worry yourself sick and still not be able to change it. I may or may not be able to change the situation, but I'm not going to worry myself until I'm sick. I handle stress differently. Better. Trust me when I say that I'll figure it out on my own. If I do need advice or want to vent, I'll come to you."

Alyssa's gaze drops away from mine, a sure sign she's hurt. She doesn't seem to know what to say. "So, you don't think I can be trusted with whatever's going on to upset you?"

If it weren't for the threats from the Giovanni family, I would've told her already. I reach across the table and lay a hand over hers. "I do trust you, Alyssa. And if I think you're able to help or give advice on something that's bothering me, you'll be the first place I go. Always. But in this case, I need to handle it on my own, and I don't want you to worry about it."

I don't want Alyssa to feel guilty for something she can't change, so until I figure out a plan of action and things have settled, I'm going to keep the problems to myself. I'll do whatever I have to if it'll keep her safe and allow her to face the world with me instead of being confined to the house living in fear. Even if it might mean I lose her in the end, I'd rather let her live free than see her living in fear like this.

She drops the issue and focuses on her food after that. I start in on mine too, and I hope she'll let this go for good because I don't want her worrying.

I also don't want to think about the fact that before too long, I'll have to choose between telling her the plan Stew and I devised. It's the only way out, and I can't hold back forever. Still, until I find the right time to tell her, I'm determined to let her have at least a little space to breathe before the next thing is thrown at her.

***

MARCELLO, MY CONTACT in the other family, sits across from me in the third restaurant we like to meet at in the city. We decided to meet to discuss what's going on in Marcello's family. I need to know why they went after Alyssa despite her presence in my home and the clear signal that sends about who she's with.

My longtime friend and informant dips his chip into some queso and chews on it, contemplating how to start. He has a habit of taking his time to think before he launches into things. Finally, he takes a swallow of water and starts.

"The family isn't happy about your choice to move Alyssa in with you."

"Mine's furious, and I know why. Why is yours mad?" I cross my arms.

"Potential loss of leverage," Marcello says. "You're toeing the line dangerously, my friend. They're not going to let you keep protecting her without consequence."

"Tell them I did it to protect Timothy so he won't be caught in the crossfire, and Alyssa wouldn't let me take him without moving her too."

Marcello eyes me. "I'll tell them, but I can't promise you they'll buy it."

"Besides, loss of leverage isn't the problem here... If it were, they wouldn't have accosted her on a walk outside the property and threatened her. They don't feel my moving Alyssa under my roof means she's off limits."

Marcello looks up at me and grimaces. "I heard about that one after the fact. If I'd known—"

"I know you would've told me. I'm not holding it against you," I promise him.

My thoughts turn to how frightened Alyssa was when I came home after the attack. She took a long time to calm down. I'm still furious with her for endangering herself so recklessly without the need to do so, but I understand how the house can begin to feel like a cage after too much time confined.

"It's not just that they're unhappy about lost opportunities," Marcello admits. "It's more than that. They don't believe her family is under your protection. They don't believe she is, and they want to find a way to get past you to get to her. But it's a good thing they still believe that because if they didn't, you'd be in some serious hot water legally already. If I tell them what you said about Timothy, it'll only reinforce the idea she's not off limits."

"It's not going to happen again. They got lucky because she chose to disregard my instructions not to leave the property alone. She won't repeat the mistake." I take a chip from the basket, salt it, and eat it plain. "Do you know how they're going to get past me?"

"My best guess? They'll try to get to her at a time when you're not home. Or not meant to be. The leaders of these men aren't dumb, even if their men aren't always good at carrying out orders in a rational way." Marcello sighs and rubs his forehead. "I don't know what else they'll do, and I don't know the plans."

"You just know she's still in danger because no one's buying the live-in girlfriend bit."

Marcello spreads his hands in defeat. "Precisely. They don't buy the ruse. It's why I said something about marriage the other day. I know you hate the idea of feeling somewhat manipulative, but you have to set that aside to do what's ultimately best. And some minor emotional harm is better than a lot more inflicted due to doing what you know to be wrong from desperation."

I do hate the idea. I don't want to have Alyssa marry me simply to avoid danger. I want her to be mine because she wants to be mine.

"I know you hate it, Damien," Marcello says, reaching out for my hand. "But if you love that girl and your baby, you'll do it. Do it in a way that lets you sleep at night if you need to, but don't wait. If you wait, it'll be too late for her."

I nod. The news troubles me, but it won't do us any good to ruminate on it. "Is there anything else going on I should know about?"

"Your father's men are moving in on her father too. We've spotted some of them lurking. Weren't you assigned to collect?"

"Yes." I grit my teeth.

The waitress shows up with our meals before he can say anything further. We both force smiles and wait until she leaves to continue talking.

"So, he's given up on making you collect?"

I massage my temples. "Not exactly. He threatened to send men who would go after her if I didn't collect. He's decided to do so, tentatively."

"All the more reason to marry her," Marcello says. "If you think you can handle the legal nightmare they'll pile down on your head."

"I realize that. And I'm not worried about the legal nightmare." I take a bite of my burger with a sigh. "I love her, Marcello. I don't want to push her into marrying me simply to escape the danger she's in, and I don't want Alyssa to regret it or hate me afterward because the Giovannis publish lies that will land me in court and have her believing I've been involved with this and lying to her all along."

"Our lives don't always give us the luxury of being romantics, Damien. Find a way to show her that you love her by doing this to protect her."

I have no idea how to do that, and I have a suspicion that Alyssa won't see it that way. No matter what I say, she's going to see this as me doing something to save her out of obligation because of Timothy or out of pity. She's not going to believe it's out of love. "Thanks, Marcello."

He nods, and the two of us turn our attention to our meals without talking further about business or our families' activities.

***

AFTER THE MEETING with Marcello, I go to see Stew. I want to make sure I have everything nailed down for this next move, and I know I need a backup plan in case things go wrong. Since Stew's the only one who knows everything that's been going on, he's the best person to use as a sounding board as I sort out the details for the plans I'm going to set into motion.

He lets me into his house with an appraising look and then a nod. "You're going to tell her finally."

I smile grimly. "No better way at this point. I want to make sure I have everything rock solid for this next move, though, and if things go wrong, we need a plan for where to hide them and how."

Stew waves me in and leads the way into the den. "Okay, so what's the plan so far?"

"Marcello is going to buy us a little time by telling the Giovannis that I took Alyssa and Timothy in because I wanted to protect Timothy and Alyssa wouldn't leave without him. I'm going to ask her to marry me, but I'm not going to tell her how I feel."

He levels me with a flat stare.

I stare back. "It would be cruel, Stewart. Honesty will only end up making her question everything we have when the Giovannis follow through on their threats. I've thought a lot about it, and I won't do that to her. I'd rather she think this was just out of duty or a desire to protect our son than that she questions whether I ever loved her at all. At least then I might stand a chance of convincing I did all along later if I can dig myself out of the charges that are sure to accompany the lies the Giovannis plan to spread."

Stew sighs. "Fine. I don't like it, but I get it. What else?"

"I need a plan to get them out of the country, and I'm not going to be able to handle that myself if this goes belly up. So, I was hoping you and your contacts might help with that if it comes to it."

"You don't even have to ask," Stew says. "I'll get her out somewhere safe, Damien."

"Where?"

"You shouldn't know that. If I tell you and they torture you trying to get to her, it'll just put her and Timothy at risk. Best to have it be information that only her extraction team knows."

Not knowing where she'll be will kill me if it comes to that, but he's right. So, I nod without any protest. "Good. Is there anything I need to consider that I haven't?"

"I think you have it covered."

I meet my friend's gaze with a deep breath. "Then there's nothing left but to give her the choice and then face the world and watch it all burn."

"Watch it all burn and pray the winds blow in our favor," Stew says grimly.

That is precisely what we're doing here. The only question now is, will it all blow up in our faces, or am I going to get out of this unscathed with Alyssa and Timothy at my side?

Chapter Twenty-Three: Alyssa

I CAN'T SEEM to shake the sense that something's wrong with Damien. We've been living together for three weeks now, and he seems to avoid talking about anything related to the men who threatened me. He still insists I don't leave the house without him or a bodyguard, and I've been following those rules, but he seems more stressed out than warranted by our situation. It's like he has a secret he's keeping and it's eating away at him.

Since he won't give me answers, I go to the one other person who might know what's going on and give me a straight answer. Lucille. She and Damien are the only ones in the family who are still close to one another, and if anyone knows what Damien's hiding, it'll be Lucille.

I turn to the bodyguard who's traveling with me when Damien's not around and smile. "Could you stay out here on the porch? I'll be fine with Lucille."

He looks around with a frown, but when Lucille opens the door, he nods and takes a seat on her porch swing.

"Thanks." I genuinely do appreciate the man's protection, but sometimes, I just need a break to feel normal for a little while. Besides, this conversation isn't one I want to have with someone listening who may report everything back to Damien.

"What's going on?" Lucille asks as soon as the door shuts behind us.

I take Timothy's car seat into the living room and pull him out of the seat to nurse him. "I wanted to talk to you about Damien. You know we've moved in together thanks to the whole situation with my dad."

"Yeah...." Lucille sits across from me and rests her elbows on her knees. "And?"

"And it just seems like he's way more nervous than he should be. He told me that this would get the men after my father off my back once we'd been living together for a while. We haven't seen any more of the men lurking around since the group told me I had a week to sort out the money." I cuddle Timothy close and encourage him to nurse. "It just seems like something else is wrong, and I thought you might know what."

Lucille shifts with a frown. "You can't tell him I told you anything, okay?"

"Okay...." My stomach drops in dread. "Why? Is it really bad?"

"Well... sort of? Maybe? Look, the whole family is really upset that he took you in. Like, my dad summoned Damien to the family home while I was up visiting my mom, and I heard him shouting at Damien for refusing to collect your father's debts."

"His father still hasn't given up on that?"

"I think he has. I overheard some of the men talking about how he was losing patience." Lucille's face is pale, and she looks a little sick. "I think he might plan to send some of them to do the job, and I don't know if your being with Damien will be enough to protect you, Alyssa. That's probably what's worrying Damien."

Now I feel sick too. How could Damien keep this from me? I know he wants to protect me, but keeping secrets like this won't do that. It just puts me in more danger.

"There's more that they were arguing over," Lucille admits. "The other family is angry that Damien is harboring you."

"What? Why?"

Lucille shrugged. "If I had to guess because it means that if they go after you to get to your father, they're tangling with Damien and my whole family by extension. It's probably why my father's so angry about it. He didn't want the family name being used to protect you."

I close my eyes and hold Timothy a little closer. What kind of mess have I been dropped into? I'm glad that Damien's stepping in to help and protect me. I know I'd be a sitting duck if not for my connection to him. Still, I can't help feeling like my connection to him is also half the reason I'm in this mess. I should just disappear. Then I'd be free of all of this. "What if I just leave?" I ask softly.

"It won't help. You'll just be running for your whole life, never knowing when it's safe to stop. That's no life at all, Alyssa. Just trust Damien. Do what he asks and trust him to take care of you and Timothy."

Part of me knows she's right. The part of me that's terrified and looking for a way out still wants to run. This is even less fair to him than it is to me, though. He's only helping because he knows about Timothy and feels obligated. He feels a connection to me. I know he cares, but caring isn't the same as loving, and he didn't ask for this.

"Whatever just went through your head, forget about it," Lucille says.

I meet her gaze. "This isn't fair to him. If not for Timothy, he wouldn't be caught up in the middle of this."

"That isn't true. First, it isn't true because Damien loves you. He may not know how to say it, but he's trying to show it the best way he knows how."

I'm not as sure about that. He's never said it, and as far as I can tell, he's just fond of me. That and he likes being in my bed and having a part in his son's life. This puts us back to his feeling obligated to get involved to protect his son.

"Second, my father would've tried to drag him into dealing with your father's debts even if Timothy weren't a factor. Even if you weren't. And third...." She holds up a finger to hold back my protest. "Third, he chose to get involved. Damien doesn't do things because he feels obligated to. He does them because he wants to or because he believes it's the right thing to do. Maybe you should be talking to him about all of this instead of assuming his motives and feelings, Alyssa."

I stare down at the baby nursing at my breast with tears in my eyes. "I'm scared of what I might learn... I'm afraid I'm nothing more than a fun pastime for him and that he's only sticking around for Timothy."

"Do you love him, Alyssa?" Lucille asks.

Closing my eyes, I shrug. I'm not ready to admit to her or myself what I know deep down. I am in love with him, and I can't bear the thought of finding out he doesn't feel the same. I prefer to not know and believe he's just doing this for Timothy because it hurts less than asking and finding out that he's acting out of a sense of obligation.

"You should admit the truth to yourself," she says softly. "And then you should talk to him before your communication issues drive a wedge between you that can't be fixed."

***

LUCILLE'S WORDS ARE still ringing in my mind when I step into Damien's house. The air conditioning is a welcome relief from the summer heat, and I stand in the entryway for a moment with Timothy's car seat clutched tightly in one hand. I know Lucille is right. I know I need to confront how I feel and talk to Damien about it, but I'm not ready to yet.

The other things she told me are easier to confront and easier to deal with.

Damien rounds the corner of the hallway and stands with his hands in his pockets, watching me quietly. "You look upset."

I lick my lips and watch his gaze flick to my mouth. "I am."

He doesn't move from his spot. "You went to see Lucille. About me, I assume?"

I look away. "I needed answers. You've been tense and upset, and you wouldn't talk to me. Lucille told me that there are still issues with the other family. That your family is upset that you're harboring me. Is that true?"

"It is." He moves then, striding over and taking the car seat from me. "Let's put him down for his afternoon nap, and then we'll talk."

I nod, relieved that I'm going to get some answers now. The two of us walk in silence to the stairs. Damien pauses at the foot of the stairs and unbuckles a sleepy Timothy from the car seat. Timothy fusses a bit, but Damien cradles him close and hushes him with a soft kiss on the top of the baby's head.

Seeing the two of them always leaves a strange warmth in my chest. I realize, as I watch him carry Timothy upstairs, that Lucille was right. He does love our son. It's not an obligation so much as it is a father's love and protectiveness toward his child. I don't know if the same love and protectiveness extends to me or if he's only protecting me because of Timothy, but it makes me feel a little better about letting him help.

We go upstairs together, and I watch him settle Timothy into the crib. Then he turns to me, his stare intense and serious. He takes my hand and draws me down the hall to his bedroom. I let him, unsure if I'm ready to hear what he has to say but knowing I need to. I have to know what sort of danger we're up against for my peace of mind.

He sits down and pulls me to stand between his thighs, his hands on my hips. "I didn't want to tell you because I didn't want you to worry, Alyssa."

"Tell me anyway," I murmur.

He looks like he's fighting an internal battle with himself over what to tell me and what not to. It must be difficult for him to go against his instinct to protect those in his care, and I know I'm asking a lot. I also know that this impacts me, and I need to know how careful I need to be. I don't want to be jumping at shadows if there's no danger, but I also don't want to be blind to the danger lurking in the shadows if it exists.

Heaving a sigh, he closes his eyes and rests his forehead against my rib cage. "Okay. The other family still has factions who want to take you as a means to pressure your father to pay them. They don't believe that you're my girlfriend, and they aren't buying the whole moving-in-together bit. They think it's a ruse to protect you."

"Isn't it?" I whisper.

He doesn't look up or answer that. When he speaks again, it's to talk about something else entirely. "My father doesn't believe we're an item either. He thinks I'm just trying to hold on to you so he can't use you to pressure me into doing his bidding."

"Is that what you're doing?" I ask, throat tightening.

His grip on my hips tightens. "No."

When he doesn't elaborate, I realize there must be more to the answer, but he's not going to share. Maybe it's just as well. Knowing his motives might mean nothing but heartache, and I'm not ready to face that. Not right now with everything else going on.

"So, what's the solution? Is there anything we can do?" I rest my hands on his shoulders, needing to ground myself.

I have not just one crime family trying to use me as leverage but two, and one of them doesn't risk a war if they do go after me. I'm not sure who to be more scared of: the other family or Damien's father. "How bad is it, really?"

"My father sent other men to handle the job he wanted me to do." Damien lifts his head to look up at me, his jaw tight. "Those men wouldn't hesitate to hurt you if they thought it would bring me back into the fold, love. The situation is bad."

"But it's just your father and the other family, right? There isn't anything else, anything worse, you aren't sharing, is there?"

He brushes his thumbs over my sides and then reaches up to take one of my hands and presses a kiss to my palm. "I don't want you to be scared, Alyssa. I'm working on a solution."

I nod, but deep down, as he pulls me into his lap and holds me close, I know he isn't telling me everything. There's more, and that's what scares me the most. What could be so much worse than having two crime families after me that he can't bring himself to share? Hasn't the worst already begun?

Chapter Twenty-Four: Damien

I KNOW I can't keep hiding the plan from Alyssa. Since discovering that my father has put other men on the job to collect the debt Alyssa's father owes him, my time to enact the plan has dwindled. I have very little time left. Still, I want it to be done the right way, even if she's probably going to hate me for what I'm going to suggest. There's been no indication she's in love with me. She comes to my bed gladly and willingly, but lust and love aren't the same, and I don't think I've won her heart.

How could I have? I haven't even told her how I feel. So far as she knows, I'm just protecting her because of Timothy and some affection for her as the mother of my child. I should have been plainer about my love for her sooner, but I was scared. Now I'm probably going to pay the price.

"Alyssa?" I step inside after a long day at work, dreading what I have to do next. The velvet box with the ring I bought her a week ago is burning a hole in my pocket.

She rounds the corner from the living room with a frown. "Is something wrong?"

"No. I just want to take you out for dinner tonight. I hired a nanny to watch Timothy for tonight. All you have to do is dress nicely and say yes to the invitation."

Her frown deepens, and she walks over, putting a hand in mine. "Did you have a rough day at work? You seem tense."

I squeeze her hand with a wan smile. "Yeah. It was a long day. But I want to forget about it and just take you out to enjoy a stress-free dinner. Please?"

She lets go of my hand with a nod. "Okay. I'll go change. Thank you, Damien."

"You're welcome."

I'm tempted to tell her I'll do anything to please the woman I love, but I hold back. The Giovanni family made it clear that if I protect her, things will go badly for me.

She's going to see some horrible things if they make good on that threat, things that will make her hate me. She doesn't need me to burden her with my feelings before that happens. When the Giovanni family releases the fake documents and embroils me in legal battles over crimes I never committed, Alyssa will hate me even more if I've told her how much I care. She's going to think I told her I loved her today only to manipulate her into cooperating before the truth could come out. She'll believe I only said it to get what I want, maybe even that I said it so she'd marry me and let me take Timothy when it comes to a divorce. Telling her the whole truth isn't possible, and telling her only part of it so she can later be hurt even worse is just cruel. When I tell her I love her, I want her to know I mean it, and I don't want anything surrounding it to make her call my intentions into question.

I watch her go with my stomach in knots. She's so beautiful, and I desperately want her, but this situation we're in is making it impossible to show her that. She sees my protection as a duty I fulfill, not something I do because I love her. I can see it in her eyes. And I don't want to do anything to add to that impression, nor do I want her to think I'm using the situation to get what I want out of her rather than navigating the situation to protect her.

What I'm going to do tonight is probably going to make it even harder to convince her I'm not acting out of duty or manipulation. My heart sinks. This whole situation is causing me grief, and I'm not pleased about it. The sooner I can get it out of the way, the better. I need her safe, and I need her to be mine because she loves me like I love her, not because of some threat to her life.

When she comes downstairs twenty minutes later, I'm pacing the foyer in tense, short strides. I stop when I hear her footsteps on the stairs and look up to find her in a blue cocktail dress that compliments her eyes and skin tone. She's put her hair up and added some jewelry, and she has a little makeup on that wasn't there before.

Her cheeks flush as I stare, and she drops her gaze to the black kitten heels she's donned. "Is it not enough? I didn't think we were going somewhere really fancy."

"It's perfect. Come here." I stand still, my heart pounding, and wait for her to obey the command.

She walks to me hesitantly, her heels clicking on the entry-way floor. "What is it?"

I lean in and kiss her slowly and deeply. It's the only expression of love that I can give right now, and I wish I could be certain she would understand. Deep down, though, I know she won't. When I pull back, I stroke my thumb over her cheek gently. "You're beautiful, Alyssa."

Her cheeks flush a deeper shade of crimson. "Thank you."

"Shall we go?" I offer her my arm.

She takes it, and the two of us head out to my car. We drive in silence once she's settled in and buckled. I don't know what to say to her, and my focus is on how to break the news to her without making things any worse. I hate not knowing if she'll be furious, hurt, or relieved. I doubt she'll be happy about the idea. I still don't know for certain how she feels about me, after all. My connection to one of the families putting her life at risk isn't exactly helping my case. It will only lend credibility to the documents the other family has threatened to release, and she'll be that much more likely to believe them. If she even agrees to marry me at all, that is. With my connections, she may refuse, and those documents may never be an issue.

We get to the restaurant, sit down, and order before she breaks the silence. She swirls the wine in her glass with her lower lip caught between her teeth the way she always does when she's worried. Finally, she looks up at me. "Damien, what is it? You seem on edge and upset."

I clear my throat. "Alyssa, I have a solution to the problem we're facing...."

Her expression goes from worry to relief. "You do?"

"But I don't think you'll like it," I murmur.

The relief fades. She frowns at me. "What do you mean?"

"I didn't want to do this, but we're at a point where this is our only choice if you don't want to hide. I don't want my son to live a life on the run, and I know you won't part with him, so this is the only way I can think of to protect both of you." I grimace at the way my words are going to sound. "Marry me."

She gapes at me.

I'm about to interrupt the silence with an explanation when the server shows up with our food. It gives her a convenient excuse to hedge for time, and I can see the words are slowly sinking in as first shock then fear, and then disbelief cross her face.

"No." She shakes her head. "I can't. Not like this. And I'm not going to marry you only to have you regret it later and divorce me. You'd take Timothy. I know how much you're already attached to him."

"I won't take him, Alyssa. If that happens at all, I promise I would never do that to you."

She stares down at her plate and shakes her head again. "I just can't risk it. Not when the only reason you're offering is because you want to protect him and don't want me to die."

"I promise that it isn't a risk, Alyssa. I can't tell you all the reasons it isn't, but I'm willing to sign a prenup before the wedding if I have to. I'm just trying to do what's best for you two."

The remark doesn't gain a response, so I give her the space she needs. It isn't exactly every girl's dream proposal, after all. She doesn't even know I love her. I've told her I care, but I know that doesn't communicate love. It just tells her I'm fond of her. They aren't the same.

To her, I'm offering to shackle myself to her solely to protect her. She never wanted me chained to her, never even imagined I might want my own kid. It won't cross her mind that I might want her too, that I might be offering this because I want her, not just because we're in a pinch. I won't tell her otherwise until this is over because I won't put her through the pain of thinking I lied about something this important too.

We eat our entire meal that way. She barely picks at hers by the time I've eaten the half of mine that I can bear without feeling sick. The tension is palpable, and we're getting glances from the diners at the tables nearby. Something isn't right.

I clear my throat and come back to the question. "Alyssa, I know it's a shock, but it's the solution I have. I'm sorry... I don't want to push or make you feel like you're being forced into anything, but it's the only out I really can offer to protect you and my son. I know you don't want to run, and I don't want him to grow up on the run either. Running and hiding with a baby is going to be so much harder than running alone. This means running doesn't have to happen." It's going to cost me everything, of course, if the other family follows through on their threats. I can't tell her that, though. They've threatened worse than releasing a few documents if I breathe a word of our conversations to anyone, and I'm not ready to try to weather that sort of wr ath.

Pain lances across her face before she looks down at her food and nods. "I don't want to talk about this now. Not here, Damien. I... this isn't the sort of solution you offer just to get someone out of a pinch, and you know how I feel about you doing things you don't want to do. I've already said no."

I can't tell her I love her now. She'll think I'm lying just to make her feel better about this. Instead, I say the next best thing that I can. "I want to keep you and Timothy safe, Alyssa. It isn't something I don't want to do."

Her gaze lifts to mine, and her eyes are full of tears ready to spill at any moment. "When this is over, it won't be.... You're not asking because you love me or you want me permanently, and I don't... I just don't know if I can... I don't want a marriage where you're with me out of duty."

"I'll give you some time to reconsider the answer. Don't make the decision so hastily. We don't have a lot of time for you to think, but I'll give what I can, Alyssa. Please, just consider it." I wave down the waiter to pay the bill. "I don't want you to be on the run or in hiding. Think about Timothy and how he would fare with a lifetime of that."

She falls silent, and it's clear she's shutting down and shutting me out. She doesn't want to think about or talk about this, and I can't blame her. This whole thing has gone poorly, and while it hasn't ended with her slapping me or shouting at me in the middle of the restaurant, I almost think this hurt, fretful silence of hers is worse.

We leave quickly after paying the bill, and she doesn't speak to me at all on the drive home. She says good night very quietly when we get back to the house and disappears into her room. I let her go, unsure what to do next and how to handle the rejection. Did her response in the restaurant mean she'd say yes if she thought I wanted her for real and permanently? Or did it just mean that she didn't want it to be me, and she didn't see a future for us?

***

I TAKE A long walk by myself early in the morning before Alyssa is up. I know I'm watched. The Giovanni family and my own have eyes and ears everywhere. I can even be certain they have people trailing us to overhear what I asked in the restaurant.

As I step into the house, I square my shoulders and prepare for the fight I know we'll have when I press her for a decision. Alyssa will be getting ready to head over to Lucille's soon, so I should be able to catch her now. She'll be up and awake enough to talk, at least.

Sure enough, when I finish taking off my shoes and head into the main house, she's coming down the stairs from the nursery on her way toward the kitchen. She's already dressed and ready to go, though I'm guessing she hasn't had her breakfast or morning coffee yet. It's a weekend, and she usually gets moving late.

"Hey," she says quietly in greeting.

"Hey." I follow her into the kitchen, gearing up for what's about to happen. She isn't going to like that I'm pressing for a decision when I told her last night that I'd give her time.

"You look like you're upset. Is there another bombshell you need to drop?"

There's the faintest hint of frustration underneath the exhaustion in her voice. I feel even worse for what I'm about to do, but I've thought a lot about the situation and Stew's advice. I need to man up and just do what needs to be done. If I don't persuade her, this is going to go sideways fast. "Listen, Alyssa... I told you I'd give you time, but I don't have a lot to give you. You need to hurry with the decision. I'm—" I let out a long breath and rake my fingers through my hair. "I hate that I can't give you all the time you need to think it through, and I hate that I have to rush you on something that I know is a big deal for you, but I can't give you more than a day or two, and I do have to rush you. Getting an answer today would be ideal, but I know you might need another day or two. I just don't have it. I'm sorry."

She frowns and looks away. "You're asking a lot of me, and you said you'd give me time! I don't want to marry you... You'll decide you don't want to be with me when there's no danger anymore, and then you'll fight me for Timothy, and I'm not going to put myself into a battle I know I'm going to lose."

That's never going to happen. "I said I'd sign a prenup if it would help you decide. I meant that, Alyssa."

She still won't look at me. "I'm going to need that time to decide, Damien. I know we don't have much time, but you said you'd give me what you could, and I'm going to take those two days to think through all the ramifications of this. If we do this, and that's a big if, then you're signing that prenup. I'm going to protect me and my baby."

I hate that she feels like she has to protect herself from me, too, but it won't do any good to tell her otherwise when she's convinced my reasons for doing this all center on our son. "Okay." I clear my throat. "I'm going to go upstairs and sit with Timothy for a bit. I'll ask again in a day or two, but if the answer is no, Alyssa, I—there's not much more I can do besides sending you both into hiding and if I have to do that, you'll spend the rest of your life running even if no one's chasing because I can't know where you've ended up for your safety. There won't be anyone to call you back. You'll have to live with the not knowing and the fear, and I don't want to do that to you. I don't want my son to live that kind of life either."

She smiles weakly and puts the pot of coffee on. "I know. I'll think about that before I decide. Just go sit with Timothy for a bit. He's awake and in the little bouncer seat."

"Okay." I retreat, knowing it won't do either of us any good to keep talking about this when she's undecided.

I trudge upstairs, heart heavy and wishing I could go back to tell her I love her. If I'd known I loved her back before this whole thing went to hell in a handbasket, I could've told her. Then she wouldn't be hesitating like she is now.

But that's hindsight, and I didn't know then that what I felt was love, not mere possessiveness or the desire to have her until I was tired of her. I haven't been in love much, and I've never felt anything like what I feel for her and my son.

I find Timothy in the bouncer seat like Alyssa said he would be. Sitting down on the floor in front of him, I smile warmly at the baby. He's the one thing that might cheer me up right now and pull me out of the grumpy, frustrated mood I'm in. "Hey, little man. You're lucky you don't know what's going on right now." I reach out and let him grab my finger.

He giggles and bounces in the seat happily.

"Yeah, your life's just grand, isn't it? I'm trying my best to keep it that way for as long as possible, buddy. But we'll see what your mom decides. You think she'll come around and say yes?"

He just gives me a toothless baby grin in response, eyes so much like my own staring back at me.

"I love you, you know," I tell him quietly. "And I love your mom. I just can't tell her I do yet. There's a lot she doesn't know. A lot of things I'll tell her eventually when I have the ability and chance to. But not yet, and I know she senses that I'm holding back." I pick him up and cradle him close. "I just want you two in my life permanently, little guy. But I want you both happy and safe more than anything, and this is the only way to do it. I owed her so much better than a proposal without even saying 'I love you' to her. I owe her so much more than a rushed affair like this, too. But I can't give her that."

Timothy gurgles and reaches out to pat my cheek as if he's trying to console me. Then he grins again and giggles a little, clearly not comprehending the mood I'm in. I grin back anyway, unable to help it. If only I could keep him this innocent and sweet forever. For as long as I can, I'm going to be part of his life, protecting him and his mother. But am I going to be able to do enough, or will I lose them in the end, even if I can save them from the crime families intent on harming them?

Chapter Twenty-Five: Alyssa

I'VE BEEN UP all night thinking. Yesterday, I went upstairs to bring Damien a coffee as a way to tell him I'm not holding the bad situation we're in against him. When I did, I overheard him talking to our son. He told Timothy he loved us both. Not just Timothy, but me too. And I don't know what to do with that.

I could have gone in and let him know I was there and talked to him about it. Instead, I stayed in the hall and listened as he told Timothy what I'd feared all along—that he's hiding something. Yes, he claimed he didn't have a choice, but Damien has so much clout and money that I can't imagine how he would be without a choice. It makes deciding what to do harder than it was before because now

I know he does love us, but I don't know if it's enough when I also know he's hiding major secrets. So now I don't know what to do with Damien's offer. It's the last day I have to decide, and true to his word on the day he came home and told me I needed to decide soon, he's given me the time he can. He hasn't broached the topic again, but we both know it's hanging there between us, leaving us both on edge around each other.

While I love Damien, the thought of marrying him with all of these secrets between us leaves me feeling sick. It helps some to know he does love me and just doesn't feel he can say it for some reason, but the reasons for not saying it are now what leaves me hesitating and frightened to say yes. Part of me wants to say yes anyway because I want him. The other part argues that when this is over, I'm probably just setting myself up for a world of hurt when all the secrets come out, and I'm not sure I can handle that. Not to mention how unfair it would be to Damien.

So, I go to the one place I can think of for help. My mother. I can't keep talking to Lucille about her brother, and I know what she'll say. She'll tell me that Damien loves me and that I should trust him to play my knight in shining armor. My mother's more real and less romantic at heart. She'll give me solid advice that doesn't center around conjecture or wishful thinking like Lucille's belief that it will all just work out somehow. She might be right about Damien being in love with me, but I can't be sure if those feelings will last, and feelings might not be enough to let us weather whatever storm descends when he tells me the whole truth.

I pull into their cracked concrete driveway and park the car. Then I get out and go to the front door.

My mom opens it before I can knock. She's expecting me, and her smile makes me feel warm in a way I haven't for months. I know she can't protect me, not like Damien can, but there's nothing like a hug and smile from my mom when everything seems to be falling apart.

She ushers me inside and gives me a big hug. I melt into her, hugging her back and burying my face in her shoulder.

"I'm sorry you're all caught up in your father's mess, sweetheart," she murmurs. "You said you wanted some advice? What about?"

"About Damien. He's proposed to protect me from his family and the other family going after Dad." I pull away with a sigh. "Mom, I'm scared. I don't know what I should do anymore."

"Does he love you and his baby?"

"He's great with Timothy. I know he adores our son. And I love the way he treats us both... But I hate that he's asking me to marry him like this."

"Why?" My mom guides me into the kitchen and sets a steaming mug of hot cocoa in front of me. "Explain what's going through your head right now, sweetheart. He seems like a great guy."

"Aside from his connections to a crime family, you mean...." I take a sip of the cocoa and close my eyes. "He is great, Mom... I overheard him with Timothy, talking to him, the other day. He told Timothy how much he loves both of us, but he also said he had a lot of secrets and reasons he couldn't tell me. I'm just... If he can't even tell me he loves me because of secrets he's keeping, is it a good idea for us to marry just to get me out of this bind?"

"Have you told him how you feel or asked how he feels?"

"Of course not. I can't trust that he'd be honest when he's admitted to having secrets and told our son he can't tell me anything even if he wants to. He told Timothy he'd tell me later when he could, and I'm afraid those secrets will be more than whatever we have can survive." I open my eyes and stare down into my hot cocoa, tears welling. "I love him, but I'm afraid of what he's hiding. I'm also afraid that if what he's hiding destroys us, he'll leave and take Timothy away."

My mother reaches out and takes my hand with a sigh. "Sweetheart, the man wouldn't have done as much as he has for you if he didn't love you both, and you said he admitted as much to the baby, who can't understand or say a word. He was baring his soul to the one person who wouldn't say a word about it or add to whatever burden he was carrying for you all. A man like that isn't going to hurt you by taking your baby away, even if it kills him to let go and not be part of his child's life."

"You don't know that," I whisper.

"I suppose I can't know for sure, but I've seen a lot in my years, and I've seen enough love and mere affection or infatuation to know the difference. My opinion is that you should go through with this if you love him because he's a good man despite his family connections and because I know he loves you. You know that too now... You just have to trust that."

I stared down at our hands. "And because it's the only way to save me from the storm Dad's brought down on us?"

"That too," she says quietly. "That's a big part of it. But I don't think he's going to divorce you after. You don't know why he's keeping secrets either, and you shouldn't assume the worst when he hasn't given you a reason to. Give him a chance. Say yes, even if it's only because you love him and you trust him enough to know he'll keep you safe from what you're facing right now."

I let out a slow breath and nod. I'm still not sure. I still need convincing, but I think I'm at a point where Damien might be able to offer that much. He might be able to reassure me, at least, that he won't take Timothy when this is through, and that will be enough. If he'll sign that prenup, then I'll do this despite my misgivings about his secrets and half-truths of late. "Okay. Thanks, Mom."

***

WHEN I GET home, the house is quiet. It's late, and Damien is waiting in my bedroom when I come up the stairs. He's sitting on the bed, staring out the window at the driveway. He turns to look at me and stands as I walk inside. "You have to make a choice, Alyssa. I'm sorry, but the time's up."

I nod and set my purse on the floor by the door. "You won't take Timothy if things between us sour after the danger is over? You'll sign the prenup?"

He crosses the distance between us and cups my face in his hands. "Never, and if it will make you feel better, then yes, I'll sign it. But I don't think things will sour. We're good together."

I drop my gaze to his chest. I'm not so sure we are. Sure, we have chemistry. He's proven that over and over. But do we have what it takes to be more? To weather the secrets he's keeping when they finally come out?

"Why are you so hesitant about this, Alyssa?" He tips my chin up to look me in the eye.

I bite my lip and shrug. "I want commitment and love, Damien. Not obligations and decisions made based on risk. And even though I think maybe you... you might feel more for me, I'm afraid that it won't be enough in the end. I'm afraid that the things you aren't saying and the things I know you're carrying alone will destroy us when they do come out, and I don't want to go through that kind of hurt."

"So, it's a no?" He looks crestfallen at the conclusion.

I sigh and reach up to run my fingers over his jaw. "I don't want to go through that hurt, but I also don't think I have much choice if I'm going to do what's best for our son. So, I'll accept your offer. You just asked why I'm hesitant. It's because accepting when I'm not certain you and I can last goes against everything in me. I'm afraid of what will happen later."

"We can't predict the future... And if it's not good for us or you, then I won't make you stay if you want out later. I promise I won't." He draws me into his arms. "You won't regret it, though, Alyssa."

"You can't know that."

He smiles sadly. "Will you accept that I have a hunch? I care very much about you and our son. I'm not trying to trap you, love. I just want to be there for you both and part of your lives. This is the only way I can do that if I don't want to send you away and never see you again. I very much don't want to do that. Not now. I can't promise what will happen in the future, but I can promise the n ow."

I take a shaky breath and nod. "I don't want just words, Damien. I want... I want you to show me how it'll be good. I see how you are with Timothy. I know you love him, and I want to believe you do love me, that we're strong enough to weather whatever's going to come later on down the road. I'm just having a hard time believing it because you...you never really said it. Maybe you can't say you love me yet. Maybe I'm all wrong about us, but right now, I need you to make me believe you love me so I can forget about my doubts about secrets and love, even if it's just for long enough to accept this is how it has to be."

"Do you need me to say that I do?" he whispers, his throat working. "That I love you?"

I shake my head. "Not when there are things you aren't telling me, things that might make me... I mean, I might hate you for it later if it turns out it wasn't enough or wasn't true."

"Then I won't say it." He leans in, brushing his nose to mine softly. "But I'll try my best to make you believe it without words so you can forget about your doubts and misgivings and the secrets that are driving a wedge between us right now."

I close my eyes and nuzzle closer. The doubts are screaming at me that this whole thing is a bad idea, but I want him to silence them so that I can give in and let him protect us. I don't want to run, and I can't bear the thought of never seeing him again. That hurts more than the thought that I might marry a man whose secrets could destroy us and who may change his mind about me.

He trails his nose along my cheek and then closes his mouth around my earlobe, nipping gently. His hands go to my hips, pulling me into him. He doesn't grind against me like he usually would, though. He just holds me there as he kisses down my neck to my shoulder and then back up again.

Shivering, I let myself melt into him. He's getting turned on as we press into each other, but he makes no move to act on it. Instead, he continues to kiss, and his hands start to roam up my sides to my breasts, playing gently.

When I moan, he slides his hands under the hem of my tank top and unhooks my bra, but his mouth stays at my collarbone, feathering kisses over my skin, even as he slides my bra off.

"Damien," I whisper. I need more."

He pulls back with a wicked gleam in his eyes. "You asked me to convince you without saying the 'L-word,' love. I'm going to give you what you've asked for. When I'm done, you're going to be convinced that I'll worship you, if nothing else."

I bite my lip, glancing at the queen-sized bed behind him.

Taking the hint, he scoops me up and walks to the bed. He drops me gently onto it and proceeds to crawl over me. I'm expecting him to let things get more heated now like he usually does, but instead, he strips me of my shirt and goes back to kissing my neck.

His kisses trail lower to the swells of my breasts, and his tongue swirls over my skin. The sensations are maddening, and I'm lost when his fingers start to stroke and dance along my rib cage and then over my breasts as he presses open-mouthed kisses to my jaw.

My fingers slide into his hair, and I pull his head up to claim his mouth with mine. He laughs, but he doesn't stop me. Instead, he lets his hips drop into mine, grinding slightly to give me the friction I'd been seeking earlier.

I almost sob in relief at the way he feels against me. He's still wearing too many clothes for my liking, but the slow pace and the teasing build into the usual burning inferno between us is new. It feels more tender and, like he promised, more like he's worshiping me, taking his time to memorize every inch like a lover would.

As he slides down my body to pull off my jeans, I'm reminded all over again how much I do love this man. The seduction of my heart and body is in everything he does from moments in bed like this to the moments when he's holding me tenderly or comforting Timothy when he's fussy. And in this moment, I find myself asking myself for the first time if maybe he could love me enough that his secrets might not break us after all. What if it's my love that isn't strong enough? On the other hand, maybe I'm thinking about this all wrong. What if my mother's right and more comes of this than I ever thought possible? Am I ready for that?

Chapter Twenty-Six: Damien

I'M IN MY office working through reports when the door bangs open, startling me. I look up to find Alyssa standing behind my red-faced father, and she looks a bit frightened. I can't blame her. He looks like he's on a war path.

The barging-into-my-office routine is getting old, though, and I stand, crossing my arms. "Father. What are you doing here? You don't have an appointment."

"I don't need one. Tell the secretary to get lost." He stalks in and takes a seat.

I glance at Alyssa, who looks upset now. He knows full well she's not just a secretary anymore. She's going to be mine as soon as I can sort out the details. If he can't handle it, that's his problem, but I'm not going to stand for him being rude to her. "The secretary is my fiancée. Whatever you have to say to me can be said with her present."

"I don't see a ring, and no, it can't." He glares back at me, unwavering.

Sighing, I nod to Alyssa. "We'll be rectifying the problem of the ring soon. Alyssa, I'll handle this. You can go back to whatever you were doing before my father so rudely interrupted. I'm sorry for his continued refusal to observe the protocols for meeting with me."

She smiles a little uncertainly. "It isn't a problem."

"It is." I pin my father with a hard stare. "As is his blatant disrespect of the woman who will be my wife. I think it would be best if he and I discuss this in private, though, so if you don't mind, could you close the door?"

Alyssa nods and withdraws, shutting the door behind her quietly.

I turn my attention fully to my father. "How dare you barge in here and treat her like the dirt under your shoe?"

"Because that's exactly what she is!" He scoffs. "You're so infatuated you can't even see that you're marrying the equivalent of a gutter snipe. I gave you numerous high-class women you could've picked from, and when you finally choose, you choose that?"

My anger begins to reach a boiling point, but I shove it back down. Now isn't the time for a loud argument over this. Not with Alyssa sitting right outside. "I am not infatuated."

"You think you're in love, then? Or are you marrying her out of pure pity?" His lips press into a thin line of scorn.

I don't care what he thinks, though. I'm marrying her because I want to protect her, but more importantly, because I love her. I wouldn't do this for just any woman, even one I did want to protect. I shove my hands into my pockets with a thin smile and keep my voice low when I reply. "No. I do love her. Enough to make sacrifices to protect her. I have a son with her too, and I'm not willing to let you use either of them to get to her father. I'm certainly not going to let you use either of them as a tool to force me to join you."

He gives me a grim, angry smile. "You'll do what you're told one way or another, and you're going to marry someone more suitable. She isn't the right one."

"No." My voice is low and deadly. "I will not marry someone else. You don't have to be at the wedding if you don't approve, but I'm doing this."

His cheeks redden further, and the red creeps down his neck now too. "How dare you? After all, I've done to set you up well, this is how you repay me? I forbid you to marry her!" His voice rises. "I forbid it. She's street trash, and I don't care if you have a son with her. I can make that problem go away if need be, but you'll marry a woman who isn't beneath you."

"You mean I'll marry one that will help solidify family crime ties." I leash my anger and sit back down at my desk. "That isn't going to happen."

"You don't get to defy your leader, boy!" my father shouts.

"You're yelling, and half the building will hear. Half a building of law-abiding citizens who won't hesitate to tell the cops what they're hearing. I'd be smart about what you say," I drawl.

His jaw clenches, and I see a muscle ticking, a sure sign of his fury. "That girl goes, Damien. One way or another. Don't force my hand."

"I'm not forcing anything. You choose if you're going to behave like a thug trying to make me bend to your will or like a father who will let his son choose his own path."

"I have responsibilities to the family," he hisses. "Responsibilities that include raising an heir to take my place. There isn't anyone else."

"That's unfortunate," I say coldly. "You'll have to hand it off to a distant cousin or whatever else is normally done when there's no heir."

"Do you want to be disowned and treated like you're dead to this family?" His voice lowers even more, and he almost looks hurt.

"I don't want to cut ties to a degree that I never see my mother or sister again, but if I have to for the good of my family, then I will."

"We are your family." He clenches his fists at his sides. "Don't you understand that?"

"You're the family whose blood I share, but blood isn't what makes a family a real family. It certainly hasn't made ours into one."

He glares at me. "I've taken care of your mother and sister and done my best to raise you to be the right kind of man."

"Only if the right kind of man is one who has no problem using an innocent woman and child to get his way." I wave at the door. "Leave. I'm marrying Alyssa. It isn't up for discussion, no matter how you feel."

My father gets up and stalks off, slamming the door shut behind him. I sit at my desk for a long moment, waiting for my pulse to slow and the anger to fade. When it does, I return to work. He'll either accept this or he won't, but whatever he does, it's not going to change my decision.

***

ALYSSA WON'T SAY it, but I can tell she needs some time to herself to sort out how she feels about her choice. So, I suggest she invite Lucille over, and then I take Timothy so she won't have a reason to object. She agrees, so I take him with me over to Stewart's to talk. Alyssa isn't the only one processing what's happening.

Stew ushers me in with a grin, cooing at the baby as I enter. He likes kids as much as Alyssa does, and he hasn't met Timothy yet. I let him take Timothy out of the car seat and hold him while I flop into a chair across from the sofa.

"So, how did things go with Alyssa?"

"She's agreed," I tell him. "But she's struggling with her choice. To be honest, she's not the only one. I feel terrible. It's like I'm using this as an excuse to ask her to do what I've wanted since I first found out she was the mother of my child."

Stew raises a brow. "You feel guilty for marrying her?"

"Well, not exactly." I frown. "I feel guilty for not telling her that I love her and asking without this sword hanging over both our heads."

"I see." Stew gives Timothy his pacifier as the baby begins to fuss. "And why haven't you told her you love her yet?"

I stare at him like he's crazy. "Because if I told her when I asked, she'd think I was just saying it to get her to cooperate. I don't want her to think I don't mean it, Stew. When I tell her, I want her to know I mean every word."

He purses his lips. "Okay... that makes sense, I suppose. Is she upset about marrying you?"

"I don't know if she's upset, per se. But it isn't what she'd do if we didn't have this threat to handle. I know it isn't. She doesn't believe I love her, and she doesn't want to marry someone who doesn't love her."

"So, she loves you but feels you don't love her."

Where would he get that notion? "She's never said she loves me. I don't know why you'd assume she does from what I just said."

"She was hesitant because she doesn't want to marry someone who doesn't love her. Did she say she didn't want to marry you because she wasn't in love with you or because you weren't in love with her?"

"Because she doesn't think I'm in love with her," I say slowly.

"So, she probably does love you, or at least has feelings of some sort for you. It won't be a disaster. You can sort out how to tell her you do love her later."

"That's what I keep telling myself, but I don't feel any better about this... I can't back out just to save my conscience on this. Not with her safety and Timothy's on the line. But I feel terrible for how this is playing out."

"You're taking charge of the situation, Damien. You're doing what you need to for her."

"I know that... I do." I stare over at the baby's serene expression with a sigh. "I won't lose her when this is over."

"Says the man who won't tell her he's in love with her."

I cough, cheeks warming. "Okay, but I will eventually. I'll tell her when this is over."

"Then it sounds like you've already made up your mind what to do. You're just afraid she'll hate you for it later." Stew stands and brings the baby back to me. "For whatever it's worth, I don't think she will. She's confused and scared right now, but when it's all said and done, she turned to you for protection. That means she trusts that you can h elp."

I take Timothy from him with a tired smile and hold the baby close as he fusses at being handed off. "I certainly hope so."

"You want my advice?" Stew asks, going back to his seat.

"It's one reason I'm here."

"Don't wait too long to tell her how you feel. If you do, you might lose her in the end, and you'll have no one to blame but yourself. But don't try to parse out whether she'll hate you or not when it's all said and done. You can't control that, so worry about what you can control."

I nod. That's what I've been doing. Focusing on the things I can fix, the things I can change, the things I can control. It doesn't mean I don't worry about her, though. I'm not usually a worrier. I'm grumpy, sure, but not a worrier. She's the first I've ever cared enough to worry about like this. But, while it drives me mad to be unable to predict how she'll react when she knows I love her and asked her to marry me more for that than because of the danger we're facing, I think she's worth it.

My gaze drops to the little boy sleeping in my arms, and I'm struck all over again by how worth it they both are. Even if my conscience is bothering me over asking her to marry me while keeping my emotional involvement a secret, I'm not going to back out. I do feel bad for lying about my motives and failing to tell her I loved her soon enough to avoid the risk that she'll think I'm saying it just to make her feel better. But I don't feel bad enough to change my mind.

Stew is right. I'm going to have to be honest with her. When the time is right, she'll need to know how I feel. The question is, how do I know when the time is right?

Chapter Twenty-Seven: Alyssa

I CLIMB OUT of my car and meet Damien in front of his before we head to the cake tasting. I still can't believe I told him yes. He got me a ring to seal the deal last weekend, and now we're going through the process to make it all look real. Since it needs to be done sooner rather than later, we're not having a big wedding. The thought of marrying him with unresolved secrets between us still scares me and overwhelms me, but I said yes, so I have to do this.

He glances over at me with a frown as we stop at the front door. "Are you okay? You look a little pale. If you don't feel well—"

I paste a smile onto my face and shake my head. "I'm fine. We need to do this. It's for the best for Timothy, and I don't have the luxury of doing this later."

If I do it later, there's every chance I won't be able to go through with it. We need to sort this out and do it quickly. Before I have time to think about how real it's all getting, preferably.

Guilt flashes on his face for a brief second before it vanishes. "I know it's a lot to take in, but let's just go in there and have fun with it. Think of it as an escape from the reality of the situation?"

Except it's not. For me, it's the train of reality blaring down on me, and I can't outrun it. I stare down at my feet with a weak nod. "Okay."

He opens the door and puts a hand on the small of my back to guide me inside.

I know we need to make this look real enough to convince everyone outside the house. Thankfully, there's enough between us for it to look convincing even though I still have my doubts. I'm glad now that I overheard him talking to our son because if I hadn't, I don't think I could've gone through with this at all. I'm still struggling, but at least my doubts don't center on whether or not he'd rather be doing this with some other woman.

His hand is warm on my back as he guides me to the counter where the woman doing our tasting is waiting. "I'm here with my fiancée for the cake tasting. Damien Darino. I scheduled."

Her bright red lips part in a friendly smile. "Of course! Right this way. You're going to love the selection. We have a wide range of choices to fit nearly every need or desire. You really can't go wrong. Congratulations on your up-coming wedding, by the way!"

I want to curl into myself and hide. It feels too real and overwhelming. I wish I dared to ask Damien to tell me everything before we get married, but I don't because with all the thinking I've done, I've realized I really can't stand the idea of losing him or of living life on the run, so I shove my hands into my pockets and try to cover my dismay with a bashful smile.

The woman eyes me in momentary confusion, and I can tell I haven't convinced her of anything. She doesn't stare for long, though, and soon she's back to chattering about the cake options. If we were a real couple, in love and giddy with joy, perhaps this might be exciting. Instead, I just feel as though I'm living out my prison sentence and waiting for it all to be over.

All it would take from Damien to make things better would be an assurance that he genuinely loves me like he told Timothy he does and an end to the secrets, but if our tumble in the bedroom when I accepted his proposal is any indication, the secrets and reasons not to tell me anything are big enough that he's never going to do that. Not before we're married, anyway.

At this point, I'm not even certain if hearing him confess his undying love would help or make it worse. I need to know what he hasn't told me more than anything, but I have a sinking suspicion that if he told me that, things would go from bad to worse in a heartbeat. His hand goes from the small of my back to my hand, and he interlaces our fingers before giving my hand a small squeeze. I try to smile, but I'm not able to get past the mounting misgivings and uncertainties plaguing me.

He looks concerned, but there's nothing we can do now with the woman leading us to a small space in the back with chairs and plates with silver forks to taste the options. Instead of saying something, he helps me into my seat and then sits across from me.

"Now, why don't you two look over our options and let me know which types you want to try first? I'll give you a moment." She steps away once we're seated and bustles off to see to something else.

Damien doesn't look at the menu immediately. He eyes me instead. "What's wrong, Alyssa?"

I shake my head. It's silly to be like this when I was the one who said yes. It doesn't mean I can turn off how I feel, though, and I'm not about to give him that window into my soul when he can't or won't tell me the truth. This doesn't need to get any more real. If it does, I may struggle to separate reality from the things I dream of, and when it all comes crashing down, I'll be the one to fall apart.

He doesn't press the issue further, though I can tell he wants to. We wait until the woman comes back with cakes to try, and I try to swallow down the things I'm feeling.

But as she sets the cakes in front of us, the fight I overheard between Damien and his father comes flooding back, adding to my anxieties and misgivings. Even if this were being done just because we were in love, his family wouldn't approve. Would they try to stop this? I don't know how I feel about that. I would be terrified of their disapproval if we didn't have everything against us surviving as a couple anyway. Strangely enough, I do feel a bit of fear that they'll take him away even though I know full well Damien and I have so many secrets building between us that we're unlikely to survive as a couple.

That is the last straw I can take. I push away from the table and grab my purse, standing quickly. "I'm sorry... I'm sorry... I just need to... I'll drive home." Spinning around on my heel, I hurry out the door and race to my car.

I hear Damien apologizing to the woman doing our tasting as I rush out the door, and then it shuts behind me, and I hurry to my car. I'll go home and hop in the shower. Maybe the hot water will ease the headache coming on, and I'll have the fortitude to go on with this after.

***

I'M IN THE shower when the bathroom door opens. I sniffle and try to stop crying. It's probably Damien. I was hoping he would let me be, but it seems I was hoping for a pipe dream. Not that I'm surprised. After all, he always shows up when I need him, even when I don't want him to

The curtain pulls to the side, and he's stripped already. He steps in and pulls me into his arms. I turn to him and bury my face in his wet shoulder. Maybe if I don't give him time to wonder why I fell apart at the shop, he won't ask. I let my fingers dance over his shoulders and down over his back.

He tenses, a breath hissing through his teeth, but he doesn't move to stop me or encourage me more.

I run my nails down over his butt and thighs, and he presses into me. What I'm doing is obviously turning him on, and I rub into him. This might be all I need. A distraction to take my mind off how I feel about this.

Damien groans and pulls me into him. "Stop it, Alyssa."

I freeze. "What?"

"I want to know what's going on. You ran out of there in tears like something tipped you over the edge into hysteria. Why?"

Shaking my head, I nip along his throat. "Please, Damien. I need this."

"No. I won't take advantage of you when you're weak and vulnerable, even if you want me to. I want to know what's the matter, Alyssa. That's all." He pulls free and reaches for the shampoo. "Let me help."

I shiver despite the hot water spraying over us and step away from him. "It doesn't matter."

"It mattered enough that you were overwhelmed enough to run home." He turns me around and uncaps the shampoo. "Don't act like it doesn't matter."

"Fine." I expel a long breath and press my hips back against his. "It does matter, but I don't want to talk about it."

He lightly smacks my rear and gently pushes me away to massage the shampoo into my hair. "We're not going to avoid this or have sex to forget about it, love."

I moan. "I can tell you want to. Please... why won't you just give me what I need?"

He leans in and presses his lips in a chaste series of kisses to my shoulder and neck. "Because it's not really what you need, sweetheart. I'm trying to figure out what it is you do need, but you don't talk to me, and I'm not a mind reader."

I close my eyes with a sigh. "Damien, I just... I can't...."

"Okay," he murmurs. "For now, we'll just enjoy these quiet moments together without thinking about weddings to keep you alive or how things are between us. We'll just take a breath and pause. God knows I have things I can't share, so it's only fair if you're allowed your secrets too."

It sounds nice. I need that, as hard as things have been lately. "Okay. We could do that," I murmur back.

His strong fingers work the shampoo through my hair and into a lather. It feels amazing, and I can almost feel the stress melting away. Maybe he's right. Maybe I don't need sex. Maybe I just need him to be here with me in a peaceful moment where I don't have to be any specific way. I can just relax and be me.

"How is that?" His voice rumbles low in my ear.

I shiver and sigh. "Wonderful. So wonderful. Keep going, please."

He chuckles. "I guess we've figured out what you do need."

Leaning back, I urge him to keep going by tipping my head further into his touch. He obliges, working his fingertips down my scalp to the base of my skull and back up. Then he reaches around me and gets the detachable shower head. The warm water sprays over my head, and he works through my hair with his fingers while he rinses out the shampoo.

We don't talk for the next few minutes while he conditions my hair. When the conditioner is lathered into my hair, he pulls me into his arms and holds me close while the conditioner sits for a bit.

I let my head fall back against his shoulder, and he kisses softly along my neck and throat. His hands don't roam, and it's the gentlest, sweetest sort of sexual contact we've had. Normally, we're more rushed or, at least, more heated. Today, he's keeping his word and not distracting me with sex. Just gentle touches and affection. It feels like he might actually love me when he does this. But he blows hot and cold, and when he proposed his focus was entirely on a way out of the problem and protecting Timothy, not on romantic gestures or indications he loves me. I'm choosing to believe that his heartfelt words to Timothy when he thought no one else could hear, were the truth, but it doesn't make me feel any better about the way he avoids telling me he loves me or about the secrets he inadvertently confessed to keeping.

When he's rinsed the conditioner from my hair, he moves on to the body wash. He pours a generous amount out on a loofah. Then he begins working it along my back in slow circles.

Once he's worked his way to my breasts and belly, I watch him work through heavy lids. He's obviously turned on, but he doesn't make a move to act on it. I can't believe he hasn't because I can only imagine how badly he wants to, but he keeps ignoring his own needs to fulfill mine. It might be the sweetest thing he's ever done for me.

He works back up my body with the loofah before he puts it away and uses the shower head to rinse me off. After he puts it away and turns back to me, I reach up on my tiptoes and kiss him slowly and gently.

"Alyssa," he rumbles in warning.

"It's just for a thank you, Damien," I murmur, kissing him once more. "For being here for me this way."

He smiles. "In that case...." He kisses me sweetly. "You're welcome. Now... I heard the baby fussing a bit when I came in here. Why don't we go check on him and then cuddle for a bit?"

I nod. "We should do that."

We get out and towel each other off. Then we dress together and head to Timothy's nursery. He's in the crib, chewing on his fingers and fussing. I pick him up and cuddle him close. "He needs to be fed."

"Then bring him to my bed. You can feed him while we cuddle."

I turn and walk back to the bedroom with Damien following. In his room, we settle onto the bed. Damien takes the baby and watches me as I slide my top up and prepare to feed Timothy.

"Why not just take it off? I don't mind, Alyssa. You don't have to feel awkward."

"Could you just pass me the throw blanket?"

He grabs it and hands it to me.

I take Timothy back and put him to my breast to feed. He latches on and starts to drink. Damien slides over and wraps his arm around my shoulders, pulling me into him. I lean back with a sigh and close my eyes.

"Is this nice too?" he murmurs in my ear.

"Yes," I admit. "Thank you."

"Anything for you."

Anything? Even keep secrets to protect me? Is it possible the secrets he's keeping aren't to keep me from running from something in his past, something related to his family, but are instead intended to protect me? What is it that I don't know? I feel like I'm missing part of the puzzle, and it's driving me mad, but I don't share what I'm thinking yet because I know it won't do any good. Instead, I just relax into him and try to enjoy the moment to let go of the stress.

Chapter Twenty-Eight: Damien

I PUSH AWAY from my desk in my home office with a sigh and get up, intending to go look for Alyssa. She's been more subdued the last week, and I can't tell if she's coming to grips with what has to happen for her protection or retreating into herself in fear of it.

My hand is on the doorknob when my phone buzzes in my pocket. Hesitating, I consider letting it go to voicemail, but after a moment, I pick up. "Damien Darino."

"Damien." It's Marcello on the other end. "How are things going with the situation?"

"They're starting to fall into place," I say, returning to my desk chair. "What's going on? You don't usually call unless you need to meet up or something's happened."

"Are you serious about marrying her?" Marcello sounds tired. "I mean, really serious. Not just to save her?"

"Yes." I don't need to think about that one. I'm positive about her, even if she isn't sure of me yet. "I'm serious about her and about marrying her, even if she doesn't know it just yet."

"I thought as much." Resignation slips into his voice. "You know what's going to happen because of this, don't you?"

"Yes." My instincts are screaming at me now that something isn't right. He wouldn't call just to ask that tiny question. He could've texted. "But you already know I do, and you wouldn't call just for that. What's going on?"

"Not everyone believes you two are the real deal, even now, Damien." Marcello heaves a sigh. "It's not just the blackmail that you have to worry about if you're going through with this. You still need to be careful and watchful over her. There are factions within our family that still think it might be worth tangling with you and your family over her, that you're just doing this to protect her, and that your father won't back you if you try to make a move against them."

"You can't be serious," I snap. "What more do I need to do to make my claim plain? As far as my father knows, I'm doing this because I love her and have a kid with her. He's not happy, but I doubt he'd stand aside and let someone hurt my wife, whatever he thinks of her."

"There's not much else you can do. Her father owes a substantial amount at this point, and some think we should make him pay it by any means necessary, even if it requires tangling with you or yours. They also think they're reading your father better than you are. I'm sorry, man."

I curse and rake my fingers through my hair. "They don't think anything good will come of challenging me that way, do they?"

"I don't know what they're thinking, but relations between our families are only thinly amicable, Damien. I would keep a close eye on her. Your family name isn't enough to keep them from hurting her."

We are so screwed if that's the case. I'm still going to marry her because at least it may discourage some of them, but it cuts me to the quick that it won't offer the protection I thought it would. Especially given what they're going to do to my good name and how she sees me. "How many are in favor of using her to get to him? Is your leader?"

"Enough. And no, not that I can tell. When your engagement was announced, he told us she was off-limits, but I have instructions to put the blackmail materials into circulation on the wedding day after you've gone through with it. He's giving you a chance to back out before he starts a war." Marcello huffed out a laugh. "You always were the sort of bastard to make trouble. There's quiet infighting going on over here over this, and it doesn't look like it's going to get any better."

"I'll keep it under advisement," I promise.

"See that you do if you want to keep that woman of yours safe."

"Thanks, Marcello." I hang up and shove my phone into my pocket with a heavy sigh. This is working out great. Just one more thing to add to my plate. I won't fail her, though. I'll keep her safe no matter what it requires of me.

Getting up, I go in search of her like I planned to earlier. I wander the first level and then find my way to the second floor. When I locate her, she's in my second-floor music room playing the piano in a slow, halting melody of pain, grief, and fear.

I lean against the doorframe and listen to her play. Have I caused the grief I'm hearing in her song? Or the pain and fear? I hope to God the answer is no to all three, but I have a feeling I've inspired all three at one point or another. If only I were free to tell her I love her, perhaps she wouldn't be so sad.

For a few minutes, she plays, and I listen. She's oblivious to my presence, and I see the unfettered longing, grief, and sense of loss she is enduring. It comes pouring out in her music choices, and I wish I could take it all away.

She's started into a second song when I shift, and she starts, her gaze flying to me. Her lips part, and she shoves herself to her feet in a hurry, stepping away from the piano like it's burned her.

"You play beautifully," I say softly. "I'd love to listen to you play more in the future, and you're always welcome to play here. I would never take that pleasure from you."

Her cheeks heat. "It was an accident. I shouldn't have come in to play. I just needed...." She shakes her head. "I needed an escape and an outlet."

"We all do at some point or another, love." I step inside and join her at the piano, tracing my fingers over the keys hers had danced on moments ago. "You can come here as often as you like when you need an escape or an outlet."

She lowers her gaze to the floor and smiles sadly. "Did you need me for something?"

"No. I came to check on you to be certain you were well and managing. Have you eaten?"

She shakes her head and bites her lower lip.

"Then let's go get some lunch. We'll come back to this later." I extend my hand.

She takes my hand with a soft sigh. "Okay. Thanks, Damien."

I squeeze her hand. "Always and forever."

I mean it too. For as long as she'll have me at her side, I'll be here to help her through these things. She just has to let me do that for her.

***

I REALIZED AFTER the moment in the piano room that Alyssa is still overwhelmed. She may not admit it or say so, but I can see it in her eyes and can still feel it in the haunting melodies that linger in the back of my mind now. She needs a break, and I can give it to her. It's the least I can do. "Love," I call across the table.

She's trying not to fall asleep over her egg. It's clear she hasn't been sleeping either, but she refuses to come to my bed when nightmares or panic strikes, so she's been sacrificing the proper amount of rest instead. She jerks upright at the sound of my voice. "What? I'm sorry. I was thinking."

"You were about to fall asleep in the egg. Let me take Timothy for the day to give you the chance to rest and relax. You need some time to yourself after everything."

She hesitates for the briefest moment before she nods with a small smile. "Where will you take him?"

"The park for a long walk, I think. I've taken him over to Stew's enough times already."

One of her delicate brows arches in question.

I wave her off. "I'll take care of him so you can rest. Really. Don't worry about it."

After another brief pause, she nods. "Okay. You can take him. Just make sure you take care of him, would you? I don't like letting other people take him places, even just for a walk. Not when I'm not there."

"I'm his father. I won't let anything happen to him. I promise." I stand and cross to her side, kneeling in front of her and stretching up to kiss her lips. "Just focus on yourself and what you need for a few hours. Let me handle the baby. I can manage."

She bites her lip, but she nods in agreement. "Okay. But just for lunch. I'll take care of him after that."

"Of course, love. Whatever you want or need." I smile up at her. "Your wish is my command."

She laughs a little, the sound warm and genuine, though strained. "Is that so?"

"Yes. Insofar as a mere mortal can grant the wish, anyway."

Another small, quiet laugh. "Just bring him back in one piece from whatever you decide to do."

"I promise to do so. Now, off you go. I'll get him ready to go on my own, and we'll be down the street at the park if you need us. The team protecting the house is also just outside if you need them." I lean in and kiss her forehead. "Enjoy the quiet time."

"Thank you."

I pull away and head upstairs. Timothy is playing with his toes in the crib, and I pick him up with a smile. "It's going to be just you and me today, little man. Your mama needs some rest."

He giggles a little, and I take him over to the changing table to get him dressed in something to go out. His diaper is wet, so I change that too while I'm at it. He fusses at me unhappily while I change him, and I hear Alyssa's footsteps on the stairs.

She appears in the doorway a moment later, worry on her face. "Is he okay?"

"It isn't the first time I've handled a baby, love. I helped with my little sister all the time. Go finish breakfast and have a nap, maybe? I've got him."

She shifts from foot to foot, eyeing us for a minute, and finally, she nods and disappears back down the stairs.

I get Timothy off the changing table and carry him downstairs, singing a song to distract him from his tears. We manage to make it to the car, and I get him buckled into his seat without any more fussing.

Then we're off. We drive down the road to the park, where I park and get out. A few minutes later, I have him strapped into the stroller and am heading off along one of the paved paths around the park.

Timothy coos contentedly in his stroller and listening to him eases some of the tension I've been carrying. Right up until I hear a familiar voice behind me.

"Son."

I stop and turn, finding myself facing my father. His lips are set in a thin, unhappy line, and his gaze falls on Timothy. His expression tightens even more with a mix of anger and spite.

"This is your son, then? My men reported to me that she'd had your kid. I didn't think I'd ever see him with my own two eyes given how closely you've been guarding them."

I step in front of the stroller to block his view of the baby, who has gone quiet. "Don't you dare bring him into this. What do you want?"

"The wedding isn't going to happen. I want to know what you think you're doing by ignoring my calls and refusing to back down on marrying this girl."

"I'm doing what I have to to protect my family. If you hadn't forced my hand, maybe we wouldn't be in this position." I cross my arms.

"The woman isn't your family. We are. You don't care one bit about us, so don't pretend you're doing this with some noble intention."

"I'm doing it to protect what's mine and the woman I love," I hiss. "And the wedding will happen, whether you like it or not. As I told you before, you don't have to be there if you're so opposed, but it will happen. Oh, and you won't be pulling my son into the family business. Ever."

"That boy is my lineage, Damien." My father's gaze snaps to mine, hard and angry. "You can't deny him his birthright."

"His birthright will be one of legitimately built wealth. It will never be one of crime."

"Is that so?" He scoffs. "It can never be that way so long as you bear ties to us."

I lift my chin, the thing that had been nagging at me for months finally coalescing into something I could put into words. Stew has often told me that I'll have to break ties with my family eventually. Now, it seems that day is here. "I'll be walking out on the rest of my ties with you all as soon as I put this business with Alyssa's father to rest. I'll never be involved, even by proximity or legitimate business ventures, to the Darino crime syndicate again."

His cheeks redden in fury. "You can't do that."

"I can, and I will." I turn the stroller around, put my back to him, and walk off.

"You'll regret it!" He calls after me.

I feel like a huge weight has been lifted off my shoulders with this. I'm going to marry the woman I love, get her and her father out of this predicament he got them into, and then I'm going to make a life for myself and both of them that doesn't involve my crooked father. Do I know for certain if it'll work out like I hope? No. But I'm willing to fight for it and find out if it can.

Chapter Twenty-Nine: Alyssa

THE DAY OF the wedding has finally arrived, and I'm a mess. I'm finishing up the final touches on my makeup with my mom's help, and I'm dreading walking down that aisle. I'm more uncertain than I have been in the weeks leading into this, and my stomach churns in worry.

"Are you sure you want to do this, darling?" my mother asks. "You seem uncertain...."

"You told me marrying him was for the best and that he'd take care of me." I straighten and pull my shoulders back, trying to put a brave smile on my face. "You were right to say so. He loves me, even if he can't say it. I don't know if his secrets will be more than we can weather, but I... I have to do this."

She sucks in a sharp breath and looks away. "I just wanted you safe. But you seem... you seem so unhappy and uncertain.... Maybe I made a mistake pushing you to accept his proposal."

I bite the inside of my cheek, worried and confused. What do I want? I know that I crave every moment I get with Damien. But I also know that I spend many of those moments wondering if his secrets will ruin us, and I don't know if I could bear that forever if he chooses never to tell me everything.

Am I making a dreadful mistake doing this?

My mother adds a last touch of blush and steps back. "Alyssa, just be honest... do you want to marry him?"

I shake my head and stare at my lap, tears blurring my vision. "I don't know, Mom. I... I don't know. I'm not certain at all."

"Oh, sweetheart." My mom sighs and drops to her knees to look me in the eye. "I'm sorry."

"I love him," I whisper miserably. "I love him, but I'm terrified of what his family is involved with and of what Dad has gotten us all into. I don't know what to do. For Timothy's sake, I should marry him."

"It doesn't have to be today, though," my mother murmurs, reaching up to squeeze my trembling hands. "Make sure you're certain about it before you walk down that aisle and say your vows, sweetheart. A man like Damien doesn't let go of the people or the things he claims easily. If he sees you as his, he's not going to just let you walk away."

"He isn't a bad man," I say softly.

"I know he isn't. But it doesn't change his nature, and his nature is to protect, and hold close the people and things he views as his and those he loves. He may not ever hurt you intentionally, but he also won't let you escape once he decides to have you. When he asked you to marry him, he decided, and he's going to have a hard time letting go, if he can at all, if you want to leave when those secrets come out."

I shiver, trying to wrap my head around that prospect. What will it be like to be one of the people he won't let go of? If I marry him and it all goes awry, something I've been afraid of all this time, will I be able to break free? Will I keep hold of myself and my son in the process?

My mother rises with practiced grace and smiles sadly. "I'll keep an eye on Timothy for you if you don't show up to walk down the aisle today. Take the time you need and be sure. It's the best advice I can give you now."

I nod, wishing I had that luxury. If I don't marry him today, will people assume I'm calling off the engagement? Will I put myself and my son in more danger? And if the secrets Damien has been keeping have been kept to protect us, could failing to walk down the aisle today jeopardize whatever he's done to protect us?

My mother leaves the room. The door bangs shut behind her, and the pit of my stomach drops. The thought of marrying him today simultaneously fills me with hope and terror. Hope because it means he's pledging himself to me and there's a chance, however slim, that we might weather whatever he's kept from me. Terror because there's a good chance he'll refuse to let go if the secrets kill whatever love is between us, and I can't stand the thought of consigning myself to a loveless marriage.

Her words echo in my mind, leaving my stomach in knots. He'll never let me go once I say my vows to him. I know she's right. I haven't let myself consider that piece of the equation, haven't dared to think about the possibility that Damien won't be able to follow through on his promise to give me whatever I want if what I want is to leave.

Now I do, and my chest squeezes. My throat tightens, and suddenly, I know I can't do this. Not today. I get up and slip on the flats I wore to the small church where we're getting married. Then I rush out the side door of the small room I'm supposed to be getting ready in.

I go straight to my car and drive blindly to the nearest place I feel safe. The hill outside the park near my old apartment is the one place I've always felt I can breathe and think. Mom will take care of Timothy until I come back in a few hours, and I know Damien won't let anything happen to him either.

I'll have to go back and face him. He'll be furious and hurt that I stood him up at the altar, but I need space to breathe and rethink what I'm doing. I can't marry him when I'm not sure that what I'm doing is the right choice. I can't marry him with doubts in my mind about whether this will work and half out of my mind with fear that I'll be trapped when it doesn't.

I know I can't put this off forever, but I need to put it off for now. Just for the moment so I can wrap my head around what's happening.

Reaching the hill, I park at the bottom lot and walk up the hill. No one's out at this hour, and I find a bench that overlooks the park to drop onto. My wedding dress is getting crumpled, but I don't care. I pull my knees up to my chest, and the tears come, ruining my makeup as I burst into sobs.

Right now, all I want is Damien and his warm embrace to reassure me, but Damien is part of the problem, and letting him be the one to comfort me won't help one bit. Not in the long run. It will only add to the terrible confusion that's weighing on me right now.

Someone takes a seat on the bench beside me. When I look up with a sniffle, Lucille hands me a packet of tissues without a word.

I accept them and pull one out to blow my nose. It stuffs right back up because I can't stop crying, but she doesn't seem to mind. She pulls me into a hug and holds me tight, the wind plucking at our hair and pulling it out of our updos.

For a long while, we just sit there like that, her offering the comfort I need and me taking it in relief. She doesn't say anything to me, and I don't say anything to her.

After a bit, I finally break the silence. "Everyone's probably wondering where I am."

"I told Damien to let me find you. He wanted to come looking, and he was pretty pissed. Everyone thinks you ran to break off the engagement. They're saying it was never real." She sighs. "What happened?"

"I realized how confused I was, and it hit me that I couldn't bring myself to go through with it without knowing for sure that it was right." I lean away and wipe my tears and the streaked makeup off my face. "I'm not breaking anything off. I just don't know if I can do this yet, and I wanted some time to sort through my thoughts and feelings."

She nods. "I understand that. It's been pretty clear how torn you are about this."

"What should I do?" I whisper, staring out across the park at the city in the near distance. "This is the only way to save myself and Timothy from the men after my father in both families. I know that if I don't do it and they catch up to me, they'll do unspeakable things.... What's wrong with me? Why can't I just go through with it? It isn't as if he mistreats me. I overheard him telling Timothy how much he loves us both. But he also admitted to having really big secrets that he can't share yet, secrets that have kept him from telling me he loves me... What if those break us?"

"You're scared." Lucille reaches out and takes my hand with a sigh. "You need just one thing in this messed up new world you're in to be sure, and you wanted it to be Damien. But you're seeing that even he isn't a sure thing, and you're running scared."

That's exactly what I'm doing. I think I knew that deep down even when I ran instead of staying and trying to work up the courage to do as I said I would. But it hasn't stopped me from running out on my own wedding and leaving Damien looking like the jilted groom at the altar.

"Is he really mad?" I whisper.

"I think he's more hurt and scared than mad, though he covers it well. It's hard to say with him. Alpha males never like to show weakness or vulnerability to others, but they're human just like the rest of us. They have fears and worries, and they don't often share them, so then they struggle in silence until it's too much for even their considerable willpower to push through."

I nod. "I messed this up, didn't I?"

"You did what you needed to. Will you go back and marry him?"

I drop my head into my hands with a tired laugh. "I know I need to, but I just want to sit here a while longer and postpone the inevitable. Does that make me a coward?"

"It makes you a human just like anyone else. Anyone would feel this way in your situation, Alyssa." She rose and pulled me up into a tight hug. "Will you go back when you've had some time to gather your thoughts and the courage you've always brought to situations like this?"

I sniffle and nod. "Yeah. Tell Damien I just need an hour. Ask him to apologize to the guests who did come and tell them that I'll be back. I just had something I forgot at home and had to run to fetch it."

"That's a lame excuse." She chuckles. "No one will believe it."

"I don't care," I mumble. "Just tell them whatever you want. Buy me an hour."

"I'll do what I can. And Alyssa?"

"Yeah?"

"When you two are alone, talk to him. Tell him whatever it was that spooked you so badly that you ran instead of talking to him. It's the only way you two will make things work." Lucille gives me one last squeeze and then pulls away. "I'm going to head back. I'll see you at the altar when you're ready to face the world with that defiant smile of yours again."

I offer her a thin shadow of that smile and nod. "Thanks, Lucille."

"Anything for my best friend." She lets my hands go and walks off down the steps on the side of the hill.

I watch her go. My heart aches, and I wish that things weren't such a confusing mess. I'm lucky to have her as a friend, though. She's always there for me no matter how awful or confusing the situation. I'm just not sure if it's going to be enough to get me through this situation too.

Chapter Thirty: Damien

I TAP MY foot against the carpet of the chapel's sanctuary platform. It is taking Alyssa far too long to show up, and Lucille even longer to come back from checking on her. Something has to be going on, but I can't go to check on her without leaving the altar and making it plain something is wrong.

People are starting to glance behind them, searching for the missing bride to appear. The pianist keeps playing music with nervous glances at me and my father, who's sitting impatiently in the front row. He looks self-satisfied like Alyssa's delay means he's been proven right about this being a mistake.

I try not to fidget. I don't need to let on that I'm getting antsy and frustrated too. It's going to be clear if Alyssa or Lucille don't show up soon, though.

The doors bang open, and Lucille comes in. She smiles faintly at the people assembled and swans her way up the aisle. I grab her arm when she reaches me and pull her close. "What's going on, Lucille?" I whisper.

"She... she needs a minute." Lucille looks a little concerned.

"So? Why do you look so worried?"

"She made me promise to tell you not to go after her."

"What?" I hiss. "Where is she?"

"She went to a park she prefers to go to when thinking."

"I know the one." I let go of her and straighten. "Lucille, she can't be out there alone. It's not safe for her. There are people after her. Bad people!"

Lucille bites her lip. "I'm sorry, Damien. She was gone when I went looking for her in the dressing room, and I had to find her. That's why I was gone for so long. I went there to check for her first and found her. Please, just... give her a minute."

"I can't do that."

"She said to tell everyone that she had to run home to get something she forgot."

"No one's going to believe that."

"I don't know what to tell you, Damien," she whispers back. "I'm sorry."

"I'm going to go find her," I hiss. "You tell the guests that she was feeling sick and needed me."

"Okay." Her shoulders sag. "I'm sorry, Damien. Don't be too angry with her. She's struggling, and she panicked."

I nod, distracted by concerns for Alyssa's safety. She's been struggling with the concept of us marrying me since the start, and I know it isn't easy. I just didn't think she'd run off without a guard and leave me jilted at the altar. It isn't a good look, and it's going to signal to everyone in both families that she doesn't want to marry me. It puts her at risk. I don't know if I can fix this. "Just keep them busy. I'll go find her and bring her back. She's not safe, Lucille."

"I know," she murmurs.

I walk down the steps and hurry to the back of the chapel. People are staring, but I don't care. I need to see Alyssa myself to know that she's safe and back under protection. I don't know if I can resolve the situation or not, but right now, I'm more concerned with reaching her before anything bad happens to her.

Walking to the men at the front door, I snap my fingers at them and walk toward my car. "You two didn't see her leave?" I snap. "How did you not see her leave?"

"Sorry, Boss.... She didn't go past us."

I pinch the bridge of my nose. While I'm sure she didn't, I'm still frustrated that all the men I have watching the venue somehow missed her leaving. "We need to find her and quick. I know where she should be, and we need to drive over there right now. Follow me and keep a sharp eye out for any trouble. She's vulnerable, and I want her back safely and in one piece. Am I clear?"

"Yes, sir," the guards say in unison.

They move to the car beside mine. I get in and pull out of the lot as quickly as I can. Then I hurry down the road toward the park near her old apartment complex. I've never been a praying man, but I consider it now as I think of all the ways things could go wrong with Alyssa's choice to walk away.

What was she thinking? Why wouldn't she stay in the venue and let me come find her? I just don't understand what's going on in her head. She's usually smart and competent, but right now, she seems to be acting on instinct and fear. I can't predict what might happen with her in this mindset, and that leaves me on edge.

My men follow behind me closely as we race toward the park. I keep asking whichever god might be listening to protect her while I can't. It maddens me that I can't be there to protect her from the danger she's in, and I won't sit easy until I know she's safe.

Finally, we pull into the parking lot of the park. Her car sits at the bottom of a hill. She used to like sitting on the bench at the top near the gazebo to watch people below and think. I don't see her at the top, though, and my heart skips a beat.

Jumping out of the car, I sprint to the steps going up the hill and begin taking them as fast as I dare. When I reach the top, my worst fears are confirmed. Alyssa isn't there. Her veil sits on the bench, and my stomach drops. She wouldn't leave that sitting here if she were returning to the venue and me. I also know she will never abandon Timothy willingly, though, so there's no way she's gone anywhere without her veil and without a fight.

My men draw up behind me, a bit out of breath.

"She was here," I tell them, turning to face them with the veil in hand. "She was here, and now she's gone. She didn't leave this behind willingly, and there's no way she'd leave it if she decided to go back to the venue. I know she'd never leave Timothy, so we better start looking."

The men nod and take two opposite directions to start searching for clues. I clench the veil in my hand and stare at the bench. Where has she gone, and what has happened to her? Is she in danger of losing her life? Will I be able to rescue her? The last question weighs on me the worst of all as I begin to look for evidence to show me where she's gone. I wish I had an answer.

***

MY MEN SEARCH the surrounding park and the woods. When the three of us have no luck locating her or any sign of where she's gone, I call in more men to search. I assumed she'd wandered on her own, but it's looking less and less like that's the case, and given the danger she's in, I head back to get my laptop from my house to try to locate her with the chip in the engagement ring I gave her. The men keep looking while I do that and collect Timothy from the church.

I go back to the church first to collect Timothy. Alyssa's mother has him, and I don't want to leave him unprotected any longer. Lucille can help me watch him while I handle the situation with Alyssa from my home office. Then I can place a guard on them both to ensure no one gets any ideas about going through her to get to my son.

When I step inside the church, I find people milling about, talking in hushed whispers. As I pass, they quiet, but as soon as I've moved past them, they resume the murmuring. No one believes that Alyssa needed to run home quickly. They're all saying she jilted me. I'm glad that I have Lucille's account of her conversation with my runaway bride to reassure me because otherwise, I'd believe she ran out on me too. Instead, I'm confident she would have returned and gone through with the wedding if she hadn't been kidnapped first.

I make my way to the front of the church where Alyssa's parents and Lucille are standing. Mrs. Jones has Timothy in her arms and is soothing the fussy baby. They all look to me in expectation when I approach.

My heart sinks as I realize I have to give them the bad news. I can't even promise them we'll get her back, though I'm determined that no other outcome will be allowed. "She was taken," I murmur. "We don't know where. I have people looking."

Lucille sucks in a sharp breath and glances at the assembled crowd. "Are you sure? She could've left to freshen up and come back here. Maybe you just missed her?"

I shake my head. "Her veil was still sitting on the bench. She wouldn't leave it if she planned to come back for the wedding, and she wouldn't run without Timothy."

All of us look at the fussing baby. He seems to know something is wrong, and he bursts into a full squalling wail. People glance in our direction, but they turn their attention away when I scowl at them all.

"It's all my fault." Lucille's eyes fill with tears. "If I hadn't left her there alone—"

"They might have taken you too." I clench my fists. "Whoever took her, we can't be sure they have the backing of the other family's don. Right now, they're wild cards, and there's no telling what they might have done to you to get to her."

"But if—"

"Lucille," I interrupt gently. "Your only mistake was not making her come back with you or calling me right away. You were trying to do your best for your friend, and you miscalculated. It isn't your fault. She knew it wasn't safe to be out there alone, and she left anyway."

"Damien, she just needed time and space to collect herself."

"And she could've had it in the safety of that powder room where she was preparing for the wedding," I snap.

Her expression crumples in pain, and I immediately regret letting my tone slip into anger. She isn't to blame for this, and I know it. It isn't fair to take it out on her, even if I am beyond frustrated and, worse still, scared in a way I've never been scared in my whole life.

"I'm sorry... I'm sorry, Lucille. I shouldn't have snapped. I'm just worried about her, and I have a thousand things on my mind. Would you watch Timothy and come back to my place with me?" I look to Mrs. Jones. "You should probably come too and stay. My men will be able to protect you as long as you stay in the perimeter. Meanwhile, your husband should start figuring out how to pay them so they don't hurt Alyssa more than they already will or have."

Alyssa's parents blanch. They *should* be scared, though. We don't know who has their daughter, and what we do know is that they're willing to take her in a public place knowing I'll come after them. That's enough to concern me, and concern is putting it mildly.

"Let's go. I need to activate the tracker I have on her to try to locate her. I can do that best from my home office. Timothy needs a nap too." I take my son from Mrs. Jones.

He settles a bit once I'm holding him, and I kiss the top of his soft head. "We're going to find her, little guy. I promise we're going to."

Lucille's eyes are wet with tears as she turns to the assembled crowd. "Ladies and gentlemen," she calls. "We're sorry to say that no wedding will be happening today. The bride is too ill, and we'll be taking her home. Please wait for the attendants to dismiss you and give us a few minutes of space to leave so she's home as soon as possible. We'll be in touch when we know the rescheduled date. We're dreadfully sorry for this!"

The crowd shifts and mutters about the situation uncertainly, but I don't stop to add my reassurances or apologies. My whole focus is on getting home, settling my son safely in bed, and then finding my fiancée. I don't have time for anything else.

My father slips out the back without a word to me, and I know from the look on his face that he isn't going to offer his help. But that doesn't concern me. I'll figure out how to do this on my own if that's what it takes.

Striding down the aisle with Timothy in my arms, I head for the doors.

Lucille races to catch up and puts a hand on my arm. "We'll find her, won't we?"

I'm not sure, but at this point, there's no reason to give up hope or to scare anyone. "Of course we will."

But if we do, will she still be my Alyssa when we do? Or will they change her irrevocably and return her to me broken and altered?

Chapter Thirty-One: Alyssa

I FIGHT THE men holding me with everything I have. We're in sight of the parking lot, and I see the cars pulling in. I watch as Damien gets out and races for the hill, but they have my mouth gagged, and one of them has his meaty, sweaty hand over the gag to make doubly certain I can't alert anyone.

Even knowing it won't do me any good, I scream into the gag and thrash in the grasp of the men holding me as we hide in the tree line. We're well away from the hill, and Damien won't see us. I need to get out into the open.

One of them jabs a needle into my neck. I feel the cold sting of something slipping into my veins, but I keep struggling. The cold spreads and my struggles grow less frantic as whatever they've given me begins to spread and work. Then I sag into them, finding that I can't seem to command my limbs anymore. Whatever they've done, I can't move.

I watch in horror as Damien reaches the top of the hill, his men racing to follow. He holds up my veil, and then he looks around. I pray he'll see me, but his gaze is roaming all the wrong places. I can't even move to alert him of where I am now.

The man holding me laughs quietly. "He's never gonna find you, lady. Not when he looks in all the wrong spots like that."

My eyes close. It's all I can manage, but I don't want to see him search frantically and then walk away in defeat.

The men drag me deeper into the woods, and I faintly hear Damien barking a command to the men with him.

"They're searching the woods," one of the three who took me mutters. "Should we get out of here?"

"Not yet." The man holding me picks me up and tosses me over his shoulder.

With the drug in my system, I can't stop him or even move a little. My face smacks into his hip. His hand lands on my rear, copping a feel as he carries me farther from the place where they caught me. I seethe and then panic as his hand slides over my butt, pinching as he laughs under his breath. I can't even move to stop that. What else will they do to me while I'm drugged?

We keep moving until we reach a parking lot in the woods on an old hiking trail in the park. I liked to come to this particular spot when I lived closer to it, and I know I've run out of hope of being seen. No one comes to this spot anymore. It's overgrown and run-down since the park management decided to close the trail. I only came here because I liked hiking the old trail even with the brush and overgrowth.

He pulls me off his shoulder and presses me against the car, his hand going to my throat as he grinds into me with a laugh. "Your father's going to pay up now, little girl. If he doesn't, I'm going to do worse than drug you and grind on you a bit. And he's going to watch."

I can't shiver, but internally I'm screaming. Even my vocal cords won't work, and my ability to close my eyes is fading too. I can only stare at him in horror as he continues to work himself up while his friends watch. They're adjusting themselves with ugly leers on their faces, and it's abundantly clear that whoever they work for, they're the bottom of the barrel. They're nothing like the sophisticated men who'd always been around when Lucille and I spent time at her family home as kids. Those men, I know now, were involved in crime, but they were much smoother and more gentlemanly. They had a code of honor, and women and children were off-limits. These men have no such code.

Tears leak down my cheeks.

He leans in and licks them away, laughing when I try to move my head and manage no more than a twitch. "Aww… I know you want to scream for me, Princess, but not yet. We'll save that for when we have you all alone and he can't help you."

A tiny whimper is all my vocal cords allow. The panic and fear build, but there's nowhere for me to go and no outlet for it. Instead, I just feel my heart rate speeding up as my heart hammers in my chest and tears continue to fall.

His hands roam while one of his men moves to watch for any sign of Damien or his men and the other watches with avid interest, his hand toying with his fly's zipper. I wish I could close my eyes so as not to see what else he chooses to do as the man heading this up yanks the skirt of my simple bridal gown up around my hips and forces my legs around his hips.

He presses me back into the car. It's the only reason I'm not entirely limp as he continues to use my body for his enjoyment. I say a prayer it won't go further, that he won't strip me and go as far as to rape me.

"Boss." The man on lookout comes back just as the second man is unzipping his pants with a smirk. "They're starting to search farther down the hill. We'll get caught if we don't g o."

The man reaching into his pants scowls in annoyance, but he zips back up as his boss pulls away from the car with me and carries me to the back seat. He shoves me in and buckles me up with a leer, pinching my thigh before he finishes. "We'll finish this later, sweetheart."

I want to close my eyes and forget where I am and what's happening, but I still can't force any of my limbs to cooperate.

He snaps his fingers at the man who was on lookout. "Hand me the other syringe. We don't need the paralytic wearing off before we get where we're going, and we don't want our little princess trying to memorize the way back."

I make a tiny mewling noise and try to force my heavy limbs to move so I can escape them, but he just laughs when nothing happens. Then he has the syringe out and is slipping its needle into the vein of my wrist while I sit there, unable to stop him.

He massages the puncture site after removing the needle and leans in to kiss me, biting my lip just enough to cause pain. Pulling away, he tugs off my ring and tosses it into the grass next to the car. "Just in case he's got a tracker on it. We don't want our fun spoiled too soon, Princess. Your father's going to pay. That's for certain."

I try to force words out past the drug and my gag, but nothing comes out. He hops into the driver's side, and his men get in too. The one who had his fly down climbs in next to me and begins to run his hand along my barely quivering inner thigh.

We take off. My panic must be making the drug move through my system faster, though, because this time I start to feel the effects faster than I did with the paralytic. My vision blurs and darkens, and then someone shuts my eyes, and I fall into darkness.

***

WHEN I COME TO, I can move again. My arms are chained to a concrete wall above me, and the place is chilly. My skin is pebbled with the cold, and I realize in horror that they've stripped me. I fight the cuffs holding me to the wall, but I can't pull free, and they scrape painfully at my skin, so I stop.

Instead, to calm my panic, I look around at my surroundings. A single bare bulb hangs from the ceiling, dimly illuminating what appears to be a basement. Wherever they have me, I'm in a basement, and no one is going to ever know I'm down here. The wall behind me is concrete, but the other three walls and the ceiling are padded with something I assume helps to muffle or dampen sound.

The floor is stained with what looks like blood, and there's a metallic stench in the air. This place has been used to hold someone before, and judging by the smell, that someone didn't survive their stay. My whole body shakes uncontrollably, and I swallow past the lump in my throat. Are they going to kill me too?

The door at the top of a staircase opens, flooding light over the previously shadowed stairs. The men who took me tromp down the stairs, and the last one pauses to lock the door behind him.

The leader stands in front of me with arms crossed and a smirk on his face. "What do you think, Princess? Want to scream for me now?"

I flinch away as he comes closer and trails his thick fingers over my rib cage. If it were Damien doing this, I'd be turned on right now. He was right when he warned me this was what would happen if I didn't take the threat seriously. In my panicked desperation to get space to rethink marrying him, I put myself in this situation, and now I'm paying. "Please," I whisper hoarsely. "Please, you don't have to do this. Whatever you want, Damien will pay it. I promise he will."

The leader scoffs. "I don't want your fiancé's money, doll. Your father's going to pay for his refusal to pay up, and you're going to be his payment." His fingers find my breasts and begin to toy with me.

My lower lip wobbles. I try to pull away, but I'm still woozy and weak from the doses of drugs he gave me in the park.

"Maybe I should give you a smaller dose of the paralytic again. Not enough to stop your pretty voice from working, but just enough to keep you from fighting me." He slides his fingers down my belly and between my legs, which are tied to either side of a block of wood. "Would that be fun, Princess?"

The other two men take seats at a small card table in the corner I hadn't examined and watch lazily while their boss toys with me. One of them grabs a bottle of something on the table and tosses it to the man touching me. My captor catches it and flashes it in front of me with a grin. "He's being nice today."

The third man pulls a camera and tripod out of a bag I could barely see behind the table legs.

He sets it up on the table and points it in my direction, setting the camera atop the tripod with a grin. "Bet we could get a pretty penny off selling this once we're done, Boss."

"I bet we could." My captor opens the bottle he's holding and squirts the contents out onto his fingers before he goes back to playing with me. "There. That's better. Feels nicer, doesn't it? I think dear old Dad would feel worse if he thought you were enjoying what I'm going to do to you, don't you? He'll know you don't want it later, of course. And maybe, just maybe, seeing this will convince that fiancé of yours not to bother looking. Wouldn't that be a bonus?"

I shake my head from side to side, tears leaking down my cheeks. "Please, whatever you want... he'll give it to you."

"I'm going to have whatever I want anyway. I'm taking it right now, aren't I?" He moves away and tugs off his shirt, exposing the tattooed expanse of his chest and abs.

Everything is rock solid muscle, and I realize I never stood a chance fighting them even without the paralytic. I don't stand a chance fighting them now, either.

"He'll pay you three times what you could make off my father or that video," I say desperately. "I know he will. You just have to return me. That's all. Return me in one piece."

He chuckles darkly and returns to let his fingers play along my inner thighs and between my legs without concern or haste. "Darling, I'm not the kind of man who works with empty promises, and this isn't about him. It's about making your father pay, and this is how I'm going to do it."

His chest presses to mine, and he leans in to trail his mouth along the column of my throat. I try to thrash, but he growls and pins me more firmly to the wall, pinching my thigh in warning. I close my eyes and fight the cuffs in a vain attempt to free myself.

"Don't worry. I'm not going to take everything now. Not yet, Princess. I will eventually if he doesn't pay up, but for now, we're going to take our time. I might let them play too, though they're not going to take what's mine if your father doesn't pay." He strokes his free hand through my hair with a wicked smirk. "Don't fight me on this. I'll just make it hurt worse, and I have been nice so far."

He must see the moment I realize the truth of his claims because he begins to toy with me in more earnest. I hate that I know he's telling the truth, and I hate even more that knowing he's being kinder than he needs to be makes me stop fighting so quickly.

I'm afraid, though. I'm afraid because I know he's being kind. If I fight him, what will happen will be far worse than what he's doing to me now. He already has worse planned, and I don't need to hasten it, however much I despise myself for letting him take things this far.

What choice do I have, though? If I fight him, will it do me any good? I glance at the dried blood on the floor, and it hits me that I have more to worry about than whether he'll rape me. Will I even make it out of this alive?

Chapter Thirty-Two: Damien

THE SIGNAL ON Alyssa's ring shows that she's in the middle of the woods at the park where she went missing. I don't know what that means because as far as I know, there's nothing out there, and I'm internally trying not to panic as the thought occurs to me that they could have killed her and left her out there to send a message to her father. Maybe they knew she had the tracker on her, and they dumped it so I couldn't find her. That's a possibility too. She doesn't have to be dead in a ditch somewhere.

I grip the steering wheel of my car more tightly and drive along the access road the groundskeeper pointed out. He told me there's a small overgrown hiking trail and parking lot out here that no one uses anymore. Maybe they used it to get her out of this place unseen.

In the trees ahead, I spot the cracked pavement and overgrown parking signs of the parking lot, and I pull in quickly. There's some fresh oil on the ground, and I spot the glint of metal near it. Jumping out of the car, I hurry over to the spot and kneel to retrieve Alyssa's ring.

Relief mixes with frustration as I realize both that she wasn't killed here and that I now have no concrete way to find her. What is she going through? I hate to even think about how scared she must be or what the men who took her might be doing to her. If the people who took her are affiliated with Marcello's side or mine, as I suspect, then the things happening to her are probably unspeakable.

I pocket the ring, my jaw working as I fight to control the anger boiling inside. I need to talk to my father. If his men don't have her, then he's going to help me track her down. After all he's put me through and the part he played in sending her running because of my family's criminal involvement, he owes me this much.

Going back to the car, I climb in and take a few deep breaths to calm myself. Before I talk to my father, I need to tell Lucille and Mrs. Jones that I haven't found her and that they'll need to watch Timothy a little longer. I also need to talk to Lucille again about what Alyssa said to her to make sure there isn't anything there that might help. I doubt there is, but it's hard to know for certain.

There's a small possibility that my sister interrupted them while they were threatening her and that it escalated to kidnapping only after they panicked about her saying something about their visit to me. Maybe Lucille didn't know they were there, but that doesn't mean Alyssa hadn't if they were there before Lucille arrived.

I drive as fast as I think I can get away with, eyeing the clock and knowing every minute wasted is another minute Alyssa is suffering whatever horrible things the men who have her decide to mete out. I can't live with that.

When I finally get home, Lucille comes to the door to greet me. Her face is pale, and her hands shake. She hasn't been eating much in the day since Alyssa was taken, and I know she won't be able to eat or sleep well until we have her best friend back. I'm in the same boat, but I'm forcing myself to eat, if nothing else, so that I can stay strong for Alyssa. I need to find her, and I can't do that if I don't take care of myself.

"Have you eaten yet today, Luc?" I ask quietly.

"Did you find her?" She looks past me at the car, and her eyes fill with tears. "Tell me you did and you just had to leave her at the hospital overnight or something."

"I didn't find her yet. I'm sorry, Lucille," I murmur, opening my arms for her.

She accepts the hug, sobbing into my shoulder. "It's all my fault. What if she's dead, Damien?"

"Don't... don't say that or even think it. I found her ring. They must have known it was a tracker or else didn't want to take the chance, and they left it in a run-down parking lot no one uses anymore. We'll find her, Luc."

"How? How will we find her when your only lead is gone?"

I don't know, but I'm going to find a way. "I won't give up on her. I'm going to talk to Dad. He threatened to send men after her, and if he didn't send them himself to stop the marriage and pressure her father to pay, then I'm going to make him help me find her."

"He won't help." Lucille pulls back and wipes her eyes. "He hates her, and he hates you for marrying her against his will."

"I'll find a way," I tell her firmly. "He's not the only one who can choose not to take no for an answer."

Alyssa's mother rounds the corner with Timothy in her arms. When she sees my grim expression, her lips pinch and her eyes fill with tears just like Lucille's did. Unlike Lucille, she doesn't bother asking. She just nods and retreats quickly, knowing that I don't have good news or her daughter to return to her.

I turn my focus back to Lucille. "As things stand, there's still a high likelihood that she's in the clutches of either our family or the other family her father owes money to. We'll get her back, Lucille."

My sister nods and swallows back her tears. "I just hope we'll get her back the same as she was when we lost her."

I can see in her eyes that the hope is one she only holds to tenuously, and I don't have the heart to tell her that the longer she's gone, the less likely that is. So, I just nod and give her another hug before I go back to my office to make some calls.

***

MY FATHER TAKES a seat in my home office and crosses his arms. He's annoyed I've summoned him, but he's here, and that's all I care about.

"Well?" he demands roughly. "What do you want?"

"I want to know if you have her."

"Excuse me?" His face reddens. "You think I'd go that far? When you were marrying the girl, you think I'd risk pushing you entirely away from the family by kidnapping her?"

"I think you hated her and didn't like that I might leave any possibility of joining you behind for her. In your view, you think she's the reason I'll never join you now, not my refusal to get involved in crimes." I cross my arms too and stare at him coldly. "So forgive me if I think you're entirely capable of taking her. Do your men have her?"

He scoffs. "No. No, they don't. Are you happy now? Can I go if you're through tossing accusations around?"

"I'm not done." I stand and press my fingertips to the glass surface of my desk. "If you didn't take her, then you may know who did. I spoke to Lucille, and there's nothing in the conversation she had with Alyssa that would help me locate her or who took her. But I think you have connections I don't."

"And you want me to use those connections to find her?" His voice rises an octave. "I'm not helping you with this, Damien. You're on your own."

"I understand that you don't care what happens to her, but I do. I care so much, in fact," I snap, "that I will burn your entire operation to the ground by going straight to the police if you won't help. Now, I think you know who has her or know how to find out, and you're going to help."

He blanches, but the fury still burns in his gaze. He knows I'm serious about the threat, though, and finally, he looks away. "I don't have her. I don't know where she is, either. The other family probably took her. I heard rumors they were planning to."

"Does the head of the family know about this?"

"I don't know." My father glares at me. "I don't know, and I don't care. Deal with it on your own just like you deal with everything else."

I stare at him in disbelief and laugh. "Like I deal with everything else? I deal with everything else alone because you won't lift a finger to help me without getting something from it. I do it all alone because if I accepted your help in any way, I'd be just as bad as you are. I'd be taking blood money, and you don't offer any other help, so forgive me if I choose to do it on my own."

His face mottles with red. "You're an ungrateful, rebellious child who never grew up enough to recognize all the ways I provided for him! I did what I had to so you could live this fancy life of yours and moan about how I conduct my business. You could at least show a bit of damn respect and appreciation! I'm not helping you with this. End of story."

"I told you what would happen if you didn't help," I hiss. "I mean it."

He gets up with a shake of his head. "Are you going to condemn your mother and sister to jail too? Your mother knows what goes on and doesn't stop it. Your sister knows now too, thanks to your woman. She can't stop it. They're both accessories to crimes I've committed. If you don't mind getting them put into prison along with me, then go ahead and tell the cops whatever you like. Otherwise, I recommend you keep your mouth shut and sort this out on your own."

I clench my fists at my sides and watch him walk out without a word. He's right. I can't follow through on that threat when I stop to think about my mother and sister. They didn't ask for the life they're living, and there's nothing they can do about it. Women in my father's world are helpless to stop the violence or the crimes happening around them. They're lucky if they have any power at all over their lives.

Deflating, I sit back down and run my hands through my hair. I'm not any closer to finding her after that, and my last possible connection is refusing to help. I'm going to have to find another way, but right now, I can't think of one.

There's a soft knock on the door. I look up to find Lucille standing in the doorway and am reminded all over again that I can't use my father's crimes as leverage to help Alyssa because it would hurt Lucille.

"I'm not in the mood to talk to you," I mutter.

She comes in and sits anyway. "I heard what he said about you talking to the police... I know you probably hate me right now for being the thing between you and making Dad help."

I exhale slowly. "I'm not angry at you. I know it isn't your fault, Lucille. I'm just angry and frustrated in general, and I hate feeling this helpless when the woman I love is in danger."

Lucille reaches across the desk and takes my hand. "We'll find her, okay? We'll bring her home, and we'll help her through it, no matter what state she's in. You can't give up on her, and you can't let go of hope. I know that you'll make this happen. If you can't, no one else could."

I squeeze her hand with a sigh and a soft smile. "Thanks for the reminder, Luc."

She gets up and walks to the door. "I'll leave you be. I just wanted you to know that you don't have to do it alone like you usually do. If you need anything, I'm here, and I'll do whatever I can."

I nod, acknowledging the support for what it is. "Thanks. I'll let you know if I need something."

With a smile, she turns and leaves the room. I'm alone with my thoughts, and I wish more than anything that I could bring Alyssa home with just a thought. Instead, I remain alone and miss her so badly that my heart feels like it's breaking. When I do get her back, the first thing I'll do is tell her the one thing I should've told her before. I'll tell her how much I love her until she believes me. But will it be in time, or have I missed my chance entirely?

Chapter Thirty-Three: Alyssa

I'M FINALLY FREE from the chains. The men decided I wasn't going anywhere anyway and let me free from them. My wrists are still bound, but at least I can move freely around the basement which serves as my prison.

I don't know any of their names. They're always careful to avoid using those around me. So, I've given them names of my own. The one who usually touches me and seems to head up the trio is Scar because of the ugly, jagged scar along his left palm. The one who watches whenever Scar has me on video to send to my father is just Watcher. It's not creative, I know, but I'm not in the mood to be fancy with the names. The other one is just Twitch. He's the nervous one in the group, and he doesn't seem as awful as the other two.

The door at the top of the stairs opens, and I scramble into the opposite corner of the table, hoping they'll leave me be this time. It's been a week, and they haven't said yet whether my father has paid the money they want or not. I still haven't figured out for certain whether they're with the family my dad owes or some other group that wants to squeeze money he doesn't have out of him. I don't even know if they've sent the videos they've made of me so far.

Time passes slowly down here, and I'm not even sure what day it is anymore. I only know that it's been seven days, roughly because they always feed me at least one meal a day. It's not consistent, and I never know when I'm going to get it or what I'll get, but at least it's a way to mark that a day has passed.

The three men tromp down the stairs. Scar leers at me. "Hiding isn't going to help you, Princess."

I cower into the corner further, shivering. I'm always cold these days. They still haven't given me any clothes. That's probably a good thing, though, because they'd just collect more dirt than my skin has and end up smelling worse than I already do. I'd give almost anything for a shower right now.

He takes a seat at the table. Watcher sits too, positioning himself so that he has a good view of me. Twitch joins them slowly, seeming more reluctant than usual.

"Boss, maybe we shouldn't keep this up. We could drug her and leave her somewhere for them to find. She doesn't know our names or nothin' else."

"No. We're going to send the notes to her father and fiancé to get the money." Scar rubs his hands together with a laugh. "And the videos. What I wouldn't give to see their faces when they learn what's happened to her."

Watcher joins him in laughing. "Maybe for the next one, if they don't pay up, we should go the rest of the way and ruin her for him permanently? I bet if we both had her, she'd never look at him the same."

Scar grins. "How about it, Princess? If they don't pay up, maybe you'd like to pay us another way so we treat you nice."

I flinch back, unable to stop myself from reacting. The reaction is what they want. It amuses them. I know that, but I still can't control the fear or my instinctive reaction to their threats of sexual violence. Not when I've already endured some and know what they're threatening they'll do if there's no payment.

"I think she likes the idea." Watcher snickers.

Twitch glances at me and looks a little sick. "Stop it. We don't need to go that far. Just tell them we'll kill her."

"That won't squeeze extra out of Damien Darino. What will is showing him what'll happen to his woman every day until he pays what we demand." Scar leans forward. "If you're having second thoughts, I can help you with that."

Twitch flinches back. He's as afraid of Scar and Watcher as I am. "What will the family's don and our capos say about this when they find out?" he whines. "We're not sanctioned to be doing any of this."

"You let me handle that. You aren't here to think. You're here to keep an eye on her and keep your mouth shut. We'll send the photos, notes, and videos out tomorrow morning. For now, let's give our pretty guest a long overdue bath. I don't like my women to stink."

Part of me perks up at the mention of a bath, but then I consider what I'll likely have to endure to get one, and my stomach curdles.

"Are you going to be good for me, Princess?" Scar asks. "If you will, I'll take you upstairs and let you have a real bath. If you can't, I'll get buckets of cold water and a scrub brush and clean you with that."

As much as the thought of what he's going to do if he takes me upstairs terrifies me, the thought of freezing cold water and the abrasive scrub brush scares me more. "I'll behave," I whisper. "I promise. I'll behave. Please let me bathe."

"All it took was a few days to break you in." He snorts and gets up, walking over to me. "I'm surprised. I thought you'd have a little more fight to you."

I don't remark on it. Back-talking just gets me slapped or otherwise hurt. I've learned to stay quiet, and that's my form of rebellion. When they want me to make noise, I keep quiet no matter how hard or agonizing it is. If they think I'm broken, they'll assume I won't try to escape.

"What if they won't pay up for her, Boss?" Twitch asks shakily.

"Then we kill her." He hauls me to my feet with a smirk and tugs me towards the stairs. "Don't worry, Princess. No one's going to see you in your birthday suit. There's no one for miles around."

***

I COOPERATE WITH Scar for the entire ordeal that is my bath. He stays true to his promise that he's not going to force himself on me entirely until we know if the ransom will be paid, but he takes every other liberty with me. At least this time I get a hot bath, lavender-scented soap, and a bed out of it.

They don't take me back down to the basement this time. He was telling the truth when he said we were in the middle of nowhere. I can't see anything but miles of trees and the barest hint of a country road outside the window of the bedroom where they've left me. There's a tree growing just outside my window, and I start to formulate my plan with the time I have until my meal.

I haven't seen the sun in so long. At least, that's how it feels. So, I stand naked in front of the window and soak up the warmth. It and the bath are the first warmth I've felt since the kidnapping. My thoughts drift to my son as they often have in the last few days of hell. Is he safe? If they had him, I'd know. They wouldn't miss the chance to use him as leverage against me. Damien will make sure he's safe.

I need to get back to him, though. He must be missing me, and Damien will be going out of his mind with worry about me. He's going to flip when he gets the video, pictures, and note that the men plan to send.

Escaping is my best hope of getting back to my son in one piece. I don't know if Damien and my father will pay the ransom. Damien will, but my father doesn't have the money, and I'm sure they're watching to make sure Damien doesn't try to pay both ransoms. They've made a big deal about my father paying up.

Leaving in broad daylight isn't smart, though. I'll be caught right away. So I go back to the bed where Scar threw me after the bath and then went about his daily ritual of humiliating and violating me in whatever ways he could without breaking the one promise he'd made me. I know that if my father doesn't pay up, he'll make good on his promise to take things the rest of the way, and I don't plan to be around for him to do so. So, I curl up on the bed and start to plan for my escape.

Sometime in the middle of the planning, I fall asleep out of exhaustion and lack of proper food for days. When I wake again, it's dark aside from the lamp illuminating the dresser and a plate of food. They didn't wake me. It must have been Twitch who brought the food. The others wouldn't care that I was asleep.

I get up and grab the plate, devouring what they've left me. It isn't much, but I'm going to need what I can get if I want to survive until I can find help. When I'm done, I swallow down the tepid water in the cup on the dresser and then grab the sheets off the bed and begin tying them together to put out the window. I just need enough to drop to the ledge of the window below so I can drop safely to the ground. It's not quite a story between the roof of the window seat on the floor below and the ground. I shouldn't break anything.

Settled on my plan, I make sure the knots are secure, and then I toss the blankets out the window and pray that the men downstairs won't notice. Then I climb out the window and down the rope. It's difficult going because of my unused muscles and overall weakness. My vision blurs a few times as a wave of dizziness washes over me, but I keep going, determined to get back home to my son.

Finally, I make it to the roof of the window. I peek over the edge to see if the window is lit from inside. It is. I'm going to have to hope they don't look out the window or notice me, but I can't stay out here in the chilly night air on the roof all night. That's sure to get me caught.

So, I let out a shaky breath and jump. I hit the grass below with a thud and suck in a sharp breath at the jarring pain that shoots through me as I bend my knees and roll to absorb the force. I did it clumsily thanks to my lack of exercise or food in the last week, but I didn't break anything.

I get up and pick my way across the lawn towards the trees and the road I could just barely see beyond them from my window earlier. My escape is going well until I make it to the tree line and a familiar, cruel voice calls out.

"Where do you think you're going, Princess?" Rough hands follow the voice. One fist in my hair, and the other grips my throat, cutting off any hope of struggle or escape. "Escaping isn't nice or obedient, is it?"

I don't respond. The whimper clawing at my throat wants to escape, but I swallow it back down, unwilling to give him that satisfaction.

He sighs as if he's sorry he has to deal with this. Then he throws me over his shoulder and slams a hand down on my rear. "I see it'll have to be back to the basement for you. We'll have to do some more work to make sure you learn your lesson."

"Please...!" The thought of the basement again makes me sick, and I start to struggle even as I beg. "Please, don't put me back there. Please. I'll be good. I swear."

"You had that chance, and you chose to do this with it. Sorry, Princess." He pinches my thigh. "It's obvious I've been too easy on you, and there are other ways besides what I've been doing to get you to fall in line."

I tense in dread, not wanting to think about what those ways might be. We make it back to the house, and he takes me inside, heading straight for the basement. I thrash on his back, beating my fists against him. He lands another cruel, hard slap on my thigh this time, followed by a flurry of others that land all over my upper thighs and leave me crying despite my best efforts not to let any sound escape me.

Then he dumps me on the hard-packed dirt of the basement floor and shackles me to a support pole by the ankle and one wrist. He doesn't touch me again after that. He just walks away, leaving me with too little chain to shift off my now-blazing rear, and then the lights go out, and I'm back in the dark. I begin to cry as it hits me that I might never get out of here. Am I ever going to see my son or the light of day again?

Chapter Thirty-Four: Damien

I SLUMP DOWN on the park bench next to Marcello and stare out across the pond at the ducks. Everything feels like it's ground to an agonizing halt. I don't have any leads, and I don't know what to do next. Marcello is the last chance I have of finding out what's going on inside the other family without going to my father and begging. I don't beg. That's the one lesson I did take from my father; a Darino doesn't beg. A Darino demands, acts, and requests, but he never lowers himself to letting another person know he needs them.

Where has that gotten me, though? I've always thought it made me strong. But because of my belief that I could control everything and make everything work in my favor, because of my fear of emotional vulnerability and admitting some level of dependence on another, I never told Alyssa I loved her. I thought I'd have all the time in the world to do it, and now she's gone. I may never see her again, and I hate that she's been taken away and never knew I loved her.

"You look like a mess, my friend," Marcello says after a moment.

"Thanks," I mutter.

"Have you been sleeping and eating?"

"Eating, yes. Sleeping hasn't been working well." I stare down at my clasped hands. "I can't get to sleep knowing she's out there somewhere, scared and alone.... I keep wondering if I'm going to get a note. If I'm going to get something to tell me she's at least alive. Have you heard anything at all, Marcello?"

Marcello gives me a pained look. "I'm sorry, Damien. Our don has warned us all to stay out of this, and there's no information going around. I don't know if he's aware of who has her, let alone if he's the one who approved her kidnapping. Everything's locked up tight. If he knew I told you even that much, I'd be dead. I can't help you."

I bury my face in my hands and let out a heavy breath. "Okay... okay, I get it. I don't want you to risk your life when you have a wife and a kid, Marcello. Go. If there's nothing else you can tell me anyway, get out of here before someone who knows us reports you."

Marcello stands and squeezes my shoulder. "I am sorry, my friend."

"I know." I get to my feet and extend a hand to him. "Thank you for doing what you could."

He shakes my hand, and then he turns and walks away, leaving me with no information to work with and no closer to finding my kidnapped bride. I wish more than ever that I'd damned the potential consequences and told her I loved her. I should have.

Turning on my heel, I stalk back towards my car. I'll go home and get another PI working on it with the one I already have. Maybe they'll turn something up. On the slim chance that the don didn't order the kidnapping, the men who took her can't have done this without any mistakes. Somewhere, they'll slip up, and we'll find her. I have to believe that.

A young boy is standing by my car in a message boy's hat with a satchel slung over his shoulder. He's pulling out a parcel and setting it on the hood. I break into a run, my focus on the boy and intercepting him before he can run off and leave the package behind with no further information. He might be connected to the kidnappers.

He spots me and takes off, darting down a path away from the lot. I chase after him, desperate to find out why he's dropping a package and if he knows something. But when I make it to the path, he's disappeared into the woods, and I'm left panting and with my heart hammering in my chest.

It's a lost cause. I'm not going to catch him now. Instead of trying, I turn and go back to the car to see what he's left. The parcel isn't large, and a brief examination of it doesn't indicate that there's anything dangerous inside. Besides, packets of anthrax or bombs aren't the other families' style around here.

I open it and shake out whatever's inside. A handful of photos fall out first. One drops onto the hood face up. It's Alyssa. She's chained to a wall with her hands above her head, and she's naked. Her body is covered in bite marks and bruises. Whoever did this is touching her in some of the other photos, but his hands are all that show. Whoever's done this is smart. They're not giving me anything to work with.

The next thing in the packet is a DVD. I can't play it in my car, so I set it aside, my stomach churning. No doubt it's worse than the pictures they've sent.

The final piece in the package is a typed note.

If you want her back, bring one million dollars to the park where you received this and leave it in the trashcan by the duck pond. You have two weeks. We're being kind since we know this kind of money is hard to withdraw, but you'd better figure it out fast. Until the time is up, we'll refrain from going all the way with her, but I wouldn't be late if I were you. Once we have received your payment and her father's, you will receive further instructions. If you don't want to pay, we're happy to keep her and finish what we started in the video. Any sign of the police or your father's gang, and she dies.

I feel sick at the implications, and the last thing I want to do is watch the video, but I pocket everything and climb into the car. Driving home, I drive just barely within safe limits to avoid being pulled over.

Lucille greets me at the door with Timothy, but she takes one look at my face and steps aside without a word. I kiss my son on the head, but then I go straight to my office and shut and lock the door. Then I put the video into my player and watch in horror and guilt as what's been happening to my fiancée unfolds.

Once again, the cameraman has angled it so that I can't see the face of the man who's with her, but I can see his hands as he violates her, and I can hear the barely there whimpers as she fights not to make a sound. When the cameraman zooms on her face, her eyes are squeezed shut as if it might block out what's happening.

The fear and pain I see there break me. I will do anything, anything at all, to get her back. Even beg and make promises to the devil. I know if I pay them, her father still won't be able to, and the note made it clear that we both have to. I suspect now that we're being watched, and at the end of the video, words scroll across the screen.

You both pay, or I finish what we've started here. He pays his share, or I finish what we've started here. We know you can pay. You'd better hope he can.

My stomach is in knots, and I want to be sick, but I force myself under control. I'll go to my father. Maybe he can't help me retrieve her, but I can try to convince him to get me the information I need to retrieve her. Because I know full well that her father will never be able to pay his part of the debt, and unless I get to her first, those men will make her pay off his debt by raping her and then, if they're bored of her after, by selling her. I'll never get her back or see her again if that happens.

***

I STEP INSIDE my father's office and thank the butler for showing me in. He nods and shuts the door behind me.

My father spins his chair around, abandoning his view of the grounds in favor of looking at me. He smirks when he sees that it is me standing here in his office. "Last time you were in here, you told me you'd never be back. Yet here you are."

I clench my fists in my pockets and remind myself that I need his help. I can't appear to beg because he'll refuse simply because I'm weak. He hates weakness, and he hates it in me even more.

"What do you want?"

"I want you to help me find and retrieve Alyssa." I stalk to his desk and pull the note and the photos from my pocket. As much as I hate to let him see my woman in this state, I know he doesn't believe in mistreating women and children. If anything will convince him to help, it will be these.

He flips through them, his expression full of stony anger. Then he drops them back on the desk and glances over the note. "They shouldn't have done those things to her."

"Help me find her, please."

My father raises a brow. "Please?"

"I know how to use manners when it will get me what I need."

"It won't be enough to get you what you need or want here. Will you come back into the fold if I help you get her back?" He crosses his arms.

I shake my head immediately. If I do that, Alyssa will never come back to me, even if I save her from the thugs who took her. "Not if it isn't legit business you want me running. Dad, it doesn't do me any good to get her back just to sacrifice my principles and go do something she'll hate me for, something I'll hate myself for."

I'm desperate enough to agree to something I'll hate myself for, but I won't rescue her only to lose her because of what I have to do to pay back those who helped me.

"Then we don't have anything to talk about."

"We do. I can make you just as much money, maybe more, by taking your businesses legitimate and legal. I promise.

You've seen how much I've done with mine." I cross my arms and widen my stance to communicate nonverbally that I won't budge on this. "If you can save Alyssa, I'll take over the two you've had me on the board for, and I'll turn them legit. Then I'll get them working and running more efficiently so they can make the same kinds of money mine do."

My father shakes his head and laughs. "No. Crime pays far better than anything you do could, son. I won't be taking the family businesses legit, and I'm not going to help you rescue her if you're not willing to bargain with the one thing I want. This isn't a negotiation. You're either willing to give me what I want to get what you want, or you're not. Right now, it's obvious that you're not."

I grit my teeth, but I know he means it, and he's right. I'm not willing to give him what he wants because what he wants means losing the one thing I want more than anything right now. I need Alyssa home to have what I want—her—but it won't do me a lick of good to bring her home if I ensure I'll lose her again in a worse way before I even rescue her.

So, I nod and turn away.

"You know, I may feel you're a disappointment as an heir," my father says quietly. "But I can't say you're a disappointment as a man. At least you stand by your convictions, annoying and high and mighty as they may be."

I swallow hard at the rush of emotions that brings. Anger, pain, hurt, relief. My father has never once told me he's proud of me in any context, and this is the closest to it I suspect he'll ever come. It shouldn't bring me any relief or gratitude, but it does. "Thanks, Dad."

"If you change your mind about the work, you know where to find me."

Opening the door, I stride out. There's only one path left now. I have to get more PIs and men on the job to find her before it's too late, and I know just the man I want heading all of this up. John Newsom, a former friend of mine in college, runs a PI and security firm that's made national headlines for its successful negotiation of situations like this. Now that I know it's a kidnapping and that my father won't help, he's my next call. Can he perform the miracle I need right now? I'm not sure, but I'll pay him anything he asks to give him the chance.

Chapter Thirty-Five: Alyssa

THINGS ARE GETTING worse for me. I've been locked in the basement down here without food or water for a while, and I can just manage to stand without toppling over. The men who have me leave unchained now because they think I don't have the strength to make it up the stairs anymore. I let them do whatever they want to me now without protest. I just go somewhere else and escape them by imagining that it's Damien's hands. It's not like they know where my mind is or that it's not them I'm thinking of. It's the only way I can survive this.

Reality is starting to feel tenuous and uncertain, and I think about Damien and Timothy more with each passing day that I'm stuck down here. Where is he? Is he even going to come for me?

The door at the top of the stairs opens. I don't move. I just lie in a ball on the cold floor and listen to the steps creak as the men come downstairs. It's all three today, which probably doesn't mean anything good for me. When they're all down here, it usually means they're worried about something or planning to play with me together. Scar still hasn't let anyone take that last step into full-on rape, but it wouldn't matter to me anymore. They've done their worst on me by now, and a little more pain is just a drop in the bucket.

"I'm telling you, they'll pay the ransom. Give them until the two weeks are up and quit whining. It's been barely a week, and you know full well how hard it can be to withdraw that kind of money. We gave extra time for a reason. But to be honest, I sort of hope he doesn't pay up so we can finish things with her and then make an example out of her and the wife to make sure everyone knows what happens when they cross our don." Scar drags a chair over and sets it next to me. He sits down and leans over to dance his fingers over my belly. "Do you think you're in the mood today to behave for a trip upstairs again? Maybe this time, you won't run. Of course, I don't think you have the energy or strength left to make it down the roof again."

I close my eyes, my mind wandering to Damien. He used to run his fingers over my abdomen that same way. It was one of my favorite things he did before he turned things heated and wicked. I shiver, the memory leaving me a little turned on despite my drowsy, dizzy state. Hunger and dehydration are starting to win the battle.

"Grab me a water bottle from upstairs," Scar snaps at the other two. "And be quick about it. She can't last much longer if we don't start giving her water again."

They've been giving me water on and off every few days. Just enough to make sure I don't die of dehydration before the ransom can come. I haven't bothered to tell them that if Damien hasn't paid the ransom by now, he's not going to. I'm just not sure if that's because he's given up on me or because he's still looking for another way and is getting closer. I've chosen to believe it's because he's close and knows it, so he won't pay them when he can get to me.

Any day now, that door at the top of the stairs will open because he's coming to get me, and this nightmare will be over. I'll be safe.

"Come back here, Princess," Scar drawls. "I'm a little tired of you shutting me out by closing those pretty eyes. Are you imagining him when I touch you? If I forced myself on you, would you still try to imagine him? I wonder if you'll be able to stand having him touch you when he finally pays up." He laughs as if it's hilarious to him that his abuse might make me hate the man I love.

It won't happen. I know the difference between them and Damien. Damien cares about me. I don't know what secrets he's keeping, but I know he loves me and that I love him. With all the time to think down here, I've realized that's enough.

"Look, Boss," Watcher grouses, "Darino's not going to pay, and her old man can't pay. We're waiting for nothing. Why don't we just screw her, then slit her throat and dump her in the Hudson somewhere?"

"Because that won't pay us back for our trouble," Scar snaps. "You'll pay us back other ways, won't you, Princess?"

"You're only saying that because you're not thinking with the right head." Watcher eyes us both with a leer, his hand toying with his fly.

I watch him back, my stomach lurching.

"Eyes back on me, Princess. I don't care if he unzips and plays. You pay attention to me." Scar pinches my hip sharply, drawing a croak of pain from me. "How am I thinking with the wrong head?" His voice is casual, but I hear the threat of violence behind it. "She could make us money. Sell a few of the unedited tapes, and then sell her off to the kinds of men who'll make sure she's never free again, and we'll make plenty of money."

"Not enough to risk the wrath our capos and the don will bring down on us when they find out."

"How would they find out?" Scar presses his thumb between my legs and begins toying with me.

I don't bother to fight him. It doesn't do any good. It'll just make it hurt worse. I let my eyes shut.

He's too engrossed in his argument with Watcher to care, and he lets me drift.

"We need to get rid of her, Boss." Twitch returns with the water.

He's eyeing me nervously when I open my eyes again, and now Scar's watching my face too, irritation in his eyes. He pinches a particularly sensitive spot, letting me know he saw that I'd closed my eyes and tried to let my mind wander to Damien again.

"You promised us that's what we'd do if we didn't see any sign of the ransom being paid."

My gaze fixes on the water bottle, and I part my lips in an attempt to beg for it, but the sound doesn't make it out of my parched lips. If they don't feed me soon, I'm pretty sure I really will die, whether they decide to kill me or not. But the water will at least stave off death a little longer. Just a little longer so Damien can find me.

Scar snatches the bottle out of Twitch's hands and twists the cap off. He pulls me into a sitting position roughly by my hair and puts the bottle to my lips. "Sip it, Princess, or you'll just throw it up."

I nod weakly and do as told, thankful for even a few sips of water to alleviate the dreadful dryness in my throat and the thickness in my mouth.

"Fine," Scar snaps. "Fine... if we don't get the money from her father and Darino at the end of next week, we take what we want from her and kill her. Then we dump the body, and no one knows it was us."

I tremble in his grip, realizing the enormity of what they're saying. I'm going to die if Damien can't get to me before the end of this next week or find a way to get my father the money to pay his part of the ransom. I'm never going to see Damien or my son again.

That isn't acceptable. I want to see Damien again. I have to tell him I love him, even if he may not say it back. I have to hold my son close so that I know he's safe and that I'm safe too because I'm there with him and his father. I need those things like I need the water I'm slowly sipping at again.

I'm going to escape. I'd rather die trying than sit and wait for death. Pushing weakly at the water, I cough and try to speak again. "A bath... please..." I plead, letting a note of the misery I feel creep in, hoping they'll believe I'm entirely beaten. "Please...." When the tears start to fall, they're not a show. I'm entirely exhausted, scared, and worried that I might not be able to escape in this state.

Scar contemplates me before handing the water off to Twitch with a nod. He scoops me up and carries me toward the stairs. "Don't disturb us. I'll take care of her. You two don't touch her until I give the order, you hear? I'm still in charge."

The other two grumble about it but agree before he turns and carries me up the stairs. I close my eyes and try to imagine that it's Damien carrying me out of the basement to freedom, but the smell of him is all wrong, and I can't do it. I sniffle and cry noiselessly against Scar's chest. All I want is for Damien to be freeing me and then holding me, reassuring me that all is okay and that I'll be fine. But I can't have that now. Maybe not ever if I can't get out of here tonight.

***

SCAR STAYS WITH me as night falls. He lets me stay in the same room I was in before. I'm not sure if it's out of pity or if it's because he wants a bed while he plays with me, but I'm not going to complain about the soft warmth of the mattress and sheets against my bare skin.

He hovers over me with a smile that I would call affectionate if I didn't know how psychotic he is. He doesn't have an affectionate or tender bone in his body. He's all cruelty and manipulation. He's the embodiment of evil. "You're going to be good for me, aren't you?"

I turn my head away, but I don't try to get away from him otherwise. He doesn't remark on it or stop me. I hear his belt buckle come undone and tense. So far, he hasn't touched himself in front of me, though Watcher seems to take a perverse joy in doing so. Usually, Scar is under tight control, and he only uses his hands and mouth to try to force my body into betraying me. I know he must take care of his own needs later because I've seen what torturing me does to him, but he's never gone there in front of me.

"Look at me," he whispers.

Shivering, I force my gaze to his, studiously avoiding looking anywhere but his face. He leans in, and I feel him against me as he brings his weight down.

"You promised," I hiss, starting to panic.

I thought earlier he couldn't take anything worse, that it wouldn't matter if he did this too, but it does now when I'm in the moment.

"Shut up. If I want to screw you, I will. But I'm not going to go that far. I just want to play. I won't actually push in."

His frankness and the crude smirk on his face leave my stomach in knots, but not in a good way. I want to be sick, but I force myself not to react as he reaches into the drawer of the bedside table and pulls out the tube of lube he uses when he's being nice.

The sight of it fills me with dread. He says he won't go that far, but if he's not planning to, then what does he need that for?

"Please, stop. Please... don't do this...." I push at his chest, wanting him off me and desperate to get his body angled so he's not between my legs anymore.

"Fight me, and I'll change my mind," he snaps. "Stay still."

I close my eyes on a sob and do as told because I don't want him to change his mind or make this any worse. He lets me get away with it, not pressing the issue like he did earlier in the day. Instead, he opens the lube, and then I feel his fingers playing like they always do. I work a few deep breaths in and out of my lungs and retreat into my imagination like I've done before.

It's not Scar's fingers pressing into me. It's Damien's, and it feels nice. There's nothing scary about the situation. We're at home, and he's trying to take away the stress because he knows I've been working too hard and worrying myself sick about silly little things. He's good at distracting me and relieving the stress.

My body starts to relax a little. The soft bed and sheets against my back help the fantasy along, and I start to breathe easier. I'll get through this. I just have to hold on to that dream, that imagined moment with Damien where I'm there, not here.

And it works. Scar doesn't pull me from the fantasy by demanding my attention on him. He just uses my body to get himself off and then rolls off me. True to his word, he doesn't screw me. He just touches us both until he's satisfied and spent, and then he leaves me there, covered in his mess and the lube.

I turn my back on him and curl into a ball, not bothering to worry about everything I'm covered in. It doesn't matter. I'm leaving tonight.

He doesn't stay once he's recovered. He gets me a wet cloth from the bathroom and leaves me with that. The door slams shut behind him, but I don't hear the lock turn. He's confident I'm not going anywhere because I'm weak and because he took things much further tonight without much fight from me. He thinks I'm broken.

I'm not. I get up once I've waited long enough to hear him snoring through the thin wall separating this room and the next. He was right to assume I couldn't make it down the roof again. I'll have to go through the house, which means more risk of being caught, but I'll do it. I'm not going to stay for whatever happens next.

Creeping out the door, I tiptoe down the stairs, wincing at the slightest creak. No one intercepts me, though, and when I make it to the door, I think I've finally made it. I put my hand on the door's knob, my fingers trembling.

Twitch's angry voice hisses from behind me. "Where do you think you're going?"

Then his hand is tangling in my hair, and he drags me away from the door, yanking viciously. "You've caused enough trouble, you brat."

I grab onto the doorframe of the hallway into the living room, panic and desperation fueling me. Kicking and hissing, I try to lash out at him. He slams me into the doorframe, and my shoulder pops. I scream as white-hot pain lances through me.

"What's going on down here?" Scar's furious voice booms down from the stairwell.

"Caught her trying to escape again, Boss."

"Did you?" Scar sighs loudly. "Oh, Princess... that was stupid. Very, very stupid. And when they don't pay the ransom, you know you're going to pay, don't you?"

And I did. I closed my eyes as a sob strangles in my throat. *I tried,* I think, wishing Damien and Timothy could hear me. *I tried to come home to you both. I loved you... I wish I'd told you that when I had the chance, but I do. I loved you, Damien Darino.* And I hope he'll figure that out from what's been left behind, but have I left anything that will communicate that message, or will he always wonder how I felt?

Chapter Thirty-Six: Damien

HIRING JOHN WAS the best decision I've made on this whole disaster. Within the first week, I'll have to rescue her or pay the ransom, but he finds a lead. It takes a while, but he has contacts I don't have within the various crime networks as well as with investigative bureaus, and he manages to discover that a small faction of Marcello's family has gone rogue and acted without the sanction of their don or their capos.

So, on that information, I'm marching straight into the lion's den. Well, sort of. I've muscled my way past Don Giovanni's secretary to see him, and I'm going to wait here until he sees me, whether he likes it or not. My men and John are waiting to back me up if necessary, and I mean to get his help to get my woman back one way or another. If I have to start a war, I will.

He looks up when I bang through the door into his office and frowns in irritation. "Damien. Your father raised you better. What are you doing in my office building without an invitation?"

"I'm here about my fiancée. I know your men took her, and I also know they did it without your permission or the sanction of their capos at your command. As a result, I'm extending you the courtesy of asking that you help return her to me rather than coming in guns blazing." I cross my arms and stare down at him.

He stands and straightens his jacket with a sigh. "You youngsters are always so pushy and hasty. Do you realize you come across as though you're coming in guns blazing when you march in here like this? I presume you brought back up."

It isn't a question, so I don't bother to answer. We both know I did. I don't want a fight, but I'm prepared for one if it comes to it.

Giovanni sighs. "You realize her father owes me a great deal of money. Why should I stop them from getting it using her?"

"You should stop them because if you don't, you're going to have a war on your hands. I'll go to my father and inform him that your men took her. He may not like my future wife much, but if he knows your men took her as an act of aggression when the two families are meant to be at peace, he won't look on it kindly."

He doesn't need to know that the only way my father would agree to go to war for me is if I agree to join his side. I'm never going to do that, and I certainly don't have the resources to wage war on the family to get her back.

"That and because your men defied you and acted without permission. If that gets noised about and you permit it, you're going to have men thinking they can do whatever they want without consequence. We both know that would spell the end of your rule."

Giovanni's gaze narrows. "Are you threatening me, boy?"

"I'm doing whatever I need to right now to get the woman I love back. Do you think I don't know you'd do the same if the situations were reversed?" It's a bit of a low blow, but it's no secret among the mafia and crime families that Giovanni dotes on his wife, who is his only real weakness. "Look... You'll get your money. I'll pay his debt, and you'll help me get her back. Then you won't go after her again. He can even be the one to hand off the money if that's what needs to happen to let you save face, but I'm not losing the woman I'm going to marry or her father to this. You'll drop the threat to blackmail or harm me if I help her in exchange for working with me to get her back before they do worse and the money he'll pay you. I'll even pay you a little extra for the help and agreeing to leave us alone."

He looks away, jaw tightening. "You make a persuasive argument. I don't need a war with your father. These men didn't act with my permission. I'll put you in touch with their capos. They may know where their men would hide out with the girl. When you find them, you'll let my capos bring them in for me to mete out justice the long and hard way. Otherwise, you won't get my cooperation. I won't be undermined or made to look weak in this."

I hold out my hand with a sharp nod. "You have a deal. I'll work with your men to get her back, and you'll have them. They deserve whatever they get for what they've done to her."

He frowns. "I suppose they sent proof they took her?"

"Plenty of it." My jaw tightens as I think about the video. "They've been sexually abusing her, and I have no doubt it's far worse than what they sent me. If I don't find her before their deadline for the ransom is up she's either going to die or be sold off to the sex trade. I don't think I need to say more to communicate the urgency of this."

"No. They will pay for this. The Giovanni family does not deal in sexual abuse or sex trading, and my men know I do not tolerate the abuse of women or children." His fists clench on the desk until his knuckles turn white. "They'll answer for breaking my family's code and defying my orders. That I promise you."

I nod sharply and turn on my heel. "Then you have yourself a deal, Don Giovanni. And my gratitude."

"I'll send you the contact info this afternoon. Be there at the time and place I send, and don't be late. I hope you reach her in time, Damien."

I smile grimly. So do I. Because if I don't, I might rethink my stance on crime long enough to help Giovanni and his men make those thugs pay for taking her from me.

***

IT TAKES A few days before the capos I speak to have anything for me. I spend those days with my mind on Alyssa and what shape she'll be in when I find her. I miss her with every fiber of my being, and I need nothing more than to have her in my arms to hold where I know she's safe.

My phone rings while I'm at work, but I pick it up, abandoning the spreadsheets I was reviewing. I care more about making sure I don't miss a call that could lead to Alyssa than I do about anything in my company. I'd sell my soul if it meant getting her back. The only thing I won't do is jeopardize my chance of helping her recover from whatever's been done to her by selling my soul to my father and the crime families that have hurt her so badly.

It's one of the capos, Mario. "Darino," he says when I pick up. "We know where she is. We can go in to get her, but they're holed up well, and we don't want to risk her or our men."

"So we need a plan." My mind goes to Stew. He's good with plans, and he'd agree to help in a heartbeat if I asked.

"We do. My don won't provide more than three or four men to retrieve her. He doesn't care if those men live for long so long as we leave them alive enough to die slowly. He also doesn't care much whether we extract the girl successfully. We're not risking our lives for a woman we don't know. We're going in there to make our men face punishment for their disobedience." His voice is apologetic. "We have families too, though, and she's not our priority."

I understand, though I hate hearing it. If I were in their position, I'd do the same. Their lives are full of enough danger without putting themselves into more trying to put a stop to a hostage situation they're not trained to deal with. "I'll have my men there too. All I need is for you to listen to them if they ask something of you. John will do his best to get everyone out alive."

"Good man, John," Mario says gruffly. "We'll do what we can. Let us know the plan."

"I will." I hang up and call John first. "John," I say when the line picks up, "they've found her location."

John chuckles. "Then it's showtime. We'll make them pay for this, Damien. I promise."

"We'll get together with Angelo. Mario called me, but Angelo heads everything up. He'll know more about the location, and we can plan from there. I want to bring Stew in on it too."

"A good idea. His security teams would be able to back us up if necessary. I'll see you tonight at the usual meet point?"

"Yes. I'll send Angelo a text, and we'll meet there."

"We'll get her back, my friend," John says quietly. "But you should prepare yourself because we might not get her back in one piece mentally or physically."

I swallow past the lump in my throat and close my eyes, recalling her face and the way she looks when she smiles. It isn't something I've let myself think too much about, but I know John's right to be concerned. I can't trust that I'll get her back in one piece mentally or physically. "It doesn't matter," I tell him. "I won't lose her, and we'll find our way through whatever we have to once I have her back. I'm not letting go, and I'm certainly not going to keep my feelings a secret anymore. She's going to know she's loved, even when the days seem so dark she doesn't know how she'll make it."

"She's lucky to have you," John says. "I'll see you tonight."

The line beeps as he hangs up, and I tap out a quick message to Angelo before I shove my cell back into my pocket. Then I get up and head out to find Stew. I need my friend on my side for this because tonight, we plan a war.

***

WE ALL MEET up at the agreed spot in silence. I'm the first to speak once I'm sure no one's followed us and that we're alone in the park with the night and the animals. "Angelo, what's the situation with where they're keeping her? How hard will it be to ambush them and make a rescue?"

Angelo grimaces. "We've scoped out the place. They're staying fairly alert, but they're more nervous than anything. They aren't being as strict about the watch as they should be to keep us out. If we go in under cover of night, I doubt we'll run into much resistance."

"And once we're in the house? Do we know where they're keeping her?"

"Basement, I think. I haven't seen any signs of her." He crosses his arms with a scowl. "Orders from above are not to risk any of my men trying to get her out, and I have to follow them, but I'll do what I can to give you a good chance to get to her. There are only three of them, so if we take the upstairs with the four of us from the Giovanni family and you, John, and Stewart handle the rescue, you should be able to get her out. Be ready with a team to back us up. We'll go in the front."

"And which entrance is closest to the basement?" I ask.

"The back. You go through there, and the basement is right off the kitchen." He looks at the other three men on his side. "We handle our men, and we handle them efficiently. Keep them contained, and make sure they don't get to any of these three or the girl. Am I clear?"

They all nodded.

"That's the best I can do for you, Darino."

I nod. It's something, but will it be enough? I don't know, but somehow, I'll have to make it enough.

Chapter Thirty-Seven: Alyssa

I STIR AT the faint pop of gunshots upstairs just outside the door. The soundproofing along the walls helps to keep the sound outside from filtering in, but the door isn't soundproofed quite right, and I strain to catch every sound.

My body is battered, weakened, and starved. I don't have the strength to pull myself to my feet or to drag myself to the stairs, so I lay in a ball on the cold floor and listen instead. My heart pounds in my throat, and I don't dare to let myself hope that it might be a rescue. It's probably something to do with the men upstairs, and the people shooting likely don't even know I'm down here.

The door creaks open, and footsteps pound down the stairs. I close my eyes. This is probably the end, but I don't have the strength to fight it. Is it Scar or Watcher coming to put a bullet in my head? Or maybe it's Twitch. He doesn't seem a likely candidate, but who knows?

My body feels light, and my mouth has gone dust dry from lack of water. Maybe tomorrow would've been the usual day to give me a few bottles throughout the day. I don't know anymore. I haven't left the basement since I was caught trying to escape the second time. I've been too weak to fight Scar or Watcher on anything they wanted to do. The one saving grace is that my increasingly out-of-it state seemed to turn them both off, and they've left me alone for a while now.

Strong hands run over my body, and I imagine that it's Damien. Scar must be desperate if he's feeling me up in this state. What changed his mind after he left me chained up in disgust last time? I vomited on him from lack of food and trying to drink water too quickly, and he didn't touch me again after that.

"Alyssa?"

I tense. Damien? I have to be imagining it. It can't be him. He's not here. It's just my fever-addled, half-starved brain making hallucinations to help ease my trauma. Even so, a hallucination of Damien is better than no hallucination of him. I open my eyes to see him above me, shining a flashlight over me and staring in horror at my body.

"Don't be upset," I croak. "Don't be. You're just a hallucination, and I want you to be happy, not upset."

Someone behind him curses, their voice low and angry.

I start to tremble. "Don't be angry," I slur again. "Please. Don't hurt me."

"Alyssa, love...." Damien crouches next to me and pulls off his jacket to cover me.

It feels warm and real, and it smells like him. Man, my brain is good at coming up with things. It's crazy how realistic it all feels. "Am I dead?" I ask suspiciously, the words rasping uncomfortably through my dry throat. Maybe I've died and gone to heaven. That would explain why he seems so r eal.

"No, darling. No, you're not dead. I found you before that could happen. I found you." There's a catch in his voice, and he gathers me up into his arms to hold me close. He smells like Damien, and his arms are strong and warm.

"I kept thinking about you when he touched me. I imagined it was you. Now...." I cough on the dryness in my throat. "Now I must be hallucinating all the time. It's nice, you know."

"You aren't hallucinating either," he whispers in my ear. "I'm here. I swear to you I am, Alyssa."

"I heard gunshots," I mumble.

"We had to fight our way in. Someone wasn't where we expected, and we had to shoot. He's being handled." He shifts me a bit and then stands with me in his arms. "We're leaving this place, Alyssa. It's going to be alright now. They're not going to hurt you again. I swear that to you."

I press my head against his chest with a sigh. Is it possible this is real? Could he really be here? I don't want to believe it because I'm afraid it will all be a lie and that it'll disappear.

He carries me up the stairs and out of the basement. The house's interior is dark, and I can hear shouting and thuds upstairs. Damien doesn't stop. He keeps walking until we're out of the house and under the night sky.

Lifting my head, I see the stars. It's then that I realize this is real. He is here, holding me and rescuing me. I'm not dead or dying. I'm safe.

I start to cry as that fact sinks in. I'm safe. They aren't going to hurt me anymore. It's done. I'm safe.

Damien holds me tighter. "Please, don't cry, Alyssa. Please. I'm here now. You're safe. We're going home, baby girl. Home, okay? Right now. You don't have to be scared."

I shake my head with a sob. "You're really here. Really, for real." I throw my arms around his neck and cling to him tightly. "I was afraid you might not find me or that you might not come for me. I tried to keep believing, but I was so scared. They were going to kill me." My voice cracks thanks to the lack of water, and I start coughing.

He hurries to the car and sits me in the front seat before grabbing a water bottle and helping me take sips. "Did they do anything to you that requires immediate medical attention?" he asks.

My arm hurts from where it was dislocated days ago, but there's nothing else besides the memories and pain in my mind. It isn't dislocated anymore, though. They popped it back in so that they could manage me without me screaming in agony. "No. I just want to go home. Where is Timothy? I need my son."

"He's at home, love." He kisses my forehead gently and then pulls back to buckle me in. "That's where we're going now. You'll be safe there, and you can see Timothy then. Just rest for me, okay?"

I nod and sink back into the seat with a sigh, my eyes slipping closed. It's been too long since I've slept and felt safe doing so. Now that I know I'm safe, I let myself slip into sleep, trusting Damien to get me home safely.

***

WHEN WE GET home, Damien wakes me and takes me inside himself. He doesn't let me walk on my own, and even if he had, I doubt I could manage it. I'm too weak and dizzy from my ordeal. I cling to him as he carries me inside.

Inside, he takes me straight to his room and settles me on the bed. "We're going to get you dressed first. I'll have Lucille bring the baby in here for you, but you're still tired and weak from what happened."

I nod and curl into his touch. "Don't leave me. Don't go. Please, don't go."

He takes my hand and gives it a hard squeeze. "I'm not going anywhere. Let me look over your injuries, Alyssa. I'll tend them for you."

"I want to hold Timothy." I need to see my son, to reassure myself that he's safe and that I'm here and safe as well.

"You will." He pulls his phone out of his pocket and dials Lucille. "I'll call her and ask her to bring him up right now for you, okay?"

I nod and settle down, resting my head against his shoulder. His scent is reassuring and grounding, and I trust him to do what he's promised. This is real. I'm not imagining or hallucinating, and I'm free. I'm safe.

The door opens a few minutes later, and Lucille comes in, carrying Timothy. She gasps when she sees the state I'm in, her eyes welling with tears. Timothy wiggles in her arms and starts to cry too, and I suck in a sharp breath at seeing him. I need him in my arms, and I try to get up off the bed to reach him. My legs gave out, and if not for Damien grabbing me, I would have hit the floor.

Damien pulls me back up onto the bed. "Stay here. I'll bring him to you."

"Do you want me to get her some clothes?" Lucille recovers her voice, but her gaze shifts away from me.

"Please. I'll help her bathe. Can you get the bassinet for Timothy? I'm sure she'll want him where she can see him while I try to get her cleaned up."

"Of course." Lucille hands Damien our son.

He takes the baby and brings him to me. My arms tremble when I try to take him, and I realize I don't even have the strength left to hold my son. I start to sob, overwhelmed at the inability to pick back up where I left off when I was taken.

"Hey, hey...." Damien shakes his head. "Love, don't cry. Lay down for me, and I'll put him on your chest so you can hold him."

I do so, tears still sliding down my cheeks and dripping into my hair. He helps me situate myself up against the pillows and then lays Timothy on my chest. I wrap my arms around my son, and my whole body starts to relax.

Lucille retreats, shutting the door softly behind her. Damien climbs onto the bed with me, and he wraps me up in his arms, watching both me and Timothy.

"You're home, Alyssa," he whispers in my ear. "You're home, and you're safe. They can't touch you anymore, and they never will again."

I press a kiss to Timothy's head, still crying silently. It's hard to believe it's all over, and I don't want to let go of Timothy for fear that this will all disappear, and I'll be back in that basement alone and dying.

"You need a bath, love," Damien says softly. "And food and water. You're too thin. Did they starve you?"

I close my eyes, trying not to go back to that basement or the things done to me there. "They gave me water every few days to keep me from dying, and they fed me less often than that after I tried to escape and come home twice."

His grip on me tightens, and I know he's angry, but I don't have the strength to reassure him right now. After a minute, he says, "I need to take a look at your injuries and tend them. Will you let me do that if Timothy's in the bassinet within reach?"

I open my eyes and stare down at my baby. He's settled in and is sleeping peacefully again. I'm not sure I can bring myself to let go of him, but I know if I don't, I won't be able to eat. I need to recover for his sake so that I can take care of him.

"You can hold him again just as soon as you're cleaned up and have a bit of food in your stomach. I promise. I'm not going to take him from you."

I sniffle and nod. "Damien?"

"What is it, love?"

"When I was down there, the only thing I could think about was coming home to you two. Both of you. I should have told you before it was too late, but I love you." I look up at him, afraid of what I might see.

"We'll talk about it later," he whispers gently. "When you're not as stressed or in need of some pampering and care. Let tonight be just about you and coming home mentally, not just physically. Okay, Alyssa?"

I nod, not because I want to postpone telling him how I feel but because I know he's right about needing time to recover. So, when Lucille brings in the bassinet and sets in the bathroom before leaving quietly again, I don't protest Damien's leaving to run the bath.

I let him take me and Timothy into the bathroom and allow him to take Timothy from me while I hold on to the sink to stay upright. Then I let him put me in the tub and try to remember that it's him bathing me this time, not Scar or Watcher, and that I'm never going to go through what I did in that basement ever again. I do what he's asked, and I make tonight just about coming home. But will I ever really feel like every part of me has come home, or is some part of me going to be stuck in that basement and house forever?

Chapter Thirty-Eight: Damien

IT TAKES A week before I'm sure Alyssa can be left by herself to rest, but once I'm certain she'll be okay and won't panic with me gone, I head out to my father's home in the countryside. It's time to tell him that I'm through with this. The paperwork I've brought on the assumption he won't agree to take the business legit is burning a hole in the satchel over my shoulder, and I can't wait to be done with this.

I pull into the driveway of his mansion-like home and park before walking to the front door. This time, I wait politely. I don't need a fight, and I want this taken care of quickly and quietly.

My father meets me at the door and ushers me inside his study instead of the imposing office where he normally conducts business. "I hear you got her back, and that the other family has cleaned up the trash."

My jaw tightens. "No thanks to you."

"You knew what you had to do if you wanted my help."

I pull the satchel strap over my head and sit down. "I'm here because I have an ultimatum for you. Either you take family business legitimate, or I won't have any part of it."

He scowls. "We've been over this. You can't walk away from your birthright, no matter how much you might want to. You're part of this family, and one day, you're going to act like it."

"I didn't say I'd tell the authorities about you." I pull the paperwork out of my satchel. "We're past that point. I can't do that to Mom or Lucille. Not in good conscience."

His eyes narrow, and he sits back, folding his hands over his belly. "Then what are you saying?"

"Exactly what I told you. I'm through with this if you don't make it a legitimate business. No more illegal dealings, money laundering, or drugs, Dad. None of that. I won't be involved in it, and neither will any of the companies I manage. I've gone over the books in my time waiting for word on Alyssa, and I know you're using the companies I've had my management team running to clean your cartel money. That's over."

"It certainly isn't. It's my money you used to start that business and the others. Do you think you can walk away from dirty money by making me take it legit or... what? You'll sell them all off? You can't do that without approval from the board, and you only have a fifty percent interest to control here."

I push the paperwork across the desk. "I'm aware. That's why I brought this. I'll keep the business I built with the money I made from my investments and hard work. You'll take back the ones bought with family money. I'm signing all my shares over to you, and we're going to be through. I have a woman I'm going to marry and a son with that woman to think of, and I'm done playing this back and forth with you where you try to force me into the life you live, and I push back and refuse. I won't have them caught in the crosshairs of that either, and if I don't do something, they will be."

My father snatches the papers off the desk and flips through them, his expression going stony. "You'd really give up all this money and your companies just to avoid being involved in your family's business?"

"It wouldn't be my first choice, but you're refusing to take the road I'd prefer. So yes." I pull my satchel back over my head and stand. "I don't want to see you or talk to you again."

"Does that extend to your mother and Lucille too?" he asks coldly.

"Lucille is always welcome at my home. So is Mom. It's you I have an issue with. Stay away from me, my home, and my family."

His jaw tightens, but he doesn't say a word or try to stop me when I turn and stalk out of the room. I have other places to be and one more stop to make before I can go home and spend the rest of my day helping Alyssa to come back to me fully.

***

MY FINAL STOP before I return home to Alyssa is at her parents' run-down home in the poorer suburbs of the city. I walk up their cracked driveway and knock on the door. Then I wait.

Her father answers the door. He looks broken and twenty years older than he did before his daughter was taken. The reality of what he got his family into has taken its toll, and the weight of guilt is far heavier than it was before the incident. I've had a hard time finding it in me to forgive him for what he's caused, but for Alyssa's sake, I've found a way.

"We need to talk," I say.

He steps aside and lets me in. "I got your message that you found her. Is she... will she be okay?"

"She's alive and will live. I don't know yet what mental state she's in entirely." I shove my hands into my pockets. "I'm not here about her. Just for her. You're going to go into the program my charity runs for gambling addicts. You need help, and I need to know nothing like this is ever going to happen again. Are we clear?"

He bows his head. "I know... I know I need help, and I know it can't happen again. I hate myself, Damien... what I caused... what happened to her..."

I wish I could feel more sympathy, but seeing what happened to Alyssa because of him, I don't have an ounce of sympathy left. "Just sign the paperwork." I dig it out and hand it to him. "Then go and stay in the program. Get help so she won't pay for your addiction again. I'm not connected to my family anymore. I won't be able to save you again, and the next time, I can't guarantee I'll be able to save her either."

He nods and takes out a pen, scratching his signature across the paperwork that will gain him admittance to the program my charity runs. "Thank you for taking care of her like I should have," he says quietly.

I put the papers away and nod. Then I turn and walk out of the house, returning to my car. Now that I'm through with all of this, I want to be home with Alyssa and Timothy. I'm as desperate to keep her close as she is to have me and Timothy within reach, though I'll never admit that to anyone. I keep waking up thinking she's gone and reaching out to her side of the bed to reassure myself she's not. We're both slowly overcoming the trauma we went through, and I can see in her eyes that she's not there yet any more than I am. She has further to go, though. She's been through far w orse.

Driving home, I think about all I want to tell her, all I need to tell her. She's already told me she loves me, but we haven't spoken about that since she told me the night I brought her home. We need to, but I don't think either of us has been ready to. Soon, we'll face that hill too, and get everything out in the open. For tonight, I just want to spend time with her.

I make it back to the house and go inside to look for her. My sister has gone home, so it's just me, Alyssa, and Timothy again. When I go upstairs, I find her curled up in bed with a book, Timothy already in his crib so I moved to the master bedroom.

For what I want to do with her tonight, I don't need my son as an audience, so I step inside and crook my finger at her to indicate she should follow me. She sets the book aside and gets out of bed with an anxious glance at Timothy, but she follows me after a moment.

In the hall, I shut the bedroom door softly and pull her into my arms. "I didn't want him to wake up or hear anything."

She bites her lip and lowers her gaze to my chest. Her hands come to rest on my chest, and she shifts slightly against me. "Why not?"

"Because what I want to do to you isn't something a baby or child should witness." I lean in and kiss her forehead and then her mouth. "But if you're not in the mood, we don't have to do anything. We can go back in there to cuddle while you read."

Her fingers curl into my shirt and pull me closer. "I don't want to be treated like glass, Damien. I won't be able to get back to myself or who I was if you treat me like I'm fragile or like they broke me."

I sigh. "I just don't want to trigger any traumatic memories, sweetheart. I'll understand if you don't want to do anything."

She tugs me close and presses her mouth to mine in a desperate, heated kiss. "I want you to stop treating me like I'm broken and start helping me to mend the cracks. I need you to erase what they did." Her voice breaks. "I need more than just the fantasies I fled to when they were abusing and hurting me. I need the real you. All of you."

I nod. "Okay. Okay, Alyssa. I'll gladly give it to you. I promise." Picking her up, I silently urge her to wrap her legs around my waist. When she does, I carry her to the guest room where I shut the door behind us and then deposit her on the large four-poster bed.

She shivers visibly in the thin nightgown she's wearing. I can see that she's turned on as much as she is cold, and I'm relieved that this isn't frightening her.

"What do you want me to do, sunshine?" I ask, my voice a low gravelly murmur.

"I want you to make me feel whole again." She reaches down and pulls the hem of her nightgown up and over her head, exposing the whole of her body to me.

She's still too thin, and I can see the bruises in the faint light of the moon shining through the window. But she's right. I have to stop treating her like she's fragile and could break at any moment. So, I prowl forward and join her on the bed. I run my hands over her shoulders and then down her sides before I pick her up and set her onto my lap.

Her reaction is one of relief and need. She leans into me and begins to press closer, her hips working in slow circles. I groan and grip her hips more tightly, urging her to continue.

She does. I let her take what she wants. Tonight is about giving her back the power that was stolen from her, not just about me reminding myself that I haven't lost her. She needs this moment as much as I do, and I'm not afraid to let her have control if it will help her. But when this moment is over, will she come back to me, or will she find she still has pieces missing, pieces I can't give back?

Chapter Thirty-Nine: Alyssa

WHEN I WAKE up, I'm in Damien's arms, and we're back in his bed instead of in the guest room. I don't know when he moved us back, so I must've slept like the dead, but I needed the rest, so I'm glad he didn't wake me. Timothy is sleeping peacefully in his crib, so I turn into Damien with a contented sigh.

He drapes an arm over my hip. "How do you feel this morning?" he asks.

"Better. Damien, I want to talk about us. About how I feel and how you feel. About the secrets you're keeping." I prop my head up on my hand and stare at his handsome features, my stomach fluttering. "I need to tell you exactly how I feel, please. I just... I can't go back to how I was if

I don't face what happened and what I've realized. And I can't go back to how things were between us either."

He lifts a hand and strokes my hair out of my face with a nod. "I know. If you're ready to talk about it, then we'll talk."

My shoulders relax. He isn't going to shut this down like he did last time. "I meant what I said the night you rescued me. I love you. I wasn't delirious."

He stays quiet, waiting for the rest.

"I realized while I was down there that the thought of never seeing you again and never being able to tell you how I felt was worse than anything they were doing to me." I drop my gaze to his bare chest with a sigh. "I thought I would die without ever having the chance to tell you, but I vowed to myself that if I lived to be rescued, I'd tell you as soon as I could."

"I'm glad you have," he murmurs.

"Damien, I need to know everything from you. All the things you're keeping from me... I know you are because I overheard you talking to Timothy the day you told me I had two days to decide if I'd marry you. I know you love me if you were being honest that day, but I also know these secrets you have could ruin us, and if we're going to be anything, I need those out of the way."

He reaches out and tips up my chin, and his expression is stern. "I kept secrets because I had to if I wanted to protect you, and I didn't tell you I loved you because one of those secrets was that the Giovanni crime family threatened to release false documents implicating me in criminal activity if I stepped in to protect you. They would have released them as we were saying our vows, and I didn't want to say that I loved you only for you to doubt me later. That would've been too cruel. Had I told you any of this, they threatened to do worse than release documents that would tangle me up in legal troubles for years to come." He brushes my hair out of my face with a sigh. "But that's over now. They'll back off, and I've cut ties with my father. We're not in any danger now, and it's safe to tell you that I love you more dearly than anything in this life, except, perhaps, my son. I'm relieved to hear that you love me in return. To be honest, I was concerned you didn't, and when you ran, it only solidified that notion. I wish I hadn't proposed marriage then, that I hadn't needed to.... It must have seemed like I was taking advantage."

I laugh in relief as it sinks in that the secret was never something that would ruin us. My fears were for nothing. "Taking advantage? No. Not once I overheard you talking.

I thought you didn't love me and were only doing it out of obligation until then or that you were doing it to get Timothy. I wish you hadn't been forced to keep it to yourself."

He sighs and rakes his free hand through his hair. "I'm glad you see it that way. Was I wrong not to tell you I loved you? I wanted to, but I couldn't bear the thought of you being in more pain later for wondering if I'd lied all along about it just to convince you to marry me to get Timothy."

I chew on my lower lip and think about the statement. Then I nod with a grimace. "I definitely would've reacted that way if they'd gone through with the blackmail. I would've doubted everything I knew about you."

"So, I'm glad kept it to myself to tell you when you'd be sure to believe me," he murmurs. "It was hard to do it. We said it wouldn't be serious, that we weren't going to keep sleeping with each other. But it was never casual for me, and I always intended to have you in my bed as mine permanently."

I reach out and cup his cheek in my hand. "I'm sorry you went through all of it alone, but I'm so grateful I found a man willing to do all of that for me. Thank you."

He leans in and kisses me softly and slowly, the caress of his mouth against mine communicating the emotions he didn't know how to share.

I shifted closer and wrapped my arms around his neck, taking in the kiss gladly and relishing the peacefulness of the moment. "If we would've been more straightforward with each other at the beginning, we never would've gone through what we did," I mumble. "It wouldn't have mattered about the blackmail as much because I would've known already how you felt."

He groans. "I know.... In the future, let's be more honest?"

"I think that would be a good idea." I trailed my way down his neck and chest with slow kisses, and I was rewarded for my efforts with a shiver. "Damien?"

"Hmm?" He sounds a bit dazed and distracted, probably by what I'm doing.

"I'm glad you found me."

"I am too, love. I am too."

"Are you going to propose to me properly this time? With all our feelings out in the open?"

His eyes open to watch me. "Do you want me to do that? You ran away from me and left me at the altar last time. You cried at the cake tasting and ran then too."

I sat up, guilt washing over me. "I was overwhelmed, and I'd heard the fight with your dad. He doesn't approve, and it hurts. I was afraid, and I made bad choices."

He reaches up to cup my cheek as I straddle his waist. "I know, baby girl. I know. But you don't have to be afraid anymore, so be honest with me... what do you want? My father isn't in the equation. Not anymore. I took him out of it when I signed over every business he's invested startup capital in and every business he owns with me that has been laundering money behind the scenes without my knowledge or approval. We're free."

Tears fill my eyes. Free. I never thought I would come to value that word so much, but I do. I'm free in ways I didn't know I could be, and I'm happy. "I want a proposal, and I want a wedding done the right way. I want my parents to be happy for me instead of worrying they've made the wrong call pushing me to marry you. I want to have my own family with you and Timothy."

He nods. "Then that's what you'll have. I'm sorry we couldn't do it right the first time around, sweetheart."

"Me too." I smile down at him sadly. "But we'll do it right this time, won't we?"

"Of course." He leans up and kisses me more insistently.

"I thought you didn't want the baby to hear or see anything."

He pulls back with a grin and gets out of bed before scooping me up. I don't get a chance to protest before he's striding to the bathroom with me in his arms. "We'll make good use of the shower. He won't hear a thing."

I flush and laugh, burying my face in his shoulder. It feels good to be with him like this. It's good to be home where I'm safe and can start to heal. I'm not there yet, but it's a little easier to breathe when he's with me to help me through the dark moments.

The sunshiny attitude I had before my kidnapping isn't back just yet, but it feels good to laugh, even if I don't see the bright side of everything like I once did. I'm a different person than I was, but Damien still loves this new me, and he's not going to walk away.

Things between us aren't perfect. There are moments when they feel strained and uncertain. He doesn't know how to confront what happened to me or how to help me. Even though I tell him it isn't his fault—and we both know it isn't—I don't know how to help him see he isn't to blame. But at least we're in this together. We're facing it as a team, not separately like we did while I was chained up in that basement.

Knowing that is enough for now. Will it be enough in the future? I can't know that for certain, but I can trust that it will be enough for tomorrow, and that's all I need.

Chapter Forty:
Damien

WITH THE KNOWLEDGE that Alyssa wants a proposal in mind, I waste no time finding a ring I know she'll love. It's simple but elegant, just like her, and I'm looking forward to giving it to her. I don't have anything extravagant planned, but I want to help her overcome what happened at her favorite park, to reclaim some of her own power. Maybe it's a bad idea to propose there, but I want her to have a better memory to associate with the place.

I take her by the hand as we sit in the car and smile at her encouragingly.

She's staring at the hill where she was taken with a mixture of pain and anger. "Why did we have to come here?" she asks.

"I wanted you to have a chance to reclaim something you love that they tried to take from you," I murmur, lifting her hand to my lips and kissing her fingertips gently. "If you don't want to, we can go home."

I can propose to her anywhere. But I wanted to do it here if she was willing to give me the trust to turn something bad into something good again.

She lets out a shaky breath. "Okay... how are you going to give me that chance? All I see when I look at that hill is how much pain and suffering I went through."

I smile and lean in, grasping her chin and gently turning her head towards mine. Then I kiss her, slowly and gently. This is about new memories that are pleasant and safe, not about indulging myself. Though, at the moment, I'm certainly indulging. I want her to be in the right frame of mind when we go up there, and pleasure is an excellent tool to get her there.

She sighs softly into my kiss and then kisses me back. Her fingers slide up my arms and neck to tangle in my hair, and she leans into me. I let her set the pace. We have time. Lucille knows that this might take a while, and she has time to watch Timothy for us. All day, if necessary. Her words, not mine.

When she pulls back, her lips are slightly pinker than usual, and her cheeks are flushed. "That's a good start. Are we doing more of that up on the hill?"

"I hope so." I climb out of the car and go around to open her door.

She lets me help her out of the car, and I lock it behind us as we start up the hill. Her grip on my hand is tight, and I know she's nervous. Stopping, I pull her into me and kiss her again for a long moment. Then I whisper in her ear, "Don't be afraid, Alyssa. I'm right here, and they can't hurt you ever again. This is your favorite place to go when you're stressed, and they're never going to ruin it for you again. We'll find a way to make it yours again."

She nods with a soft smile. "Thanks, Damien."

"Of course." Taking her hand again, I pull her up the hill with a playful smile. "Besides, I have a surprise at the top."

Stew helped me set it all up a few hours before I brought her out here, and it's all waiting. That's one reason I was hoping she would agree to come up here. I have everything set up in the gazebo for the perfect surprise and proposal.

"A surprise?" She trails off as she catches sight of the rose petals strewn along the pathway heading up to the top of the hill and the gazebo and bench there. "Why are there rose petals everywhere?"

"You'll see." I tug her onward with a laugh.

We make it to the top of the hill, and she finally sees the gazebo with the battery-powered string lights draped and wound around the gazebo's rails. She puts her hand over her mouth and turns to me, tears filling her eyes. "It's... it's beautiful. Did you do all this for me?"

"I did." I let go of her other hand and drop to a knee, pulling out the ring box and opening it for her to see. "You said you wanted a proposal, and your wish is my command, love. Will you marry me?"

She nods, laughing and crying all at once. I slide the ring onto her hand, a sense of pride and adoration welling in my chest. This wonderful, brave, strong woman was going to be mine for the rest of our lives. Standing up, I draw her into another kiss, taking my time with the moment.

"This certainly helps to put a different cast to the place," she whispers against my shoulder as we stand there in one another's arms.

"I know it can't fully erase what happened here, but I hope it's a start," I whisper back.

"It's a start," she agrees. "Can we call my parents and tell them the news?"

"Of course." I pull back and let her pull her phone from her purse. "We don't need to tell mine. Things aren't good between us now that I've decided to cut all ties with my father, and they're not going to be as happy for us as yours will be."

"Okay." She dials her parents' number.

We wait together as it rings and then connects.

"Alyssa?" her mother says. "What's going on, sweetheart?"

"Mom, Damien just proposed." Her voice is tight with joy and tears. "We're getting married. This time for real."

"That's wonderful news!" Her mother sounds ecstatic. "I knew you'd find your way with each other, and we're both very happy for you. Your father's here, too, if you want to say hi."

"Hi, Dad," Alyssa says quietly.

"Congratulations, sweetheart," her father says, his voice choked up. "I'm so glad this news came before I left for rehab. If I can be present for the wedding, I will."

"I know, Dad. Focus on getting back to a good place where you aren't gambling, okay? That's the best gift you could give me." Alyssa's gaze connects with mine, and she smiles warmly. "We have to go, Mom and Dad. Talk soon, okay?"

"We love you, honey," her mother says. "Talk soon."

They hang up, and Alyssa looks at me. "There's one more thing we should do to make this day complete."

***

ALYSSA DRAWS ME into the courthouse. We made a quick stop back at the house to collect documents and to let Lucille know we'd be gone for the rest of the afternoon. Alyssa wants to make it official that I'm Timothy's father and to do that, we have to get the birth certificate corrected.

"Why didn't you put my name on the birth certificate to begin with?" I ask, genuinely curious.

She sighs. "I don't know. I was scared, I guess... I thought if your name was on there, it increased the chances that you'd decide to take him from me if you ever found out about him. Without the certificate with your name on it, I thought you wouldn't be able to do it without a lot of effort."

I hate that she felt that way, but I can't blame her for doing everything she could to hold on to our son. Timothy is a bundle of joy, and I can't imagine what it would be like to lose him. How much worse would it be for her? She'd carried him in her womb for nine months, alone and fighting to protect him without any help from me. Then she'd been dealing with the newborn for months before I came into her life again, and she hadn't once complained or considered coming to me for help. "You'll never have to worry about that again," I tell her quietly.

"I know." She leans up and kisses me. "If I thought I would, we wouldn't be doing this."

"Well, I'm glad we are." I kiss her back before pushing open the door to the court office for records. "And equally glad you trust me enough to do this."

"We're getting married. If I didn't, we'd be in for a lot of trouble."

It hadn't crossed my mind earlier that my name might not be on the certificate or that I should ask her to put mine on his birth certificate. I wouldn't have broached the topic with her, most likely. It touches my heart that she thought of it anyway. "Thank you, love. It means a lot to me, you know."

She squeezes my hand. "Then let's go make it official, shall we?"

I grin. "Let's."

This woman is so much more than I ever imagined I would find, and the fact that we have a wonderful baby boy together only makes it that much better. My future is far brighter now than it was before she came back into my life, and while I fought it at first, I'm not fighting it now. There's no guilt or shame at the thought of her being mine for the rest of our lives, and I'm glad to be giving her all of me in exchange. I have everything I ever wanted right here in the woman beside me.

Epilogue: Alyssa

OUR WEDDING TAKES place in a blur. I know I'm supposed to remember things because I'm the bride and put it all together, but the truth is, the only thing I'm focused on the whole time is Damien. I can't wait to be his in every sense of the word, and I'm certainly eager for the honeymoon.

We've left Timothy with my mother for a week so that we can go to Italy. I've always wanted to go, and now we are. Currently, we're sitting on the private plane in Damien's room in the back. He's lounging on the bed, and I'm sitting beside him.

I have news to share with him, and I hope he's going to be happy about it. Right now, though, I'm more focused on our first night as a married couple.

He reaches up and pulls me down to kiss me with a smile.

I reciprocate, sliding my body against his and then straddling him. His hands find my hips, urging me to move in slow, hard circles against him while we kiss. There's not much between us besides his boxers, and every movement sends a wave of need and sensation through me.

His hips grind into mine until I'm certain I might explode with the need without doing anything else. He trails his mouth in hot, open kisses along my neck and down to my collarbone. Then he's tugging my shirt off over my head to expose me to his gaze.

His fingers play over my now-bare skin, leaving me to set the rhythm for both of us. I speed up the slow circles against him, needing more.

He groans, but he doesn't stop me or try to change the pace. Instead, he lets me play while his hands roam over my body and his mouth follows.

I close my eyes with a sigh. This is heaven, and I have a lifetime to enjoy it now. He's not going anywhere, and that knowledge brings me a sense of security and calm that I value more than I knew I could.

Leaning in, I press my chest to his and murmur in his ear. "I have something to tell you."

"What is it?" His voice is a low, husky growl.

"You're going to be a father again."

He stops and pulls me back so he can look me in the eye. "You're pregnant again?"

I nod with a smile. "About three weeks along."

His mouth claims mine, and that's all the answer I need. He's happy we're adding to our little family, and I know that this time, I'm going to have all the support and love I need to bring this child into the world.

***

A FEW MONTHS after the honeymoon, we go to visit my parents. My father is working for Damien's real estate firm as a salesman now. He's cleaned up his act, and he's not gambling anymore. I've never seen my mother look so relaxed or happy, and the two seem more in love than ever.

We haven't told my parents I'm expecting yet. We wanted time to enjoy the knowledge ourselves, but now we're here to share our joy with them. I know my mother's going to be happy. She's always wanted a lot of grandchildren.

They greet us at the door with broad smiles and usher us in. My mother quickly takes Timothy from me, and I smile at her gratefully. Morning sickness and exhaustion have started setting in at this point, and I appreciate all the help I get.

We settle down on the sofas in the living room, and Damien and I share a glance and a smile. He's left it to me to tell them, and now seems as good a time as any.

"We have news for you both," I say.

My mother straightens and looks up from playing with Timothy.

"We're expecting another baby. I'm three months along."

My mother gasps, and my father grins. Then my mother is enveloping me in a big hug, and my father is shaking Damien's hand with a word of congratulations. I'm surrounded by the warmth and love of family, something that hadn't been possible before Damien came along and changed everything. My family is whole for the first time in my life, and I couldn't imagine being more blessed or happy than I am now.

Printed in Great Britain
by Amazon